JARED'S RUNAWAY WOMAN

BY

JUDITH STACY

MILLS BOON

First published in Great Britain 2008
by Mills & Boon, an imprint of Harlequin (UK) Limited,
Large Print edition 2011
Eton House, 18-24 Paradise Road, Richmond, Surrey TW9 1SR

© Dorothy Howell 2006

ISBN: 978 0 263 22400 9

Harlequin (UK) policy is to use papers that are natural, renewable and recyclable products and made from wood grown in sustainable forests. The logging and manufacturing process conform to the legal environmental regulations of the country of origin.

Printed and bound in Great Britain
by CPI Antony Rowe, Chippenham, Wiltshire

It was the stranger, the man she'd kissed in the alleyway.

But he was more than that.

Kinsey saw the stranger and Sam in profile. Same chin. Same nose. Same black hair.

They both turned to her. Eyes and mouth. Nearly identical. Sam's features were soft. The man's were hard, straight and rugged. This was what her son would grow up to look like.

Kinsey's blood ran cold.

Jared Mason had found her.

Judith Stacy fell in love with the West while watching TV Westerns as a child in her rural Virginia home—one of the first in the community to have a television. This Wild West setting, with its strong men and resourceful women, remains one of her favourites. Judith is married to her high school sweetheart. They have two daughters and live in Southern California.

JARED'S
RUNAWAY WOMAN

To David, Judy and Stacy—who else?

Chapter One

Colorado, 1887

Kinsey Templeton watched the passengers file out of the stagecoach at the depot across the street. Horses and wagons passed between them kicking up little swirls of dirt. She squinted her eyes against the bright afternoon sunlight and craned her neck for a better view.

A husband and wife. Two women and a young boy. A man traveling alone. All tired and dusty, probably hungry, stretching their legs and drawing fresh breaths of the clean air.

Since arriving in Crystal Springs several months ago, Kinsey watched the arrival of nearly every person who set foot in town. The task had grown more difficult lately. The stage came more frequently now. The railroad had made the town a regular stop on its line, bringing even more new faces. She had her job, too, at the boarding-house. Kinsey was probably the only person in Crystal Springs who arranged their day to match the stage and train schedules.

She was probably the only one who needed to.

With a quick glance around, Kinsey checked to see if any of the merchants she knew on Main Street or her friends going about their business seemed ready to stop and chat. No one did. No one at the stage depot took notice of her either.

She was all but invisible to everyone arriving in Crystal Springs. Twenty-five years old, her brown hair tucked beneath a bonnet, she wore the same sort of clothing as all the women in town. She looked as if she belonged there.

No one noticed that she watched the stage passengers, scrutinizing their appearance, their clothes and manners. Even if anyone commented about her odd behavior, Kinsey wouldn't have changed her ways. She couldn't. She had no choice.

Because she knew that still, after all the miles, all the towns and all the these years, someone would come after her.

How would she recognize him? A family re-semblance? Maybe. Maybe not. More likely his clothing. Eastern. Well-cut and expensive. His appearance would be out of place here in the West. He'd have the look of a dandy. A thief.

A predator.

Kinsey turned her attention to the husband and wife in front of the depot. The two of them talked for a few minutes before he pointed to the White Dove Café down the street. The couple was passing through, Kinsey decided, and focused on the two women and young boy who were now speaking to the express agent. She dismissed them as quickly, realizing they were, like so many other travelers she'd seen, inquiring about their layover time. She settled her gaze on the man who'd been the last to exit the stage.

His back was to her as he gazed westward down the street. Tall, wide-shouldered and long-legged. Hours on the cramped stage had surely been difficult for a man his size.

He wore dark trousers and vest, and a pale blue shirt. His black hat covered most of his equally black hair. A pistol was holstered low on his thigh. He carried a small satchel in his hand.

The man seemed to fit in, in dress and manner, at least from what she could see from across the street. Yet a unease crept over Kinsey, as if—

He turned quickly to answer the shotgun rider

who'd called to him from atop the stage. Kinsey's heart rushed into her throat.

Good gracious, he was handsome. Clean-shaven and carefully groomed despite the long stage-coach trip, yet somehow displaying a rugged air at the same time. Long limbs, stolid, sturdy. He carried an air of confidence, perhaps bordering on arrogance, as he spoke. A man used to being in charge.

The shotgun rider tossed down a valise and he caught it easily. He was staying in Crystal Springs. Kinsey's stomach fluttered unexpectedly and her heart thudded harder until—

"Mama! You're squeezing me!"

Kinsey gasped and leaned down to her son, easing her grip on his hand and pulling it up to plant a kiss on his tiny fingers.

"Mama's so sorry, Sam," she said, watching the little frown disappear from his face. "Let's go into the store. I'll bet Miss Ida has a treat for you."

He darted ahead of her in typical five-year-old fashion, scooting through the open door of the MacAvoy General Store before Kinsey could catch his hand again. She smiled with motherly pride. Sam was a beautiful child, with dark hair and blue eyes. He was a joy. Smart, too. Miss

Peyton had allowed him to start school already. The townsfolk had taken to him—and Kinsey—immediately. Crystal Springs felt like home now, despite the short time they'd lived there.

Kinsey headed into the general store, knowing she'd find Sam sitting on the counter, Ida Burk presenting him with a peppermint stick from one of the glass display jars. But at the doorway she turned back and cast another look at the stage depot. At the man.

In that instant he turned her way, and for a second their gazes met and held. Kinsey's breath caught. Her heart started up its thumping again and her stomach gave a quick lurch. He stared right back at her, frozen, as she was, for a few seconds.

Kinsey came to her senses with a little gasp and dashed into the general store, leaving the stranger staring after her.

What the hell was he doing.

Jared Mason gave himself a mental shake, silently admonishing himself for blatantly ogling the woman across the street. True, she was pretty; he could tell that even from a distance. And true, he'd been cooped up on the stage for days—and before that, weeks on the train—and this was the first woman who'd caught his eye, so he guessed he owed it to himself to enjoy the view.

Yet that wasn't what he was here for.

Jared adjusted his grip on his valise and satchel, and headed down the street toward the hotel the shotgun rider had told him about.

Walking, stretching his legs felt good. Jared kept his pace steady, more interested in looking over the town than getting to the hotel.

Crystal Springs, Colorado, seemed like a prosperous place. Jared spied stores, restaurants, a bank, a hotel and several other businesses. Men in suits roamed the street alongside cowboys carrying guns on their hips, miners with long beards, women in gingham dresses. The town looked clean, and from the talk he'd heard on the stagecoach, the place was growing.

Another new face among the townsfolk wouldn't draw much attention, Jared decided, and that suited his purpose well. He needed to blend in, to look like he belonged. The element of surprise was essential. He'd known that since he set out on this trip, several weeks and thousands of miles ago.

After crossing the Mississippi, Jared had abandoned the private railroad car and sent it back to New York, continuing the journey in the cars with the other passengers. Over the next weeks at some of the train stops, he'd slowly changed his appearance.

Suit, silk shirt and cravat exchanged for Levi's trousers, vests and cotton shirts. Italian leather shoes gone, replaced by boots. A wide-brimmed black Stetson hat. He'd bought a pistol and shoved it into the holster on his hip; he had yet to fire it but he did know how to load it.

The transformation of his appearance had been completed somewhere in Kansas. Jared didn't recall exactly where now. The train depots, the small towns, the scenery had blurred a long time ago.

In the town of Cold Creek, about fifty miles to the east, Jared had abandoned the train. He couldn't take another day of cinders and smoke blowing in through the open windows, the clacking of the rails, the relentless swaying, the screaming whistle. He boarded the stagecoach bound for Crystal Springs.

Jared glanced down at the satchel he carried and the technical journals tucked inside. They'd saved his sanity, along with the newspapers he'd bought along the way.

All he'd been able to do for the duration of the cross-country trip was read. And think. Think about what he'd lost. And what he'd come here to get back.

At the corner he stopped and eyed the Crystal Springs Hotel across the street, suddenly anxious to get inside, book a room, get cleaned up and grab a few hours of sleep. But his gaze swung to the general store down the block and the spot where he'd seen the pretty woman standing in the doorway. She was gone now, but her image lingered in his mind.

She'd had a market basket on her arm so she was probably shopping. For supper, maybe? For her family?

A raw surge of emotion ripped through Jared. A cozy home. A warm kitchen. A good meal on the table. Someone special waiting.

"Damn…"

Jared bit off a worse curse as the painful reminder of why he'd come here twisted inside him. He trudged on toward the hotel, as anxious as ever to get this job done. Once more he silently vowed he wouldn't go home empty-handed. And after this long, arduous journey, he wasn't particular about how he accomplished his task.

But he wouldn't fail. He'd head back east quickly. As soon as he got what he'd come here for.

Chapter Two

"That's not what I heard," Lily Vaughn said, raising her eyebrows.

Kinsey glanced up from the two pans of frying chicken on the cookstove and looked at her friend at the worktable beside her. Lily was only a few years younger, pretty, with a head full of wild golden curls she struggled to keep contained in a bun at her nape.

"What did you hear?" Kinsey asked.

Lily looked around the kitchen, causing Kinsey to do the same. The big room held enough cupboards, cabinets and workspaces to provide the two meals a day necessary to keep the boardinghouse residents happy. Kinsey had come to work there, cooking and cleaning, shortly after arriving in Crystal Springs.

"Well, I heard that after church last Sunday, the two of them went for a walk down by the creek and—" Lily leaned in and whispered in Kinsey's ear.

She gasped and pulled away. "My goodness, she—"

"Are you two girls gossiping again?"

Nell Taylor came through the swinging door from the adjoining dining room, giving them a stern look.

"Because if you are," Nell said with a sly smile, "you'd better wait until I get in here so I can hear it, too."

Kinsey giggled, at ease in the Taylor home. Not only had Nell given her a job but she also allowed her to live in a room off the kitchen at the rear of the house. It was small, but plenty big enough for Kinsey and Sam. Nell had given Lily a room up on the third floor of the big house next to her own when the young woman had come to work for her a few weeks ago.

Nell's husband, the woman was fond of saying, did things in a grand way, except save money. He'd died, leaving his widow nothing but the house. Nell had converted it into a boarding home and managed quite nicely with Lily and Kinsey as hired help.

"I was hoping Kinsey would have some gossip for us, Nell," Lily said, returning to the biscuit dough on the worktable. "Did you hear anything more about that hateful old Miss Patterson while you were in town this afternoon?"

"Some people prefer to think of Bess Patterson as set in her ways," Nell pointed out.

"I think she's mean and completely unreasonable," Lily said. "What sort of woman would hold a church hostage—just to get her own way?"

"It's *her* money," Nell said. "She can decide what she wants the church to look like."

"I still say it's shameful," Lily declared.

Kinsey thought the same but didn't say so, as she stirred the pot of potatoes boiling on the stove. The town's only church had burned to the ground and Bess Patterson, the wealthiest and, some said, most peculiar woman in Crystal Springs, had offered to pay for its rebuilding—provided the structure met her specifications. So far, none of the plans met with her approval.

"I didn't hear anything new on the subject at the general store," Kinsey offered.

Both Lily and Nell looked disappointed. Nell got a stack of plates from the cupboard and headed back into the dining room.

"So what *is* new in town?" Lily asked, cutting biscuits from the dough.

The image of the stranger from the stagecoach

bloomed large in Kinsey's mind. He'd lurked in her thoughts ever since she'd hurried into the general store this afternoon to avoid his gaze, and once again his memory made her stomach a little jumpy. But just why that happened, she wasn't sure.

"Well?" Lily prompted.

"Nothing," Kinsey said quickly. "Nothing's new in town."

"Not a thing?" Lily asked hopefully, as if it might prompt her to recall something.

Stalling for time and struggling to put thoughts of the stranger aside, Kinsey glanced out the window at the boys playing in the neighbor's yard. She spotted Sam quickly, running and waving a stick alongside the Gleason boys. Dora Gleason had four sons; one more child in her yard didn't matter one way or the other, she'd said. Sam was close to the same age as the Gleasons and they all got along well.

"I saw Isaac in town," Kinsey said softly.

Lily's spine stiffened. "Sheriff Vaughn, you mean?"

"I mean your husband."

Lily jammed the biscuit cutter into the dough and, after a few minutes asked, "Did he say… anything?"

"He said—"

"No. Never mind. I don't want to know."

"Lily, you know I've stayed out of the business between the two of you but—"

"Please, Kinsey...." Lily closed her eyes and turned her head away.

Kinsey wiped her hands on her apron and touched her friend's arm. "I understand."

Lily turned to her again, tears welling in her eyes. "It's hard enough dealing with...what happened..."

"I know."

"Oh, just look at me carrying on so." Lily pulled out of her grasp and swiped at her tears with the hem of her apron. "And in front of you, of all people. I'm so sorry, Kinsey. How thoughtless of me. Here you are a widow with a little boy to raise all by yourself. You've lost your husband and you probably resent the way I'm treating mine."

"It's all right," Kinsey said, because, really, it was.

She hadn't taken sides in the Vaughns' marital problems but she understood the situation well enough to know there was no easy answer.

"Do you miss your husband terribly?" Lily asked.

"Well..." Kinsey lowered her lashes and drew

in a breath, trying to appear brave, as she always did when the matter of her dear departed came up.

"It's hard for you to talk about him." Lily shook her head. "I'm sorry. I shouldn't have said anything."

Kinsey pushed her chin up. "It's…difficult."

"Why don't you go on over to the White Dove?" Lily suggested, seemingly anxious to get off the subject of husbands, both living and dead. "Saturday is their busiest night and if you go over now, you can get a jump on those dishes and get home early, take your time getting ready for services tomorrow."

On Sundays the boardinghouse didn't provide meals for its residents, other than a cold breakfast. It was the only day Kinsey, Lily and Nell could call their own.

"But I'm not finished here," Kinsey said, waving toward the boiling and sizzling pots and pans on the cookstove.

"I can do it," Lily insisted. "You run on. And don't worry about Sam. I'll make sure he comes back from the Gleasons before dark."

"Well, if you're sure," Kinsey said, feeling a little guilty.

"Of course I'm sure," Lily said.

Kinsey exchanged her apron for her wrap, bonnet and handbag and went out the back door. Her gaze settled on Sam still playing with the other boys, and immediately all troubling thoughts left her. She called to him and he rushed over, still clutching the stick in his hand.

"Having fun, honey?" she asked, kneeling in front of him.

"Yeah, Mama," he said breathlessly, bouncing on his toes and waving the stick. "I shot 'em all."

She smiled and smoothed back his damp bangs. "Mama's going to the White Dove now. Miss Lily will come get you in a little while. You stay right here with the Gleason boys. Understand?"

"Okay, Mama," he said, glancing back at the boys still running through the yard.

"Give Mama a hug."

She opened her arms and Sam launched himself against her, his smooth cheek resting on hers, both arms curled around her neck. Kinsey held him to her, soaking up the treasured moment.

Then he pulled away and she managed to get a quick kiss on his cheek before he dashed back into the fray, shooting the Gleason boys with his pretend gun.

Kinsey rose slowly, her heart aching a little.

Until Sam came along, she hadn't imagined the depth of love she could feel for another human being.

He'd changed everything. Given her purpose, given her a passion for life she thought she'd lost years ago. Her love for the child had awakened a fierceness that she'd not known she had. Maybe no woman knew she possessed it until she had a child of her own. A child she'd lay down her life for.

A child she'd kill for.

Tears welled in Kinsey's eyes, and the intensity of her feelings hardened her stomach into a tight knot. She'd keep Sam safe.

No matter what.

Jared settled into a chair beside the front window of the White Dove Café and tossed his hat into the empty seat beside him. The holstered pistol pulled against his thigh, annoying him. He wasn't used to wearing the thing. He'd even forgotten it in his hotel room just now and was halfway down to the lobby when he remembered it and had to go back for it.

The restaurant was still busy, even though it was late, and the delicious aroma of the food made Jared's mouth water. A good hot meal was just what he needed right now.

After getting off the stage earlier today, he'd gotten a room and a bath at the Crystal Springs Hotel, then lain down, intending to grab a few minutes of rest only to wake up several hours later. Staring into the dimly lit hotel room, it had taken him a while to remember where he was. He sprang out of bed and got dressed, grateful for the solid floor beneath his feet instead of the buck and sway of trains and the stagecoach.

The serving girl, a young woman with pale blond hair, approached the table carrying a coffee pot.

"Hi. I'm Dixie. Menu's up on the wall," she said, waving toward the chalkboard by the front door. She leaned down to fill his cup, resting her hand on the back of his chair. "See anything you—like?"

All he could see were her bosoms about six inches from his face, reminding him of what a long *uneventful* journey the trip from New York had been.

"Just, ah, just bring me whatever's good," he said.

Dixie's smile turned sultry. "Oh, it's all good."

She winked, then sauntered across the restaurant and through the swinging door to the kitchen.

Jared doused his coffee with sugar and sipped as he looked out the window, avoiding the gazes of some of the other diners who'd turned to stare.

The last of the sun cast long shadows down the dirt streets. Few people moved about as the stores closed for the night. Farther down the street he caught a glimpse of the Wild Cat Saloon. The place was brightly lit and already a stream of cowboys and miners passed through the bat-wing doors. Saturday night, he remembered.

His mind swept back to memories of other Saturday nights in the thirty-two years of his life. Everything from suppers in a tuxedo to grabbing for the last pork chop off the platter in the lumber camp chow hall. Jared smiled at the thoughts.

His father had built a highly successful construction business in New York and had insisted that all of his five sons learn it from the ground up. That had meant summers at lumber camps and sawmills, sweeping up offices, working as an apprentice to architects and engineers before being sent off for a formal education. It had led to Jared, the oldest son, spending most of his time away from home.

And it had led to the death of his closest brother.

A different woman—this one with gray hair and a no-nonsense demeanor—brought him a plate of hot food. He dug in, turning his attention once more out the window. Jared took the time to study the buildings along Main Street as he ate, a habit deeply ingrained in him.

Wooden structures with simple lines. Functional. Nothing fancy. But that's the sort of construction called for here. It would change, though, as the town grew and a bigger, more diversified population brought new ideas with it. Towns like Crystal Springs drew all sorts of people.

He wondered what it was, exactly, that had drawn the woman who'd run off with his brother's baby to this place.

Clark. Younger than Jared by only a year. The two brothers had been inseparable growing up. They'd stayed close, exchanging letters even during the time Jared had been in Pennsylvania overseeing the construction of a mill for his father's company, and Clark had been in Virginia doing the same for a factory and warehouse complex.

Jared had been surprised the day he'd received the letter from Clark saying he'd gotten married.

He'd been devastated the day he got the telegram telling him that Clark had died.

Jared had never met Beth Templeton Mason. No one else in the family had met her either, except his mother who'd traveled to Virginia for a visit shortly after the wedding.

No one in the Mason family knew quite what to think when the widow had shipped Clark's body home to New York, along with his personal effects, and was never heard from again. They'd been content to leave it at that until a few months ago when Jared's mother had come across a forgotten stash of Clark's belongings. Among a stack of correspondence carelessly into the crate she'd found an unfinished letter from Clark announcing the news that his wife was expecting a baby.

A baby. A Mason. Heir to the hard-earned family wealth and social position. Amelia Mason's first and only grandchild. She wanted that baby, and Jared was only too happy to take up the chore himself.

A hired investigator had tracked Clark's wife through a series of towns and menial jobs until he'd located her here in Crystal Springs. She'd done a poor job of hiding her true identity, simply giving herself a new first name and dropping her married name.

Just why she'd run off with Clark's son, no one knew.

All the family knew was that they wanted the boy in New York with the Masons, where he belonged. Jared had taken over the task himself and made the trip to Crystal Springs.

All he had to do was find the woman. That wouldn't be hard in a town this size. He silently chastised himself for sleeping all afternoon. Otherwise, he was sure he could have located her before nightfall.

Jared pushed his empty plate away and Dixie caught his attention coming through the swinging door from the kitchen. But it wasn't she who caused him to sit up in his chair. It was the woman he spotted behind her in the busy kitchen, elbow-deep in a tub of sudsy water.

The woman he'd seen across the street from the stage depot this afternoon.

Steam from the hot water made her face dewy. Tendrils of her dark hair curled around her cheeks. Her arms, exposed clear past her elbows, were smooth and a little pink as she washed dishes. Someone in the kitchen must have said something funny because she was laughing. Her face was lit up, glowing.

Jared wished he could hear her. He wished he was in the kitchen with her to listen to the melody of her voice, see her smile up close…see all of her up close.

Her bibbed apron outlined the swell of her breasts and the sash tied tight around her waist showed the flare of her hips. Sudden, strong desire claimed Jared, producing predictable results.

Dixie stepped in front of him, cutting off his view of the kitchen. She held a slice of berry pie in front of him.

"You look like a man who'd enjoy something hot and juicy," she said, leaning toward him. "You interested?"

His desire cooled a little. He took the saucer from her hand. "This will do fine," he told her.

She lingered just long enough to give him a knowing look, then disappeared into the kitchen again. Jared watched, catching another glimpse of the woman at the washtub as the door swung open, savoring the sight of her until it closed again.

Jared finished his pie and coffee and left money

on the table. He held back the urge to leave a generous tip, as he usually did, not wanting to call attention to himself. Outside on the boardwalk, he drew in a breath of the cool night air. It was dark now; lanterns burning in the windows down Main Street provided faint light.

Things had picked up at the Wild Cat Saloon. Horses were tied to the hitching posts all along the street. Piano music flowed out along with the drone of voices. Jared considered going inside, having a beer, but decided to get the lay of the town instead.

He walked past the many businesses that lined Main Street, all closed for the night. Above them, on second floors, windows glowed with lantern light. Jared imagined weary merchants and their families having supper around a kitchen table, talking over their day, planning for tomorrow.

Across the street, the sheriff left the jailhouse. He was a big fellow with a pistol on each hip, carrying a sawed-off shotgun. A lot of firepower. Jared thought the lawman might need it. Every cowboy and miner he'd seen walk into the saloon tonight carried a gun.

He dropped his hand to the pistol on his hip. Maybe he'd hire a horse from the livery tomorrow and ride out of town a ways, find a spot to target practice. He wasn't a stranger to guns, exactly, though he certainly didn't carry one with him every day back in New York. He'd hunted for deer and wild turkey, on occasion. But he'd never fired a pistol, and he sure as hell had never shot at a human being.

At the edge of town Jared spotted a number of houses lining the street. Trees and picket fences, big porches with swings. Homes where families lived.

The thought of returning to his hotel room seemed less appealing by the minute.

By the time Jared ambled his way back down Main Street, loud, raucous laughter spilled out of the Wild Cat. He stopped across the street, but his gaze wandered down the block to the White Dove Café.

The restaurant was dark now. Had the woman he'd seen washing dishes finished her chores and gone home already? An odd feeling of loss came over Jared as he realized that, if he'd hung around, he could have seen her again.

At that instant a woman stepped out of the alley that ran next to the White Dove. Faint light caught her face.

It was her.

Jared's breath caught and he took a step toward

her just as gunshots rang out. From the corner of his eye he saw several men rush out of the saloon firing pistols.

Jared ran for the woman.

The gunfire registered in Kinsey's mind just seconds before a man barreled at her from nowhere. He threw his arms around her and pulled her into the alley, pressing her back to the side of the restaurant. He held her tight against his chest, locked in his arms, shielding her, her nose buried against his throat.

Her mind raced. Was she being attacked? Or rescued?

She wasn't going to linger to find out.

Kinsey struggled against the man but she was held prisoner, sandwiched between the wall of the restaurant and the man's hard chest and encircling arms. She couldn't get away, could barely move. All she could manage was to lean her head away far enough to look up at him.

Recognition stilled her. It was the man from the stage depot. The one who'd stolen her attention, made her heart beat fast. The one she'd thought so handsome. And now here he was, holding her.

He gazed down at her, still not releasing her from his firm grasp.

"There's shooting down at the saloon," he said softly. "I didn't want you to get hit."

Kinsey looked into his eyes, lost for a moment in the effects of the soft light from the street playing about his face. She saw the hard jut of his jaw, and his clean, cotton scent washed over her. Her heart banged harder now, but not from fear. It was from—well, she didn't know what it was from.

Still holding her in his arms, the man touched his finger to her cheek, spreading a line of fire down her jaw.

"Are you…are you all right?" he asked.

No. No, she wasn't all right. Her breasts were pressed against his hard chest, and his legs were brushing hers. He held her in a way that sent her heart racing.

"Yes…yes, I'm fine," she managed to say. "Are you all—"

Jared kissed her. He couldn't stop himself. As if some unknown force had claimed him, robbed him of his good sense and free will.

His mouth covered hers, soft and moist. Slowly he worked his lips over hers, blending them together.

But it wasn't some unknown force making him do this, he realized, as a rational thought coasted through his mind. It was this woman. There was something about her....

Kinsey hung in his embrace for a stunned second, then rose on her toes and leaned her head back a little. He groaned and deepened their kiss until—

"What's going on here?" a man demanded.

Kinsey gasped at the familiar voice. It was the sheriff.

The man whirled, keeping himself in front of Kinsey, shielding her. Humiliation burned in her. What in the world had she been doing?

She stepped from behind the stranger, anxious to put some distance between the two of them.

"It's nothing, Sheriff Vaughn," she said, and cringed inwardly at her own shaky voice. Kinsey pointed lamely down the street, realizing that all was quiet now. "The shooting at the Wild Cat... this—this gentleman was just protecting me."

Sheriff Vaughn studied them for a moment, his gaze bouncing between the two of them.

"You all right?" he asked, his voice a little gentler.

"Yes, Sheriff, I'm fine."

"Run on ahead," he said, nodding in the direction of the boardinghouse. "I'll catch up in a minute. See you safely home."

Kinsey hurried away, thankful for the darkness that hid her hot cheeks.

Jared watched her go, heat still coursing through him. He couldn't take his gaze off her, until from the corner of his eye, he caught sight of the sheriff and the shotgun he pointed at Jared's gut.

Sheriff Vaughn was a big man, probably not any older than Jared, but with a hard look and sturdy countenance that surely helped keep him alive in his chosen profession.

The sheriff asked his name and, after Jared provided it, asked, "Where are you from? What are you doing in Crystal Springs?"

"I'm from back east," Jared said. "Here on business."

The lawman still didn't back off, which surprised Jared a little. Small towns like Crystal Springs went to great lengths to lure new business and usually went out of their way to accommodate newcomers. Apparently Sheriff Vaughn didn't feel that way.

Or maybe he just didn't like Jared.

"We watch after our women in this town," Sheriff Vaughn said, hefting the shotgun a little higher. "Even the widows. So don't go getting any ideas. Mrs. Templeton is well thought of around here."

Jared's heart lurched. "Templeton? Kinsey Templeton?"

The sheriff narrowed his gaze at him. "You best watch yourself, Mason. I'm keeping an eye on you."

Jared stepped up onto the boardwalk as the sheriff strode away. Down the street he caught sight of a skirt swishing in the dim light.

Kinsey Templeton. The woman who'd stolen the first Mason grandchild. He'd found her.

Jared swore under his breath. He'd found his brother's wife, all right.

And he'd kissed her.

Chapter Three

The towering shade trees that had once sheltered the church lay ahead and Kinsey was never more anxious in her life to get to Sunday service. She had more than her share of sins to atone for this morning.

Already a crowd had gathered. Folks huddled in small circles catching up on news, sharing concern about the sick and shut-ins in Crystal Springs. Children in their Sunday best tugged at their mothers' hands, anxious to play with friends.

Sam did that now. Kinsey held tight, not wanting him to start roughhousing with the other boys and get dirty before services started.

The church had burned completely to the ground—thankfully no one had been injured—and everyone felt lucky that Reverend Battenfield had agreed to move to Crystal Springs to tend to their spiritual needs, especially under the circumstances. The reverend and his wife, an older couple, were a welcome addition to the town.

With the charred remains as a backdrop, the reverend preached his sermon every Sunday to the townsfolk who were seated on makeshift benches some of the men in town had built. Kinsey suspected he hoped the difficult circumstances under which he ministered to his flock would be noticed and might loosen purse strings when the building-fund collection plate made its rounds.

Nell and Lily had left the boardinghouse well ahead of Kinsey and she saw them now talking with several other women. Usually, she would have joined them. But this morning Kinsey searched the crowd for someone else.

Sheriff Vaughn.

Embarrassment rose in Kinsey once more and she tried to fight it off so her cheeks wouldn't turn red again. Good gracious, she'd been caught kissing a man in the alley. What must the sheriff think of her? He hadn't mentioned it when he'd walked her to the boardinghouse last night, but what if he brought it up this morning? How would she possibly explain it to him?

When she didn't even understand it herself.

Despite her best effort, Kinsey felt her cheeks grow warm. Because the truth was the stranger hadn't just kissed her. She'd kissed him back. And her wanton actions hadn't stopped there. She'd raised herself up on her toes—*up on her toes*. Leaned *her head back* so he could *kiss her better*.

How humiliating. How embarrassing. How could she have done that?

And what was this phantom warmth that lingered in the pit of her stomach hours later?

"Mama, can I go play?" Sam asked, tugging on her arm.

Thankfully, reality pushed all thoughts of the stranger in the alley to the back of Kinsey's mind as she turned her attention to her son. His hair was still damp, slicked into place from when she'd combed it earlier. He wore his Sunday best, dark trousers and the white shirt, that she'd helped him get into after she'd donned her own blue dress and bonnet.

"Can I, Mama? Can I?" he asked, tugging on her arms and hopping up and down.

She glanced across the crowded churchyard

and saw several of the boys Sam went to school with playing together.

"All right, you can play for a while. But don't get—"

Sam jerked away from her and raced toward his friends before she could remind him not to get dirty. As if he would have listened anyway, Kinsey thought with a faint smile.

Just then, Sam tripped on something and fell flat on his belly. A man stepped away from the group of men he'd been talking with and knelt down to help.

Kinsey headed over, not particularly concerned that Sam had hurt himself. He was a tough little fellow and had taken harder falls playing with the Gleason brothers in their backyard. She hadn't heard him scream, either, the distinctive sound that determined whether a mother responded at a walk, or a dead run.

The man helped Sam to his feet and spoke to him, bringing Kinsey to a quick halt. It was the stranger, the man she'd kissed in the alley.

But he was more than that.

Kinsey saw the stranger and Sam in profile. Same chin. Same nose. Same black hair.

They both turned to her. Eyes and mouth. Nearly identical. Sam's features were soft. The man's were hard, straight, rugged. This was what her son would grow up to look like.

Kinsey's blood ran cold.

Jared Mason had found her.

She charged across the churchyard, her search for the sheriff forgotten, as Jared got to his feet. She swept Sam into her arms. Startled, he let out a scream but Kinsey clamped him against her and dashed through the crowd. At the edge of the churchyard, she ran.

It had taken only a question or two to the men standing with him in the churchyard for Jared to learn where the woman who now called herself Kinsey Templeton lived. Luckily, the sheriff hadn't been within earshot when Jared had asked his casual questions, and none of the other men noticed when he slipped away.

He'd seen Taylor's Boardinghouse last night, he realized as he stopped in front of the big white-and-green house with a front porch swing. Well-made, structurally sound. But was it a clean, decent place for Clark's son to live?

Another swell of emotion overtook Jared. Clark's son. He'd known the minute he laid eyes on the boy. He, like Jared, favored the Mason side of the family, though Clark had not.

Even if Jared hadn't seen the family resemblance, the look on Kinsey Templeton's face would have told him who the child was. Shock. Fear. And something else.

Courage, Jared realized. The courage of a mama bear come to do battle for her cub. Under other circumstances, Kinsey would have turned and run at the sight of Jared. But she'd charged in, taken her child. He'd seen the fierceness in her eyes.

Jared wondered for the first time since starting this journey what Kinsey Templeton might do to keep her son.

The front door of the boardinghouse was unlocked so Jared walked inside. The parlor was neat, nicely furnished with two settees, several chairs, bookcases and a piano. Off to the right, the large dining room table was backed by a china hutch, its beveled glass doors sparkling in the morning sunlight that beamed into the room.

The place was silent. Jared figured everyone was at church.

Everyone but Kinsey and Sam.

He glanced up the staircase, listened for a moment, then headed down the long hallway toward the back of the house. The men at church had told him Kinsey lived and worked here so he went into the kitchen and, sure enough, spotted her in a small bedroom.

Already she had a satchel sitting on the bed and drawers open in the bureau. Sam stared up at her, grass stain on his shirt, tears on his cheeks.

Jared crossed the kitchen and planted himself in the bedroom doorway. Kinsey whirled, saw him, stepped in front of Sam and pushed her chin up. They glared at each other for a few seconds, sizing each other up.

"You're frightening the boy," Jared said softly.

"Keep away from us."

"You and I need to talk."

Sam peeked around his mama's skirt and Jared's chest tightened. His brother's child. The only thing left of him. And only one way—one *easy* way—to get him.

Jared took a step backwards. "Let the boy go outside and play. He doesn't need to hear this."

Kinsey didn't move. Not an ounce of trust showed in her expression. Jared didn't blame her. If he had a treasure like this, he'd protect it with his life, too.

"I'm just here to talk," Jared said, holding out both palms.

He retreated to the other side of the kitchen,

well away from the bedroom and the door that led outside. After a moment, Kinsey knelt and spoke softly to the boy. He sniffed and nodded. She pulled a handkerchief from her skirt pocket and wiped his eyes and nose, then lifted him into her arms and carried him to the back door. She stood there for a moment, the cool breeze blowing in, and eyed Jared hard. He backed up another step and she put the boy down, spoke to him again, then watched while he ran outside and pulled himself into the rope swing that hung from an oak tree in the backyard.

Kinsey pushed the door closed and turned to Jared, her hand behind her, still on the knob.

"You're not taking him," she said. "If that's what you're here for, you may as well leave right now."

His gaze darted to the window. "That's really him? That's Clark's son?"

She hadn't expected to hear the softness in his voice, the sorrow and longing. With some effort, Kinsey hardened her heart again.

"You're Jared, aren't you?" she asked. "Clark spoke of you. I knew you'd be the one to come."

His eyes cut toward her and Kinsey saw the hard edge, the toughness—both mental and physical—Clark had told her about. Jared, the oldest of the brothers. Biggest, smartest. The leader.

The only Mason tougher than Jared, Clark had said, was their mother. Kinsey knew that was true.

She knew, too, that she was cornered. Escape wasn't possible, not at the moment, and she'd have to deal with this man.

He shifted his weight from foot to foot, looking a little unsure of himself.

"About last night…." Jared cleared his throat. "I didn't know that was you in the alley. I saw you across the street from the stage depot and again working in the restaurant kitchen, but I didn't know who you were. I wouldn't have… kissed you, if I'd known. Sheriff told me afterwards."

Heat rushed into her cheeks. Kinsey glanced away.

"It's dangerous for you to be on the streets like that at night," Jared said.

"Worried that somebody might grab me?" she asked.

"Yes."

"Like you did?"

His gaze hardened a bit. "I only meant to protect you when the shooting started at the saloon."

Kinsey gestured toward his pistol. "I'm surprised you didn't start shooting, too, like most men would have done."

"Oh." Jared looked down at the gun. "Well..."

"So I owe you my thanks," Kinsey said. "For that."

Jared walked to the window. Kinsey turned and they stood together watching Sam in the swing. Several long minutes crept by, the silence reminding Kinsey of exactly who this man beside her was, even if she had raised onto tiptoes to kiss him.

"He's healthy?" Jared asked.

Kinsey nodded. "Smart, too. He's in school. The schoolmarm was impressed that he can read already."

"You taught him?"

"Sam's got a quick mind," Kinsey said. "Like Clark."

She saw the hard look on Jared's face soften again, revealing the hurt and sorrow that he surely still felt for his brother, and that he probably preferred Kinsey didn't see.

"His name is Samuel?" Jared asked.

"After your father," Kinsey said. "It was Clark's idea."

Another quiet moment passed before Jared spoke again.

"We need to talk this out," he said.

"No, we don't. You need to leave."

"I won't do that."

They squared off. Kinsey felt her anger rise. She saw Jared's jaw tighten, but he drew in a calming breath.

"I want both of you to come back to New York with me," he said, "and live in our home."

"We have a home."

"Sam's family is there."

"*I'm* Sam's family," Kinsey said. "I've been taking care of him since the day he was born and I don't need any—"

"You call *this* taking care of him?" Jared demanded, waving his arms. "Living in the back room of a boardinghouse? Working two jobs to scrape by?"

"I take excellent care of Sam!"

"How much money have you put away?" He edged closer. "What if he gets sick? Can you buy medicine? Pay a doctor?"

"I'll find a way—"

"What about his future? His schooling? His education?"

"I can manage—"

"You're robbing him of what's rightfully his. Did you think about that?" Jared asked. "The boy's entitled to Clark's inheritance."

"I don't need—"

"The Mason family is one of the most powerful in the East," Jared told her. "We've got money—lots of money. We've got political connections. Social position. We know important people in high places who can get things done. All of that is Sam's birthright. He'll have everything he could ever need."

"I don't want that sort of life for him," Kinsey said.

"It's too late for that," Jared said. He jabbed his finger toward the window. "He's a Mason."

She shook her head frantically. "No."

"And so are you." Jared pointed at her now. "You can make up a new first name and call yourself Kinsey, and you can drop your married name and pretend you're a Templeton again, but you're still a Mason. Still my brother's wife. Still a part of the Mason family."

Kinsey gasped and pressed her lips together,

forbidding herself to say another word. Jared glared down at her. She drew in a breath, forcing herself to stay calm, to think.

She lowered her lashes, then looked up at him again.

"You're right, of course," she said quietly. "I just need some time to think things over."

Jared backed off a little and nodded. "Fine, then."

Kinsey opened the back door and stepped outside, watching as Jared cast a last look at Sam in the swing, then headed toward town.

Her heart thundered in her chest and she wondered how she'd gotten so lucky.

Jared Mason didn't know who she really was.

Chapter Four

No trains today.

Kinsey made her way down the boardwalk, her mind whirling. No trains expected through Crystal Springs until the end of the week. No stagecoach due for two more days. She'd committed the schedules to memory a long time ago. That's how she knew there'd be no escape from the town—from Jared Mason—today.

When Nell and Lily had come home from church yesterday and inquired about her abrupt departure, Kinsey had calmed herself enough to make a reasonable excuse that they hadn't questioned. If her two friends noticed that she'd been on edge the whole evening or watched Sam in the backyard like a hawk, they hadn't mentioned it.

No one had noticed the family resemblance between Sam and Jared Mason either, thank goodness. But why would they?

She hadn't noticed it herself the first time she'd seen Jared, not even when he'd kissed her.

Kinsey had tossed and turned most of the night debating on what she should do, what she could do. Her first thought had been to run again but that wouldn't be possible right now. A few other plans had bloomed in her mind as she'd lain awake staring at the ceiling, listening to Sam's breathing from his little bed across the room. They were dangerous, foolish, probably even under ordinary circumstances.

But dealing with Jared would prove anything but ordinary, she knew.

Her saving grace was that, at the moment, he didn't know who she really was. But if he ever checked deeper, if he ever found out…

Kinsey stepped off the boardwalk and hurried down the alley beside the White Dove Café. She averted her eyes, not wanting to look at the spot where she'd allowed the man who was trying to ruin her life to hold her and kiss her, but warmth flushed inside her just the same.

This morning she'd gotten Sam off to school and taken care of her share of the kitchen chores at the boardinghouse before heading into town. Because around dawn, it had occurred to her that before she worried herself silly and ran away from a town she truly liked, she ought to do a little checking of her own.

At the back entrance to the White Dove, she went inside and found Mrs. Townsend, the woman who owned the place and let Kinsey work there two nights a week washing dishes, at the cookstove. The kitchen smelled wonderful, delicious aromas of ham, eggs, biscuits filling the room.

"How's business this morning?" Kinsey asked, pushing open the swinging door to the dining room just wide enough to sneak a quick peek inside.

The restaurant was half full. No sign of Jared yet. But she knew he'd be back. The White Dove was by far the best restaurant in town. No Mason, Kinsey knew, would settle for less. Certainly not Jared, after he'd bragged yesterday about the powerful Mason family, with their political connections, social position and their important friends in high places.

"Slow, thankfully." Mrs. Townsend shook her head. "I'm shorthanded—again."

A quick glance around the kitchen told Kinsey that once more, Dixie hadn't reported for work on time. The young woman had gained an unsavory reputation in Crystal Springs and was frequently the topic of gossip. She was family, though, and Mrs. Townsend didn't have much choice about keeping her on.

"Do you need me to help out?" Kinsey asked, cracking the door again to glance inside the dining room.

"Roy's helping," the woman said, nodding toward the window where her husband was loading up more logs from the woodpile. "We'll be fine. Dixie will be along shortly. I saw you leave church yesterday. Missed you at the service."

"Neither Sam nor I were feeling well. I should have kept us both at home," Kinsey said, surprised at how easily the lie rolled off her tongue. She glanced into the dining room again. "Anything new from Miss Patterson?"

"I heard Reverend Battenfield was planning to pay a call on her yesterday afternoon," Mrs. Townsend said, flipping eggs onto a platter and shaking her head. "He was taking the mayor with him along with Herb Foster."

"From the feed and grain store?" Kinsey asked, frowning.

"Herb is just sure he's come up with a plan for the new church that Miss Patterson will love."

Herb wore checkered trousers and striped shirts thinking himself an Eastern dandy, so Kinsey had her doubts about whether he could impress the persnickety Bess Patterson with his ideas for the new church.

"If we don't get that new church built before the hard winter sets in, we'll have to wait clear until spring," Mrs. Townsend said.

Kinsey wasn't hopeful. Already Miss Patterson had turned up her nose at three other plans for the church and had so infuriated several men in town that they wouldn't even talk about the situation anymore.

"Looks like some folks need a refill," Kinsey said, taking the coffee pot from the back of the cookstove. Mrs. Townsend smiled her thanks as Kinsey pushed into the dining room.

She made the rounds, topping off coffee cups, chatting with most all the diners and casually casting glances out the front window. Just as she'd answered the familiar how's-that-boy-of-yours question yet another time, she caught sight of Jared coming out of the hotel down the street. Her hand quivered, sending hot coffee into the saucer. She apologized quickly wondering why her first thought of the man had been that he looked handsome this morning, rather than that he was trying to ruin her life.

Back in the kitchen, she said goodbye to Mrs.

Townsend and rushed outside. From the back corner of the building she saw Jared walk by, waited another few seconds, then headed for the hotel.

Cecil Nelson was behind the desk, helping out his folks, who ran the place. The young man seemed to grow taller each time Kinsey saw him.

"Morning, Miss Kinsey," he said, swiping his bangs out of his eyes.

She had no time for small talk. Glancing around quickly she leaned toward him. "Give me the key to Mr. Mason's room."

Cecil drew back a little. "Well, Miss Kinsey, you know I can't do that."

She pulled herself up a little. "Would you like me to tell Becky Cochran's pa what I saw the two of you doing out behind the White Dove last Wednesday night?"

His face flamed and his jaw dropped. "Well—well, shoot, we weren't doing nothing but—"

"I saw what you were doing. And unless you'd like Becky's papa to know also—"

"No, no you can't do that." He shook his head frantically. "He'd fly into me something awful—not to mention what Ma would do when she found out."

"The key." Kinsey held out her hand.

Cecil fidgeted for a moment then gave her the pass key for room number four. She headed up the stairs.

"I love Becky. I swear I do," Cecil called. "You aren't going to tell, are you, Miss Kinsey?"

She stopped and looked back. "If you really love her you ought to have more respect than to put her in that sort of position. And if I see the two of you together like that one more time, I'll tell."

Kinsey hurried up the stairs, Cecil's thanks fading behind her, a little uneasy at passing moral judgement on the two young people she'd caught kissing, given what she was about to do.

The upstairs hallway was empty as she made her way to the front of the hotel and room number four. The best room in the place. Figured Jared would request it.

With a final quick glance around, Kinsey unlocked the door, slipped inside and closed it behind her. She dropped the key into her skirt pocket and fell back against the door, her heart suddenly thumping in her chest.

Good gracious, she was in a hotel room. A man's hotel room. What had become of her?

She reconciled herself with a quick look

around. Bed, bureau, writing desk, washstand, rocking chair, dressing screen in the corner. Just a hotel room.

Then her breathing quickened and a whispering sensation rippled through her.

Jared's room.

He came full force into her mind as she stood surrounded by his personal belongings. The rumpled bed linens spilling into the floor, the pillows molded to the shape of his head, his clothing hanging on the pegs beside the door, his satchel and valise in the corner. The room smelled of him, rousing a memory she'd rather forget.

The alley. Her nose buried against his throat. His body pressed close. His hot breath. His lips covering hers, drawing her in until she rose up and—

"Good gracious…" Kinsey muttered in the silent room, once more admonishing herself for her behavior. Jared had the good grace to apologize for his actions that night. Maybe she should do the same.

Except she wasn't sorry.

Kinsey gasped aloud. How could she have even thought such a thing?

She certainly didn't have time to figure that

out now. Jared was at the White Dove having breakfast, and she intended to be finished with her task here long before he scraped his plate clean.

Yet she couldn't help but touch his shirt hanging from one of the pegs. Pale blue. Cotton. Big. Clark had been a big man, too. Kinsey smiled faintly at the memory.

At the end of the peg row, she saw Jared's gun belt. Odd that he hadn't taken it with him. Nearly every man in Crystal Springs—in Colorado—carried a gun.

Yet it didn't really surprise her. She suspected that like Clark, Jared was more comfortable with a pencil or ink pen in his hand. All the Mason brothers, like their father, spent their days and nights designing and overseeing construction projects—factories, office buildings, warehouses. The bigger, the better, Clark had said with reasonable pride.

Kinsey touched the holster. The leather was stiff, new. She pulled the pistol out. It was a Colt .44 caliber revolver. The Peacemaker. Well-oiled and immaculate. She sniffed the barrel. Not fired recently, if ever.

She held the pistol in both hands, feeling its weight, its balance, then stretched out her arms and sighted through the window at the dotted *i* on the sign atop the building across the street. Kinsey knew about guns. Her mother, who'd lived through the ravage of the War Between the States, thought every woman should know how to shoot and had taught Kinsey well.

She remembered Jared's awkward reaction in the kitchen of the boardinghouse yesterday when she'd mentioned that he hadn't opened fire when the shooting began at the saloon. Something to keep in mind, she decided, as she slipped the Colt into the holster once more.

She turned to the satchel and valise on the floor and placed them on the writing desk. The valise held folded whites, and she had to force herself to dig past them to the bottom of the case, her cheeks warming as she fondled Jared's long johns, socks and handkerchiefs. But she found what she expected to find. Stacks of money. Her stomach quivered at the sight, then hardened into a knot.

She knew why he'd brought so much cash with him, what he intended to do with it. Buying her off, obviously, had entered his mind before he left New York. It was a side of the man that didn't really surprise her. Yet it still didn't give her the information she'd come here to discover.

When she opened the satchel, her heart fell. Technical journals. Pencils. The odd drawing tools she'd seen Clark work with. There was a stack of papers filled to the very margins with pencil sketches. Excellent drawings of mountains, waterfalls, flowers, buildings, portraits of old women, young children. They chronicled Jared's trip westward. She imagined him seated on the train, looking out the window capturing the passing scenery or sketching unsuspecting passengers. She'd seen in Clark the same compulsion to stay busy. None of the Masons, it seemed, could bear to sit still, their hands idle.

Kinsey put the drawings aside and pulled a large brown envelope from the satchel. A new wave of disappointment swept over her as she pulled out a stack of documents and skimmed them.

A letter from the midwife who'd delivered Sam, confirming his birth date and the names of his mother and father. A report from a Pinkerton detective tracing Kinsey's flight from Lynchburg, Virginia to Crystal Springs, Colorado, and details on all stops in between. The last item in the packet dashed all hope for Kinsey. An unfinished letter, written in Clark's own hand, advising the family of the impending arrival of his first child.

The man who'd come to her house yesterday claiming a right to Sam was, in fact, Jared Mason. Kinsey's shoulders slumped at the realization.

Lying awake in bed last night it had occurred to her that she didn't know whether the man who claimed to be Jared was, in fact, Clark's brother, even though she'd seen the family resemblance with her own eyes. The man could have been a fraud, a distant family member, wanting to kidnap the boy and sell him back to the Mason family.

Or maybe she was just grasping at straws.

But there was no doubting Jared's identity now. Kinsey shoved the documents back into the envelope and—

A key scraped in the lock. Kinsey whirled around, saw the doorknob shake.

There were only two keys to every room in the hotel. She had one of them in her skirt pocket. The other one belonged to—

Kinsey slapped her hand over her mouth to keep from screaming as the door opened.

Chapter Five

Kinsey dropped to her hands and knees behind the dressing screen just as the door swung open. She pressed her lips together to keep from betraying her hiding place with a squeal of terror.

Footsteps thudded into the room, then a mumbled curse.

Jared's voice. No doubt about it.

Kinsey crouched lower, trying to make herself as small as possible. The door closed. She was trapped.

Trapped inside a hotel room. Good gracious, what had she been thinking? Kinsey silently berated herself for her decision to come here. But he'd been on his way to breakfast—she'd seen him with her own eyes. Why would he come back?

Did he suspect her of doing exactly what she

was doing? Had he planned this, set a trap for her, somehow expecting to find her here?

Maybe he hadn't slept well. The thought flew through Kinsey's mind like a welcomed cool breeze. Maybe he simply wanted to go back to bed—

What if he went back to bed? What if he took off his clothes?

Heat coursed through Kinsey like ripples through a pond.

What if he took off his clothes?

She leaned forward—just a little—and peeked around the corner of the screen. Jared stood at the bureau, muttering under his breath, fumbling with his gun and holster.

All his clothes on.

Kinsey's cheeks flushed and she ducked back, silently willing him to leave the room. The wood floor was coarse and bit into her palms. Her knees hurt and her back had started to ache.

To say nothing of how hot the room had become.

Then, to her immense relief, she heard Jared's footsteps. The door opened, then closed. The room fell silent.

Still, Kinsey waited. She didn't dare move for fear of making a noise that might draw him back into the room. She gritted her teeth and silently counted to one hundred—twice. Unable to bear another second on the floor, she got to her feet and heaved a sigh. She pressed her hand to her lower back as she listened at the door for a moment, then, hearing nothing, slipped into the hall.

Arms circled her waist from behind and hauled her back into the room before she could let out a scream. The door slammed shut and she was dropped crossways on the bed. She bounced on the soft mattress and looked up to find Jared Mason towering over her.

Kinsey launched herself off the bed but he caught her again. Their feet tangled and he fell down on the mattress with her.

Her heart pounded as Jared lay on top of her, pinning her to the bed, one of his legs between her knees. She took a swing at him but he caught her wrists and pressed them down, inches from her head. His weight, the heat of his body, soaked into her.

Another few seconds passed before Kinsey realized that he looked as startled as she. His face, hovering just above hers, was taut. His breath quickened. His body tensed.

Then a little smile quirked his lips. "I figured

you'd do anything to keep Clark's son, but I never counted on this."

Her cheeks flamed, bringing on a wave of anger. "Oh! You think I came here to—! How dare you!"

He raised an eyebrow. "That's not why you're here?"

"Of course not! Get off of me!" Kinsey struggled, trying to free her arms and kick her feet, but he held her easily.

"I'll scream," she threatened.

"Go ahead," he said. "Scream all you want. We'll get the sheriff up here and you can explain to him—and the whole town, who'll hear about it before noon—why you're in my room."

Kinsey pressed her lips together, the gravity of her circumstances weighing more heavily than Jared atop her. She tried another tack.

"Would you please let me up?" she asked.

He held her, still, just to show her that he could, she suspected.

"You're hurting me," she told him.

Jared released her so quickly it startled her. For a man so big he moved with incredible speed, even grace, pushing himself off her and to his feet in an instant.

Kinsey sat up on the bed, yanked her skirt

down and straightened her blouse, attempting to do so with a modicum of dignity and self-respect. But when she tried to get to her feet, Jared stepped close again, keeping her in place.

"What are you doing in my room?" He nodded to the dressing screen. "I saw you hiding back there."

Heat filled her cheeks again, but she pushed up her chin and glared at him. "I came to find out exactly who you are."

That seemed to surprised him. Obviously, as a member of the powerful Mason family, Jared wasn't used to having his word questioned.

"I wasn't about to let you anywhere near Sam without knowing if you were who you claimed to be," Kinsey told him.

His surprise turned into something else—respect, maybe?—and he nodded slowly.

"Did you find out what you wanted to know?" he asked.

"Yes." Kinsey sighed. "Unfortunately."

"So you're ready to talk about you and Sam coming back home with me," he concluded.

The notion of living in the Mason's New York home, the confines of the hotel room, and Jared's great height towering over Kinsey caused everything in her to rebel.

She glared up at him. "Move out of my way."

The words came out in her sternest "mommy voice," the one that stopped Sam—and any other children with him—in his tracks. It had that effect on Jared, too, because he stepped back, more a reflex than anything.

Kinsey got to her feet and rubbed her wrists where he'd held her on the bed.

"I have to go to work," she told him, her tone suggesting that she didn't have leisurely hours to while away, as he did. "We'll talk later."

"When?"

"After dark when Sam goes to bed."

He studied her for a moment, as if he wanted to protest, but he didn't. Kinsey moved around him toward the door, but he blocked her path.

"I didn't mean to hurt you," he said softly.

Jared lifted her hand and pulled back the cuff of her sleeve to reveal her wrist. He did the same with the other wrist, holding them both in front of him.

He gazed at her and the moment seemed to stretch into forever. Jared leaned forward and brushed a kiss on one wrist, then the other. A firestorm ignited in Kinsey, threatening to consume her, but holding her in front of him.

Jared seemed unable to move either. He eased

closer. So did Kinsey. She rose on her toes, until their faces hovered just inches apart and she felt his hot breath against her lips.

Then he pulled away. Kinsey's cheeks warmed, from embarrassment this time. She darted out of the room.

How embarrassing.

Jared yanked the window of his hotel room open farther, hoping for a breeze to cool the place—and him. He stood there gazing down at Main Street, and rested his thumbs on the buckle of his gun belt.

Damn pistol. He'd forgotten it again this morning when he'd headed out for breakfast, and this time made it all the way to the restaurant before he realized it. He'd had to turn around and come back for the thing.

Embarrassing, all right. And hardly a good way to fit in on the streets of Crystal Springs. The sheriff had seen him leaving the hotel and had stopped on the street and eyed him hard. Under ordinary circumstances Jared wouldn't have cared what the lawman thought of him, but Jared didn't want to arouse suspicion—any more than he already had, that is. After the incident with Kinsey in the alley, he knew the sheriff was watching him.

Another plume of warmth rose in Jared at the memory of kissing Kinsey in the alley. It was a thought he couldn't get out of his mind. And it didn't help any that he'd found her hiding in his hotel room this morning.

When he'd come back for the gun and caught a reflection in the washstand mirror, he'd known right away that the bottom he saw in the air was Kinsey's. No question about it. He'd made a study of her backside each time he saw her.

Or maybe it was her scent hanging in the room that had alerted him to her presence. Sweet and pure, fresh.

The smell of her still wound through the room, and through him, driving his desire for her a little higher. It was a feeling that troubled him. She had been, after all, his brother's wife.

To distract himself, Jared shoved his belongings back into his satchel. He didn't bother to count the money; in his heart he knew Kinsey wouldn't have taken any of it. Clark wouldn't have married that sort of woman.

Of course, Jared wouldn't have picked Kinsey as the type Clark would have been interested in—let alone married to. Jared remembered the sort of women Clark had courted, and they were nothing like Kinsey. Quiet and demure were more to Clark's taste. Those sorts of young women were the norm in the social circle of the Mason family.

Clark could have changed his mind after meeting her, of course. Kinsey was the sort of woman who'd make any man think twice, Jared decided.

He muttered a curse. She would make a man think twice because she was so damn hard-headed. Determined and strong. Capable and independent. A wife like her could drive a man crazy, he decided.

Kinsey's lingering scent caught his nose again and Jared grumbled as he headed for the door. He had to get out of this room. He had to get out of this town, too. He had a big job waiting for him up in Maine.

And above all, he had to redeem himself for what he'd done to Clark.

Jared fought off the bitter memory and focused on getting control of this situation.

Kinsey had decreed that he couldn't talk to her until tonight after Sam went to bed. Well, he'd just see about that.

* * *

The morning had started out badly, but the afternoon had been better, Kinsey decided as she left the White Dove Café, her handbag a little heavier from the extra coins inside.

Mrs. Townsend had stopped her on the street and asked if she could help out during the midday meal service. Dixie, who hadn't showed up for work this morning still wasn't to be found it seemed. Kinsey had gratefully agreed, glad to have the extra money.

She'd been unable to meet Sam after school, though. He would walk home with the Gleason boys and was perfectly fine; Lily or Nell were always at the boardinghouse when Sam got home. Kinsey just liked being there when school ended, chatting with Miss Peyton and the other mothers, then hearing about Sam's day as the two of them walked home together.

Of course, there was no way Kinsey could tell Sam—or anyone—about *her* day. Caught red-handed inside Jared Mason's hotel room. Accused of offering favors to get him to leave town. Then nearly kissing him—again.

Kinsey cringed inwardly as she recalled the moment he'd touched her wrists, how the sight of his big hands had caused her heart to beat a little faster, how the feel of his lips caressing her skin had sent another wave of heat through her.

As it did now. Kinsey glanced around the crowded street, making sure no one was watching, and picked up her pace.

Jared had intended to kiss her again in the hotel room. She just knew it. They'd looked into each other's eyes and Kinsey had done the unthinkable. She felt herself rising on her toes, ready to receive his kiss.

Good gracious, what was wrong with her?

Perhaps that was part of his plan, Kinsey suddenly thought. Maybe he had done that on purpose to keep her off balance, keep her from thinking about the reality of her situation.

Jared Mason intended to take Sam away from her. He was smart. He'd do anything to get his way.

As would she.

Kinsey hardened her heart and pushed aside the memory of those moments in Jared's hotel room. Worry and anxiety claimed her, swift and strong. She walked faster, anxious to get home to Sam.

But her worry proved baseless when she arrived at the boardinghouse and found Sam in the Gleasons' yard, playing with the brothers. He saw her and hurried over.

"Hi, Mama."

"Hi, honey." She knelt down and gave him a hug. "How was school today?"

"We drew pictures," he said.

"I'll bet Miss Peyton liked yours the best," Kinsey said. Even at this young age, Sam showed signs of having his father's gift for drawing.

"Did you walk home with the Gleason boys?" Kinsey asked.

"Huh-uh," Sam said. "Uncle Jared walked me."

Kinsey's blood ran cold. "Who—who walked with you?"

"Uncle Jared." Sam gestured toward the boardinghouse.

Kinsey's heart pounded into her throat and hung there. She got to her feet.

"You run on and play for a while, Sam," she said, urging him toward the Gleason brothers.

Anger raged in Kinsey as she crossed the yard. Jared Mason, a man of power and privilege, so used to having everything he wanted, so accustomed to always getting his way. He'd deliberately ignored her wishes. He'd invaded her home. Turned her world upside down.

And now he'd moved threateningly close to Sam.

Kinsey yanked open the back door and stormed into the kitchen. There he stood, in the entrance to her bedroom. Kinsey's anger doubled.

"How dare you," she demanded, her breath coming in short puffs.

Jared stood still as a stone fortress, expressionless, unmoved by her anger, her outrage.

She stepped closer. "Don't you ever—ever—come around Sam again. Don't you ever—"

A smile tugged at the corner of Jared's lips. Smug. Pleased with himself.

Powerful.

Jared held up a leather-bound book.

Kinsey's breath left her in a single huff. Her world tilted.

"I'm sure you recognize this. The Templeton family Bible." He nodded toward her bedroom behind him. "I found it beside your bed."

Kinsey dug deep, hoping to muster anger. "You have no right…"

Jared stepped closer and fanned the thin pages, stopping in the center of the Bible. "This is the section where the family records are kept. Births, marriages…deaths."

Run. Run now. The thought flashed in Kinsey's mind. Yet a chill claimed her, holding her in place.

Jared consulted the page, though it was obvious he didn't need to. This was a show he reveled in.

"Beth Templeton married to Clark Mason," he read. "Clark Mason, dead. Beth Templeton Mason, dead."

Jared looked at Kinsey. "You want to explain to me how that's possible? I mean, since you're claiming to be Beth Templeton Mason, the woman I figured was using a different first name and her maiden name."

He was toying with her. Enjoying the power he had over her. He already knew the answer so Kinsey didn't respond.

"Funny thing," Jared said, forcing a little laugh and shaking his head. "According to your family Bible, there really is a Kinsey Templeton. A whole separate person. Adopted by the Templeton family. Beth's stepsister."

The weight of the past bore down on Kinsey, crushing not only the moment, but her future as well.

"I—I can explain—"

"You were never married to Clark. You were only his sister-in-law. You didn't give birth to Sam." Jared's expression turned hard and cold. "Or did you?"

Kinsey's cheeks flamed and she found her anger now. "That's a filthy thing to suggest. Clark and Beth were devoted to each other. Beth was Sam's mother."

"So you've got no blood tie to Sam at all, have you," Jared said.

Kinsey gasped, realizing what he'd just maneuvered her into admitting.

Jared stepped closer. "In fact, you've got no family relation to Beth either, do you? You're her stepsister. A stranger to the family. Somebody they took in."

"It wasn't like that," Kinsey declared. "We were sisters—as close as any sisters could be. We—"

"You're nothing but an outsider." Jared moved in, his words cutting worse than a sword. "You're nobody. You've got no standing in Sam's life. You stole him."

"I didn't! Beth begged me to—"

"You stole him and you hid him. You kept him from his real family."

Jared towered over her, battering her with his words, with his accusations…with the truth.

Kinsey blinked back tears. "You don't understand! You weren't there! You didn't—"

"I'm taking him."

Kinsey gasped and shook her head frantically. "No!"

"I'll get the sheriff if I have to," Jared told her. He gave her one final hard look, and walked toward the door.

"No!"

Kinsey whipped the gun from his holster. Jared spun around. She pointed it square at his chest and pulled back the hammer.

"You're not taking Sam anywhere."

Surprise registered on Jared's face. He shifted. His gaze bounced from her to the gun, around the room and back to Kinsey once more. She saw his mind working, berating himself for underestimating her, for letting her get the drop on him, for losing the upper hand.

"You're not taking Sam anywhere," Kinsey said again, hearing her cold, deliberate words.

"You have no idea what I've been through. And you have no idea what I'll do to keep Sam."

"Look, I—"

"Leave town. Don't come back," she told him. "Don't you ever—"

"Mama?"

The back door opened and Sam walked in.

Jared grabbed the gun from her hand.

A foolish move. It could have gone off, shot him or her, or some innocent bystander. But Jared wasn't familiar with guns. Kinsey had realized that when she'd seen him fumbling with his holster in the hotel room and it suddenly made sense why he hadn't joined in the shooting in front of the Wild Cat Saloon the night he'd kissed her in the alley.

That's how she'd known she could get his gun from him just now.

But she let him have it. She wouldn't struggle for it. Not with Sam in the room.

The boy looked back and forth between the two of them and alarm showed in his face.

"Mama?"

"It's fine, honey. Everything's fine." Kinsey knelt in front of him and pulled him hard against her. Then she glanced up at Jared and put Sam away from her. "Run on outside again, sweetie. Play with the Gleason boys a while longer. Mama will come get you in a bit."

Sam gave her a troubled look, but went outside anyway.

Kinsey rose from her feet and turned to Jared. He had the gun. He had the truth.

And now he'd have Sam.

"Make it easy on the boy," Jared said. "Explain to him what's happening. I'll come by for him in the morning. Have him ready."

Chapter Six

She could run.

The temptation, so deeply ingrained in Kinsey, sprang to her mind the instant Jared had left the kitchen of the boardinghouse. She'd watched from the back porch as he paused for a moment to look at Sam playing with her neighbor's boys, then moved along. She'd fought the urge to rush into the bedroom, pack their things and head out.

Two things stopped her. One: the stage wouldn't be through town for a few more days, the train not until the end of the week. She wouldn't get very far on foot, or even on horseback, should she turn loose of her carefully hoarded money and buy one. Asking someone in town to hide her was unthinkable, given the explanations such a request would require.

Two: Kinsey didn't want to leave town.

Realizing she and Sam were safe until the

following morning when Jared had said he'd return, Kinsey had gone about her chores at the boardinghouse as usual, helping Nell and Lily with supper preparations. Somewhere between peeling the potatoes and serving the apple pie, Kinsey had decided that she didn't want to be forced out of Crystal Springs. She didn't want to be on the run again, searching for a new home, making new friends, always looking over her shoulder. She liked it here. She liked her home, her job, Sam's teacher, his friends, the townsfolk.

Washing up the supper dishes, Kinsey had decided to stay—and keep Sam with her, of course. Now, after tucking him into bed and slipping on her bonnet and wrap, she left the boardinghouse armed with nothing more than a plan.

Yet her plans had kept her and Sam safe for five years, had brought her to this comfortable town, had held the Mason family at bay.

It surprised her a bit that Jared hadn't known who she was or that the private detective hadn't discovered it. Apparently, in Clark's many letters to his family he'd never mentioned her. But why would he? Business, the project he was overseeing, consumed most of his thoughts, as it would any man.

Now she had a plan that would insure that she

kept Sam. A plan, Kinsey believed, that Jared Mason, of all people, would understand.

Jared understood power. She'd seen it in him when she'd been in his hotel room. The way he held her arms, the way he blocked her exit from the room. Then at the boardinghouse, the gleam in his eye when he realized that he'd discovered she wasn't Sam's mother and that he'd gotten his way, that he'd won.

So if power was what Jared Mason understood, then power was what she'd show him.

Sheriff Isaac Vaughn stood on the little porch in front of the jailhouse staring down Main Street toward the Wild Cat Saloon. It was dark now and the streets were nearly deserted.

Isaac turned to her as she approached. In the dim light she saw the gentle shift in his expression, concern, worry that she was on the streets alone.

Isaac was a big man. Tall, solid. Tough, too. He had to be, given his job as sheriff. Yet Kinsey had never experienced that side of him. To her, Isaac was more an older brother. She'd gotten to know him better since Lily had come to work at the boardinghouse.

"Evening, Mrs. Templeton," Isaac said, tipping his hat respectfully.

"Good evening, Sheriff," she answered, standing next to him. "I know it's late for me to be out alone, but something's bothering me that I want to discuss with you."

Isaac shifted. His expression hardened, as if preparing himself for bad news which, as sheriff, he often heard.

"It's about you and Lily," Kinsey said.

He seemed to wither slightly, the weight of the troubles with his wife bearing down on him for so long now it seemed difficult for him to stand up under the burden any longer.

Exactly what had driven Lily from the home she shared with Isaac during their three-year marriage had been speculated about by most everyone in Crystal Springs. Everyone had an opinion—it had been the most talked-about incident in town, until the church burned down. It was common knowledge what the two of them had been through, of course, and, collectively, the town's heart had gone out to them.

Kinsey knew the whole truth, of course. She and Lily had grown close from all the hours they'd spent cooking and cleaning at the boardinghouse, and Lily had confided in her. Kinsey certainly wouldn't betray Lily's confidence by tattling to anyone and adding to the gossip that circulated through town about the couple.

"I told Lily when she came to the boarding-house that I wouldn't take sides between the two of you," Kinsey said. "You'll recall I told you the same."

Cautiously, Isaac nodded.

"I haven't said much, one way or the other, to either of you," Kinsey pointed out. "I've listened to Lily's side of things. Heard her out. Tried to comfort her, tried to be a friend."

"You've been a good friend," he said, "to both of us."

Kinsey drew a breath and straightened her shoulders.

"I think that was a mistake on my part," she told him.

"You do?"

"Yes. The truth is, I never agreed with Lily's leaving you, moving out of your home, taking a job and living in Nell's boardinghouse," Kinsey said, then added softly, "Regardless of the cir-cumstances."

Isaac winced and glanced away.

"I intend to talk to her, try and convince her to meet with you, find a way for you two to put your lives back together and get over…what happened," Kinsey said. "I wanted you to know that, Isaac."

He nodded. "I appreciate that."

"I should have done it sooner," Kinsey admitted.

It was true. She'd never agreed with Lily's decision but had held her tongue, thinking it was better to support her friend. She'd always intended to talk to Lily, make her feelings known.

Only now she had a compelling—no, selfish, she silently admitted—reason to do so.

A long silence stretched between them as Kinsey and the sheriff stood outside the jailhouse. Somewhere a dog barked. A pair of horses plodded down the street and their riders disappeared inside the Wild Cat. Lights burned in the hotel windows down the block and above the stores on Main Street.

Kinsey drew in another breath, summoning her courage.

"That new man in town," she said, trying to sound casual. "That Mr. Mason staying at the hotel?"

Isaac's shoulders straightened and his chest expanded. "Did he do something, Kinsey?"

The sheriff's tone suggested he almost wished Jared had done something. As if Isaac would enjoy nothing more than taking out his pent-up hostility over his wife's desertion on someone— anyone.

"I was just thinking," Kinsey said, fighting the urge to twist her fingers together from the outrageous lie she was about to tell, "that Mr. Mason reminded me of that bank robber from Cold Creek whose picture was on the Wanted poster outside your office about a month ago. Did…did you happen to notice a resemblance?"

Isaac eyed her sharply and one eyebrow went up. "I might have."

"I noticed the poster is gone now," Kinsey said, waving to the spot behind her where the Wanted posters always hung. "I suppose that means the robber was caught. But, well, I was wondering if the sheriff in Cold Creek is certain he got the right man?"

Isaac stroked his chin thoughtfully. "I could send a telegram, find out for sure."

"That would be prudent," Kinsey agreed. "And, I suppose, you might be concerned that, if the robber really is Mr. Mason, that he might… commit another crime."

Isaac nodded again. "Might be better if I got Mason off the streets."

"The townsfolk would surely feel safer that way," Kinsey said. "I know I'd feel safer."

"I could lock him up."

"Just until you found out for sure if he's the robber," Kinsey said. "Say, until Friday? That's the day the train comes through. You could take him to the depot, make sure he leaves town—for the safety of the citizens, of course."

"I could do that," Isaac declared, his tone indicating that he would enjoy it, too.

"But I wouldn't want him to get hurt," Kinsey said quickly. "I know that accidents can happen—anywhere."

"I'll make sure Mason doesn't have any accidents," Isaac promised.

"Good." Kinsey paused.

"And he'll be comfortable."

"Well, not too comfortable."

"I'll take care of the prisoner, don't you worry."

"And I'm going to talk to Lily tonight," Kinsey promised.

They exchanged a look, sealing their unholy bargain. Both of them were desperate. Isaac, to get his wife back, and Kinsey to get Jared Mason out of her life. People pushed into a corner would do anything, and Kinsey and Isaac were no exception, given the high stakes.

Kinsey hurried toward the boardinghouse. She glanced back to see Sheriff Vaughn heading toward the hotel.

For an instant, she almost called him back. What had her life become? What sort of person had she turned into? Arranging to have a man—even Jared Mason—locked up in jail to suit her own needs?

Kinsey's stomach ached with guilt. She didn't regret promising to intervene with Lily on the sheriff's behalf. She truly felt it was the right thing to do. But as for Jared…

The ache in Kinsey's stomach rose to grip her heart. Sam. A helpless little boy who'd already lost both of his parents. The tearful vow she'd made to her step-sister as she lay dying.

The ugly truth about the Mason family.

Kinsey drew in a fresh breath. Four days in jail wouldn't do Jared Mason any real harm. He'd have a roof over his head, three meals a day. He wouldn't be mistreated. He'd be loaded onto the train and sent packing.

And it would get him out of Kinsey's life. For a while. Perhaps forever.

Sam would be safe. Beth's dying wish would

be respected. Kinsey would have the kind of life she'd wanted since she was a child.

Her heart ached again, this time in an old, familiar way. Oh, to think that her dearest dream might one day come true...

Kinsey pushed away the thought. She headed back to the boardinghouse.

A night for celebration. No doubt about it.

Jared reared back in his chair and picked up his beer—his third, so far—from the table in front of him. Around him, the dozen or so other patrons of the Wild Cat Saloon drank at the bar, told stories, or played cards. Everyone in a jovial mood.

And none more so than Jared. He tipped up his beer, thoroughly pleased with himself. His gut glowed with the success he'd pulled off today.

He'd gotten Clark's boy back.

Winning a large contract, edging out the competition for a big job, convincing a supplier to meet the terms Jared dictated, none of his many achievements in the business world even came close to the feeling of accomplishment he felt tonight.

Jared couldn't believe his good luck. After

walking Clark's son home from school, he'd gone into the boardinghouse intending to find Kinsey and talk to her. He'd found something much more important. The family Bible that had revealed the truth of her past.

He'd been stunned. Damn Pinkerton detective had gotten a key element of his search wrong—dead wrong. No information on a stepsister, on a real Kinsey Templeton in his report. No mention of her in Clark's letters to any of the family, either.

But Jared had gotten his way, despite the mistake, and that's all that mattered.

He took another long sip from the foamy beer glass, and once again considered sending a telegram to his family back in New York with the good news that Clark's son had been found. But Jared disregarded the idea. Better to keep the situation to himself, especially here in Crystal Springs. There was plenty of time for sharing the good news after he and the child were on the train home.

And the two of them would be homeward bound tomorrow. Jared's gut ached a little as he sipped his beer. Tomorrow, he'd begin to make up for what he'd done, in memory of Clark.

Bright and early, he intended to pick up the boy and head east in a wagon he'd rent from the livery stable. From Cold Creek, he'd take the stage, then meet up with the train at the closest depot.

He didn't worry that Kinsey would run off with the boy again. Jared had her dead to rights. With no blood claim on the child, and lacking legal authority, there was no way she could justify keeping the boy any longer. Besides, the train and stagecoach were the only way out of Crystal Springs. He couldn't imagine her running off on foot, dragging the boy and her belongings with her. Jared was reasonably sure she didn't have the money to buy a horse and wagon either.

So he was set. A little smile pulled at Jared's lips. He'd be back in New York in plenty of time to get up to Maine, start the new job that awaited him. The project was a big one and Jared was anxious to get it started.

He sipped his beer and sighed contentedly. He'd made this long journey, he'd found what he'd come for and he'd gotten it.

The Masons always got what they went after.

Jared's spirits dimmed a bit as he caught a glimpse of Sheriff Vaughn pushing his way through the bat-wing doors, into the saloon. He stopped, surveyed the crowd, then eyed Jared. He headed toward him.

Jared took another sip of beer. What the hell could the sheriff want now?

Chapter Seven

High noon.

That's when the eastbound train pulled out of Crystal Springs.

Kinsey glanced at the clock atop the train depot. In less than an hour the train would leave, carrying Jared Mason with it. She quickened her steps, anxious to get to the jailhouse and get this over with.

Four days had passed since Kinsey had pulled off her underhanded scheme to keep Jared corralled until he could be run out of town—out of her life. Four days of feeling guilty, then feeling relieved only to feel guilty again.

Four days in jail. She was glad it was over, for herself as much as Jared.

Kinsey ducked into the jailhouse and found Isaac seated at his desk. The room was clean and neat, almost warm and inviting despite the gun racks on the wall and the glimpse of the barred cells down the short hallway to the left. Lily had insisted on making the place where her husband spent so much of his time as pleasant as possible. That's the sort of wife she had been...before.

Isaac got to his feet, his expression hopeful. They hadn't seen each other since earlier in the week. Kinsey knew why he was so glad to see her.

"Lily agreed to see you tonight," she said and set the market basket she carried on the corner of his desk.

The four days and nights Isaac had kept his prisoner locked up had surely been easier than the days and nights Kinsey had spent trying to convince Lily to see her own husband. It was worth it, though. In her heart, Kinsey knew it was the right thing to do.

All her effort paid off when she saw the look of relief and joy on Isaac's face.

"Come by tonight after supper," Kinsey said.

"Do you...do you think she'll come back home?"

"She's so hurt," Kinsey said, feeling the pain in her own heart. "Having your baby die is bad enough, but then..."

Isaac drew in a breath, seeming to fight off the

anger and frustration he'd lived with for so many months now.

"The whole thing makes me so damn mad—oh, sorry," he said.

"I understand." Kinsey touched his arm. "I truly believe the best way to get over this is for the two of you to be together, let your love heal each other."

"That's what I've been trying to tell her for months," Isaac said. "I can make it up to her. I swear, I can."

"Being apart never solved anything. I told Lily that."

"Thank you, Kinsey. I appreciate it."

"So, how's the prisoner?" she asked, nodding toward the hallway where the cells were located.

"Madder than a wet tomcat," Isaac said. "Prisoners usually settle down after a couple of days. Not Mason."

Probably because he wasn't guilty of anything, Kinsey thought.

"I told him this morning he's leaving town on the noon train. He's not happy about it," Isaac said.

"I'd like to speak with him."

Isaac looked surprised. "No need to explain

anything to him. I never told him you were… involved in this."

"I'd still like to speak with him," Kinsey said. "Privately."

The sheriff didn't look pleased but he nodded, then headed down the hallway to the cell. Kinsey heard him tell Jared that he had a visitor, and that he should mind his manners and his mouth.

When Isaac returned to the office he said, "Stay back. Don't get close to the bars. I'll be right here if you need anything."

At the entrance to the hallway, Kinsey paused long enough to remind herself of why she'd been forced into this desperate act. Sam. She'd done it for him.

And that was all the reason she needed.

Jared was on his feet in the middle of the cell when she walked down the hallway. His gaze impaled her with the questions she was sure were speeding through his mind: why was she here; why was he here?

She stopped in front of his cell and he walked to the bars. The four days in jail had taken their toll. His clothes were rumpled and soured, his hair unkempt. A dark, bristly beard covered his jaws. Quite obviously, he hadn't bathed.

A small trade-off for the lifetime of misery

Sam would experience if he went to live with the Mason family.

"What are you doing here?" Jared asked, clearly confused.

Kinsey looked him up and down and managed an expression of disdain, then raised a haughty eyebrow.

"I wanted to come by and see a member of the *powerful* Mason family," she told him, throwing his own words back at him.

Jared's brows pulled together and he looked harder at her.

Kinsey gestured to the empty cells on either side of his.

"But I don't see any of the Masons' *important political connections*," she exclaimed with mock surprise. "Or your *impressive social circle*. Why, where could they be? Oh, I know. They're in New York. And this is *Crystal Springs*."

Jared's eyes widened. His nostrils flared. He drew his shoulders up and his chest expanded.

He'd figured it out. He *knew*. Just as she'd wanted him to.

"*You*." Jared gripped the cell bars and fury rolled off him in waves. "*You* put me in here. It was *you!*"

He rattled the bars as if he really expected

he could tear them from the floor and ceiling, maybe even bite through them with his teeth.

His ire washed over Kinsey like a great river. But she wasn't frightened. Instead, she wanted to rush to him, tear down the bars, throw herself into his arms.

What was wrong with her?

Kinsey centered her thoughts on Sam, where they belonged.

"Yes, I'm the one behind your incarceration," Kinsey told him. "You pushed me. I pushed back. I told you I'd do anything to keep Sam safe."

"So he can live in this one-horse town?" Jared demanded.

"It's better than the life he'd have living with your mother," Kinsey told him, an old anger making her words come out more forcefully than she'd intended.

His eyes narrowed. "What the hell do you know about my mother?"

Kinsey had learned everything she needed to know about Amelia Mason one afternoon in a Richmond hotel. But she didn't intend to discuss the woman with Jared. Amelia was, after all, his mother. If he didn't know the truth, Kinsey wasn't going to be the one to tell him.

"You have no right to criticize the life I've

given Sam," Kinsey insisted. "You don't know anything about me, about us, or about Crystal Springs. You never bothered to find out. All you want to do is take him away when you don't have any idea what you're taking him away *from*."

"I know you've got no right to the boy," Jared said.

"You're leaving," Kinsey told him, refusing to reply to his accusation. "The sheriff is escorting you to the noon train and you're heading back east. Don't bother to double back because you'll just end up in jail again. And don't waste your money on another Pinkerton detective. I read his report. I learned how to hide, how to avoid discovery. It was very helpful. Thank you so much."

Jared glared at her. "You're wrong if you think I'm just going to turn tail and run, and leave Clark's son here."

"And you're wrong if you think I'll ever let you take Sam away from me."

Kinsey gave him one last look, then walked away. In the office she picked up her basket and left the jail house. She went to the school and took Sam out of class. He didn't expect to see her in the middle of the day but went happily with her when she told him about the "surprise" she'd planned.

A picnic by the creek, oatmeal cookies she'd baked fresh that morning, hours of wading in the water and sailing the tiny wooden ship she'd bought for him at the MacAvoy General Store.

No mention of them hiding in the secluded spot. No indication of Kinsey's fear that, despite Isaac's assurances, Jared might somehow get away and come looking for Sam. No word about the noon train carrying Sam's uncle eastward.

And no more errant thoughts of the man who'd kissed her so well that she'd raised on her toes and leaned her head back so he could angle closer.

Jared Mason was leaving town and that suited Kinsey fine.

Didn't it?

Nothing like four days in a jail cell to give a man time to think.

Jared paced the small cell, angry, frustrated and anxious for the sheriff to come unlock the door and let him out of this hellhole.

Four days without any sort of physical activity or mental exercise had nearly driven him crazy. No books or technical journals to read. No paper or pencil to sketch with. Nothing to do but think.

And all he'd been able to think about was Kinsey Templeton.

Jared swore and paced the cell, cursing her scent that still lingered in the air.

He'd spent much of the past four days frantic that Kinsey would leave town with the boy. The jail cell had a tiny slit that passed for a window but Jared was tall enough to look out. With the limited view, he could see down the alley beside the jail to Main Street and catch a glimpse of the stage depot. He'd watched, afraid he'd see Kinsey and little Sam hurry past, burdened with all their belongings, intending to board the stage.

That hadn't happened. Instead, Kinsey had been in Crystal Springs the whole time. At home. Content. Going about her life.

The sheriff had never told Jared why he'd been arrested. Now, the reason was painfully obvious.

Kinsey had arranged the whole thing.

She'd bested him. He had to admit it. She'd pulled off what some of the sharpest business minds on the east coast had never been able to do. She'd gotten the upper hand. She'd gotten her way. She'd won out.

And he should have been mad. He should have hated her.

But instead, he *wanted* her.

Jared swore again. God help him, when Kinsey had appeared outside his cell, gloating about what she'd done to him, all the while looking fresh and clean like a welcome breath of pure spring air, he'd wanted her. Right there and then. If he could have gotten to her, God knows what he might have done.

Amid the turmoil of Jared's thoughts these past few days, the only relief he'd known was the knowledge that Kinsey hadn't been married to his brother, that she wasn't even blood kin.

At least he didn't feel guilty anymore for kissing her.

Now he needed a new plan. Jared drew in a breath, reaching deep to ignore his anger—and the hum of desire Kinsey left him with.

Yes, she'd gotten the best of him. She'd had him thrown in jail and nearly run out of town. Jared didn't intend to give up. Not with Clark's son at stake. Yet he didn't have much time, not with that job in Maine hanging over his head.

Sheriff Vaughn ambled down the hallway, jail keys rattling in his hand.

"Time to go," he said, and unlocked the door.

Jared wanted to bolt from the cell but wouldn't give the sheriff the satisfaction.

"So what did she give you," Jared asked, "in exchange for locking me up?"

"Something you'd never understand," he replied.

"I'd understand," Jared told him.

Sheriff Vaughn's eyes narrowed as he realized what Jared was getting at. "Shut your filthy mouth."

Jared decided to do just that since he didn't want to spend any more time in jail. And he doubted Kinsey would trade her favors for the things she wanted. She didn't need to. She had brains and guts instead.

Jared walked ahead of the sheriff into the office and saw his valise and satchel sitting atop the desk. Jared figured the hotel had sent them over after his arrest in the Wild Cat Saloon.

"I guess you're going to tell me that I owe you some sort of fine," Jared said, figuring the small-town justice would exact something more than his four days in jail.

Sheriff Vaughn nodded toward the valise. "I already collected it."

So the sheriff had gone through his belongings. He should have known.

"I need to settle up with the hotel," Jared said.

"I took care of that, too, including a hefty tip."

Sheriff Vaughn picked up the rifle and gestured with it. "Get moving."

The door opened and a man walked in. Tall, blond, well dressed, close to thirty years old. Jared hadn't met him before, but what he did recognize was his own technical journals in the man's hand.

"Thanks, Sheriff," he said, and handed over the journals.

Sheriff Vaughn had the good grace to look embarrassed as he passed them along to Jared.

"Those are yours?" the man asked. "I appreciate your letting me read them. We don't get too many journals like those out here. I was a surveyor and engineer in the army."

The man extended his hand. "Caleb Burk."

Jared introduced himself and shook hands. Surely Caleb knew he was a prisoner, but didn't mention it.

"Maybe we can get together and talk sometime," Caleb suggested.

"Mason's leaving town," Isaac said. "Today."

"That's too bad," Caleb said, and sounded as if he meant it. He turned to the sheriff again. "I heard over at MacAvoy's that your wife agreed to talk to you tonight."

Sheriff Vaughn's cheeks flushed. "Damn town gossip."

Caleb nodded his understanding. "I just wanted to tell you that I hope it goes all right. You should take her something."

"Like what?"

Jared spoke up. "Flowers."

Sheriff Vaughn frowned at him. "Why the hell should I take advice about women from you, Mason? The only woman you know in town had you locked up."

"Flowers are a good idea," Caleb agreed.

"And *you're* inventing excuses to see the woman you're sweet on," the sheriff told Caleb.

Caleb bristled. "If it weren't for that crazy aunt of hers I could court her proper."

"Look, Sheriff, it doesn't take a magnifying glass to see that you're having problems with your wife," Jared said. "Take her some flowers. Don't pick them on the way over, get her some nice ones ahead of time. Go by the general store and get ribbon tied around them."

"You should listen to him," Caleb advised.

"And you should tell Miss Patterson to butt

out of your business," Isaac told him, "and court Miss Sarah like a man."

"If I do that, well hell, the town will never get a new church. You know how Miss Patterson is," Caleb told him. "Anyway, good luck tonight with Lily."

Caleb disappeared out the door, leaving, to Jared's way of thinking, the sheriff in an even worse mood, which would not help his cause. He pressed on anyway.

"Look, sheriff, if you went through my valise you saw the Pinkerton report. You know I've got family trouble of my own."

The Sheriff didn't answer so Jared kept talking.

"Just hear me out, Sheriff," he said. "That's all I'm asking."

Spending the afternoon with Sam at the creek had cleared Kinsey's mind of most every problem. Sam had that effect on her. And it was a relief, given what she'd been through this week.

Somehow, Sam still had the energy to play with the Gleason boys, so as they approached the boardinghouse Kinsey let him join the brothers in their yard. When she walked through the back door into the kitchen, Nell and Lily were both there, starting the supper preparations.

"One more eating with us tonight," Nell announced with a smile. "I got a new boarder today."

"That's good," Kinsey said as she hung her bonnet and handbag on the peg beside the door. Nell could use the money and another guest insured Kinsey could keep her job.

"He looks like a big eater," Nell cautioned. "From the size of him—oh, there he is. Come on in."

Kinsey glanced at the dining room as Jared walked in. Her mouth sagged open.

"Evening, ladies," he greeted them, then ambled across the room to Kinsey.

"Mr. Mason said you recommended the place," Nell said, still smiling.

"M-me? I never—"

"Sure you did," Jared said. "I believe your words were something to the effect that I didn't know enough about Crystal Springs, about the townsfolk and what it's like to live in a place like this."

The words she'd said to him through the jail-cell bars came back to her with frightening clarity.

Jared smiled broadly. "So here I am."

Chapter Eight

Kinsey had been jumpy and fretful all through supper preparations but, thankfully, Lily hadn't noticed. Her thoughts had been taken with Isaac's visit expected later in the evening. Kinsey caught herself watching the kitchen door that led to the dining room, wondering when Jared would walk through again. She'd run herself ragged darting to the window over and over, concerned that he'd appear outside with Sam and the Gleason boys playing in the yard.

When they'd finally gotten supper on the table, Jared still hadn't appeared. Kinsey couldn't imagine where he was. Though the food at the jail wasn't horrible, it was no feast either. He should have been hungry and Nell's boarding-house was known for its delicious meals.

Then, as was their custom, Kinsey called Sam

in from outside and they, along with Nell and Lily, sat down at the kitchen table to eat.

"I want to share some information about our new boarder," Nell said in a low voice as they ate.

Kinsey froze. Had Jared told Nell—and everyone else in town—the truth about why he'd been thrown into jail?

That Kinsey had arranged it? Had he given a reason, one that could get her run out of town?

Nell glanced around, then leaned in a little. Lily leaned in, too. Kinsey held her breath.

"Mr. Mason told me that he'd been in jail," Nell said.

"Jail?" Lily asked.

"Jail?" Kinsey echoed, hoping she mimicked Lily's startled tone.

"It was a mistake," Nell declared. "Mr. Mason said he'd been mistaken for some bank robber over in Cold Creek. But the sheriff realized it wasn't Mr. Mason so he let him go. He said I could check with the sheriff, if I wanted."

"Are you going to?" Kinsey asked, trying not to sound anxious.

"I might mention it next time I see Sheriff Vaughn,"
Nell said.

"But Mr. Mason seems like such a nice man, don't you think? Mannerly and responsible, too. He paid me in cash—for one whole month's room and board."

"A month!"

Nell and Lily jumped in their chairs. Even Sam's eyes widened.

Kinsey forced herself to calm down. "What I meant was, that's a lot of money."

"Oh, well yes, it certainly is," Nell agreed. "So, I just wanted you two to know the truth about Mr. Mason's little run-in with the law."

"You don't think there's cause for concern?" Kinsey asked, hoping she didn't sound too eager for Nell to agree with her.

"Oh, no," Nell said. "It seems to me that if Mr. Mason were guilty of something he'd try to keep it secret instead of making a point to tell me. Or he would have headed out of town, first chance."

"Makes sense," Lily agreed.

"Anyway," Nell said. "I just wanted you two to know in case you heard it in town. You know how everyone loves to gossip."

"Delicious roast," Kinsey said, deliberately changing the subject. If the conversation continued much longer about Jared Mason, she wouldn't be able to swallow another bite.

Then, as if their words had summoned him, the back door opened and Jared walked inside.

"Evening, ladies," he called, hanging his hat on the peg beside the door, just as if he owned the place. "Supper smells good."

"Go on into the dining room," Nell said.

"That's not necessary." Jared smiled down at the ladies. "I'll eat in here."

"No," Kinsey declared.

Nell, Lily and Sam all looked at her, startled by her harsh comment.

She gulped. "What I mean is, Mr. Mason is a guest and he should eat in the comfort of the dining room."

Jared's smile turned warm, almost charming. "I had a look at the guests in the dining room. I like the scenery in here better."

Nell tittered and sprang to her feet gathering a plate, coffee cup, napkin and silverware for Jared. He took the chair next to Sam.

"I guess we men ought to stick together, huh, partner?" Jared said.

Sam gave him a shy smile.

Jared looked relaxed at the supper table as he

made easy conversation with Nell. Lily, preoccupied by the impending arrival of her husband later, said little.

It was all Kinsey could do to sit still and hold her tongue. Yet she didn't dare say anything in front of Nell or Lily, and certainly not Sam. It galled her to realize that Jared knew it, too.

After supper, when she'd finished washing the dishes and Lily was busy drying, Kinsey slipped out onto the back porch and spotted Jared in the twilight standing in the yard, leaning his head back to look at the upper floors of the boardinghouse. He had the nerve to smile when she strode over, which made her even madder.

"I never told you to stay in Crystal Springs," Kinsey hissed through clenched teeth, "and you *know* it."

"Maybe I was a little confused," Jared told her, then leaned down a little. "I'd been *locked up* for four days."

Kinsey winced and looked away. "Yes, well, you weren't really hurt, or anything."

In fact, he looked more handsome than ever, she noted, though it irritated her to realize the thought had come to mind. He'd bathed, shaved, gotten a haircut and dressed in fresh clothes when she'd seen him walk into the kitchen of the boardinghouse. Now, the fading sunlight and the purple twilight only enhanced his good looks.

And sent an annoying flutter through her stomach.

"Stay away from Sam," she told him.

"Like hell…"

"I don't want you near him," she insisted.

"I've got more right to the boy than you do," Jared reminded her.

"No, you don't. I—"

Kinsey stopped as she saw Sheriff Vaughn headed through the yard toward them, flowers crushed in his fist and a ribbon trailing in the breeze.

"Evening, Mrs. Templeton," he said, touching the brim of his hat.

Isaac looked uncomfortable and Kinsey didn't know if it was because he would talk to Lily tonight, or because he'd let Kinsey down. Maybe a little of both.

Jared, it seemed, had had enough of Isaac's company at the jail these past four days because he mumbled something then went inside the boardinghouse leaving Kinsey and the sheriff alone in the yard.

"I expect you're mad at me for going back on our…arrangement," Isaac said.

"No, of course not," Kinsey said. The guilt she'd suffered these past four days still had a firm hold on her. "I was wrong to ask you to do that. I never should have suggested it, never should have involved you."

"It's all right," Isaac said. "I understand."

Kinsey wondered just how much Isaac actually knew. Had Jared told him the whole story? Is that how he'd talked Isaac into letting him go free?

"Mason told me what happened," Isaac said. "About his brother and little Sam."

Kinsey's worst nightmare twisted inside her.

"You did what you thought was right," Isaac said. "I did the same. And it wasn't right to run Mason out of town. I know you two can work out something."

Impossible, Kinsey thought. But she didn't say so. Not given Isaac's purpose in coming here tonight.

"What I said about you and Lily is true," she told him. "I think you two should be together. I won't give up trying to help."

"I know. You're a goodhearted woman. You wouldn't go back on your word," Isaac said gently. Then his gaze shifted to the boarding-house and he drew himself up, pulling in a big breath. "Well, I guess I'd better get in there."

"Let me get Lily for you," Kinsey offered. "It would be better if you two spoke out here, privately."

Isaac looked relieved as Kinsey went inside. She found Lily in the kitchen putting away the last of the supper dishes. Sam sat at the table leafing through a picture book, and Jared stood in the corner eating another piece of the apple pie Nell had served for supper.

"Isaac's here," Kinsey said softly.

Lily glanced at the door, twisting her hands together. Tears sprang to her eyes but she blinked them back.

"Kinsey, I don't know what good this will do," she said, her voice heavy with emotion. "I've said everything I can say to him."

"Then let him do the talking," Kinsey said. "He loves you so much, Lily, and I know you still love him."

"That's not the problem," she insisted.

"I know. But you two being apart isn't helping anything either."

Lily glanced away, then nodded, acknowledging that Kinsey was right. She hesitated another moment, then went outside.

Kinsey's heart ached for the two of them.

"Mama? Read me a story tonight?" Sam asked, holding up the book.

Kinsey's spirits lifted. "Of course, Sam. Run along and get ready for bed. I'll be there in a few minutes."

Sam wiggled out of the chair, taking his book with him.

"'Night, Uncle Jared," he called.

Jared looked as surprised as Kinsey felt.

"Good night," Jared answered as the boy hurried away.

The kitchen was silent except for the scrape of Jared's fork against the plate as he finished up the slice of pie.

"So what's going on with the sheriff and his wife?" he asked, putting the plate aside.

Everyone in Crystal Springs knew what had happened, so telling Jared wasn't a breach of confidence.

"I didn't live here at the time, but everyone says it was love at first sight between the two of them," Kinsey explained. "They got married, had a baby, and the baby died."

"Damn…" Jared shook his head.

"Then they had another baby, and that one died, too."

Kinsey pressed her lips together holding back the pain that always accompanied the telling—or even the remembering—of the story. "Both of the babies lived for a few days. Everyone thought the first one, a little boy, had been just a tragedy, one of those awful things that happens sometimes."

"But when it happened again?"

Kinsey closed her eyes for a moment. "The little girl died in Lily's arms. Lily was completely devastated. Absolutely inconsolable. Isaac, too, of course. But Lily…well, it changed her."

"It made her leave her husband?" Jared asked.

"When the first baby died, it brought them together. But after the second one, well, Lily simply couldn't bear it and Isaac didn't know what to do—nobody did, really. She thought she'd done something wrong, that it was her fault somehow. She thought God was punishing her. That she wasn't a good enough woman or wife. That Isaac deserved someone who could give him children. That she couldn't—"

Kinsey stopped, embarrassed at discussing such an intimate detail of her friend's life.

Jared finished the thought for her. "She can't

bear the thought of losing another baby so she doesn't want to have a…a true marriage with Isaac, fearing she'll get pregnant again."

Relieved, she nodded. "Lily thinks that's not fair to Isaac, and he insists he wants her as his wife, no matter what."

"But she doesn't believe him."

"Exactly."

"And he won't give up on her."

"That's right."

"Damn…" Jared pushed his fingers through his hair. "What a mess."

"Yes. Yes, it is," Kinsey said, then remembered that she had a mess of her own to deal with—and he was standing right in front of her.

She had something he wanted dearly: Sam. But Jared held something very dear to her in the palm of his hand: her future.

Kinsey trusted Isaac Vaughn to keep the truth of her past to himself. She wasn't Sam's mother. She wasn't who she claimed to be. She'd lied to the townsfolk of Crystal Springs since the day she'd arrived.

Isaac had learned it from Jared. She guessed Jared had told the sheriff just enough to keep from getting run out of town.

But who else might Jared tell? What other occasion might present itself that would cause him to spread the truth about her to everyone in town.

Kinsey cringed at the thought. She liked living here. She fit in. She belonged. And she'd felt that way so few times in her life. She didn't know how she'd bear it if the town turned against her.

"You don't really intend to stay here a whole month, do you?" Kinsey asked.

"My offer stands," Jared told her. "The boy comes home with me. You can come, too. I'll find you work, schooling, a place to live—whatever you want."

"I don't want anything from you, except to leave Sam and me alone."

"Then I'm staying here," Jared said, "for as long as it takes for you to convince me the boy is better off living with you."

Jared waited, as if he expected her to declare defeat and start packing Sam's things. When she didn't, he walked past her toward her bedroom in the rear of the boardinghouse.

Kinsey ducked around him, blocking his path. "I told you to stay away from Sam. Where do you think you're going?"

Jared gestured to his left and the staircase that led upstairs.

"Just heading up to my room," he said.

"You took the back room?" she asked, stunned. The room at the rear of the house—the room directly above hers—was the worst one in the place. Others were available, she knew that for a fact. She couldn't imagine why Jared, with all his Mason wealth and privilege, would want it.

"I like the location," Jared said. "Gives me a nice view of the backyard and the side yard all the way to the street. I can keep an eye on things."

An eye on her and Sam, Kinsey realized, so he'd know when they were coming or going. Or if she tried to leave—permanently.

Jared must have read the anger, the outrage, in her expression because he touched his finger to her chin and turned her face up to him.

"Wishing now you could have me thrown back in jail?" he asked softly.

His words were playful, almost a gentle dare. Warmth from his fingers spread through her, reminding her of the times he'd touched her... the times he'd kissed her.

The times she'd let him.

Kinsey pulled away, needing the distance to cool her thoughts.

"I wish I could sell you to the gypsies," she said,

"or trade you to the Indians, but none of them would want you around any more than I do."

Jared smiled and warmth flared anew inside Kinsey. He seemed to feel it, too, and for an instant, she was sure he leaned toward her.

But he pulled away and said, "I can be gone, out of your life tomorrow. It's up to you."

He gave her a nod, then headed up the staircase.

Kinsey watched him go, his long legs easily making the climb, his big shoulders nearly bumping the sides of the narrow passageway. Some part of her ached to follow him up the stairs. Make him listen. Make him leave.

Let him kiss her.

"Mama?"

Kinsey gasped and whirled. Sam stood in their bedroom doorway in his nightshirt, holding a picture book.

"Read to me now?" he asked.

She headed into the bedroom, but stopped and glanced back at the staircase. Jared's scent lingered in the hallway and her skin still tingled, for some reason.

Another thought came to her.

She'd tried everything to get him to leave town. She'd reasoned with him, threatened him, pulled a gun on him, had him thrown in jail. None of those things had worked.

Maybe she should try telling him the truth.

Or as much of the truth as she dared.

Chapter Nine

From the back window of his cramped bedroom, Jared stared out at the darkness. Tonight's thin slice of moon left much of the land in deep shadows. He made out trees, outbuildings, hills, but was left to imagine the vast expanse that stretched to the mountains westward and beyond.

The corner room—his new home—held little appeal, especially in the dim glow of the lantern across the room. A bed that looked uncomfortable, minimal furniture. The room's sole welcome features were the windows on two of the walls that, as he'd told Kinsey, let him look out at the back and side yards, the neighbor's house, all the way to the street.

And Jared planned to keep an eye on it all—that and much more.

He hadn't intended to spend so much time here in Crystal Springs. The job in Maine was waiting. It was complex. Money had already been spent. Preliminary work was underway.

When he'd planned the trip here the last thing he'd imagined was that the woman who, at the time, he'd thought was Clark's wife, wouldn't come with him to New York, bringing Clark's son with her, or wouldn't be willing to let the boy go.

Jared felt a little smile pull at his lips when he recalled the look on Kinsey's face earlier this evening. When she realized he was still in town. When she heard that he intended to stay for a month.

Fear, yes. Outrage, certainly. But something more. A challenge. As if he'd thrown down a gauntlet and she was determined to pick it up and turn things to her own advantage.

As she'd already done, more than once.

Jared braced his arm against the windowsill, feeling the cool breeze wafting in through the open window, watching the rectangle of light on the grass below him.

Kinsey's voice drifted out of her open window just below him, accompanied by a rhythmic squeaking noise. He couldn't hear her words but she talked steadily.

Who was with her? he wondered. Had Lily

come to discuss her visit with the sheriff? If so, Lily wasn't getting much of an opportunity to say anything. He wondered if the squeaking was getting on her nerves, as it was his.

A month in this place. Jared fumed at the thought. No way in hell could he stay here that long. He expected to be on his way back east long before the month was up. He'd set the time frame mostly to fret Kinsey, make her realize he was just as determined as she to get what he wanted.

He couldn't afford to be generous with his time, with the big job waiting and the Mason reputation at stake. His father and brothers had agreed to cover Jared's responsibilities while he made this trip. He was anxious to get back. Back to his work, back to his routine.

But he was in control of the situation now here in Crystal Springs. Ensconced in the boarding-house, he could keep an eye on Kinsey, watch her every move. And there was nothing Kinsey could do about it without incriminating herself and making the town aware of exactly who she was and what she'd done.

Outside, Kinsey's voice and the squeaking noise continued, winding through him, lulling him into thoughts of the past.

Clark. His younger brother. His closest brother. They'd drifted apart in the years before his death, their work taking them in different directions, letters their only communication.

At that moment, Jared realized he should have known immediately that Kinsey wasn't Clark's wife, as the Pinkerton detective had indicated in his report. As he realized earlier on, Clark would never have chosen a woman like Kinsey for his wife. Clark would have picked a gentlewoman. Quiet, soft-spoken. Delicate.

None of those words described Kinsey Templeton.

A wave of profound grief swept over Jared. Clark, married. Someone special in his life. Jared's heart still ached at the memory of the loss, and his role in it.

Jared had no delusions about finding such a woman among their social circle. In recent months he'd caught himself eyeing the women around him a little more sharply, imagining himself wed to one of them. All the visions had turned out the same: meals across the supper table from a well-bred, quiet woman, straining for conversation about the weather, invitations received, appointments to be kept.

Jared still hadn't quite reconciled himself to his

inevitable destiny but knew he had little choice. Eventually he'd have to find a wife, and he'd have to settle for a women he could tolerate, one he could live with.

Like staying here in Crystal Springs. He could live with that. Because no matter what, he wasn't going back to New York without the boy.

He didn't intend to chase Kinsey all over the country or rely on another Pinkerton detective. She was here, right in front of him. This was his best chance of getting the boy back.

Kinsey had proved a formidable opponent. He wouldn't misjudge her again. He'd have to deal with her but on his own terms.

If he stayed here at the boardinghouse long enough, he knew he could make Kinsey see that Sam belonged in New York with all the privileges enjoyed by the Mason family. Only a fool wouldn't see it—and Kinsey was certainly no fool. She'd realize that she was being selfish, thinking only of herself. That moving back to New York was best for Sam.

Kinsey's voice stopped and so did the squeaking, the silence intruding on Jared's thoughts. A few seconds later, the lantern light cast through her window disappeared.

Silence and darkness.

She'd been reading aloud. The realization startled Jared. He'd heard only Kinsey's voice because she'd been reading to Sam. The squeaking was the rocking chair he'd seen in the corner of her room.

An odd tremor rumbled through Jared as the mental picture flashed in his mind. The boy on Kinsey's lap, his head against her shoulder, her arms around him, holding him close as she read. The special moments shared by just the two of them, binding them together.

Regardless of anything else he'd thought, Jared never doubted Kinsey had been a good mother to Clark's son.

Then his imagination raced on, in an entirely different direction. Lantern extinguished, prayers said, Sam tucked into bed and Kinsey behind the dressing screen.

Jared caught himself looking down at the floor beneath his feet, as if he might see through the wooden boards to her room directly below him. Slipping off her dress, her petticoats, her stockings, her corset, chemise and pantalettes. Layer after layer, gone. Her smooth skin catching the moonlight through the window. Curves, swells. Womanly secrets. Womanly places...

He heard his own breath quicken as his body

drew tight, taut with desire. His skin warmed, coming alive with need.

Too long without a woman—any woman—Jared told himself. Kinsey was pretty. That's why his reaction to even the thought of her came so strong, wasn't it?

Then he remembered how he'd kissed her, the taste of her, the scent of her. The image of her when she'd sneaked into his hotel room bloomed in his head. Kinsey on the bed. Him above her. Their bodies melding together. A perfect fit. The heat that had sprung up between them. The blush on her cheeks and the flash of wanting he'd seen in her eyes.

Or had he just imagined it?

Jared cursed and headed for the door. Maybe he had imagined those things in Kinsey, but he sure as hell wasn't imagining the ache he felt right now. He needed some air. He needed to walk off some of his pent-up energy. He needed to chase thoughts of Kinsey from his mind.

Jared jerked open his door. Kinsey stood in the hallway.

It seemed to Kinsey that Jared looked as startled to see her standing there as she was to find herself there. Late. Dark. People—decent people—had retired to the privacy of their rooms hours ago, and here she was lingering in the hallway in front of the door of a boarder, a handsome boarder, at that.

If Nell found out, she'd fire her for sure.

"We have to talk," Kinsey said, keeping her voice low.

"Did you decide to take me up on my offer?" he asked.

"Shh." Kinsey waved her hands, as if that might quiet his words. "Come downstairs."

"Right now?"

Kinsey glanced up and down the hallway. Nell and Lily's rooms were on the third floor and the other boarders were situated on the front of the house, but that didn't mean they might not be up during the night and catch sight of Kinsey with Jared.

"Would you just come downstairs with me?" she repeated, a little annoyed.

Despite how she'd bragged to him at the jail, Kinsey knew that Jared or another Pinkerton detective could track her down again. Right here, right now was her best chance of convincing him to leave her and Sam alone. And the best way to do that, it seemed, was to simply tell Jared everything.

Well, almost everything.

If only he'd cooperate.

"I've decided to tell you the truth…about your brother and my stepsister."

Even in the darkness, she saw Jared's expression cloud.

"What are you talking about?"

"The reason I ended up with Sam," she said. "What happened to Clark and—"

"Get in here."

Jared reached for her but Kinsey drew back and eyed him sharply, almost daring him to touch her. He fumed a moment, then gestured inside the room.

"Would you come inside?" he asked, none too sweetly. When she still didn't move he added, "Please?"

Kinsey stepped into the room and he closed the door with a thud. She cringed, afraid everyone in the boardinghouse had heard the noise. Good gracious, why did being with Jared always land her in a compromising position?

"Spit it out," he told her, his words coming out harsh enough to stir her anger.

But Kinsey took a breath and calmed herself. Actually, she was glad that she had the chance to explain everything that had happened, the reasons for the things she'd done. Yet she intended to get a few things straight first.

"Did you tell anyone that I'm not Sam's mother?" she asked.

Impatient, Jared waved away the question. "I want to know about my brother."

"Then answer me."

"I didn't tell anyone," he said, though it was clear he didn't want to take the time to say so.

"What about Sheriff Vaughn?" she asked, certain now she'd caught him in a lie.

"He went through my belongings, read the Pinkerton report," Jared said. "Look, I'm just as anxious as you to keep this quiet, between you and me."

"So you don't intend to tell the whole town Sam's not really my son?" Kinsey asked.

"No."

"Or that I had you locked up in jail on false charges?" she wanted to know. Her sins were mounting and, in the town's eyes, Jared would seem the injured party.

He drew in a breath, reining in his impatience. "I'm not all that anxious to let it become known that a little slip of a thing like you managed to get me thrown in jail. So what do you know about Clark?"

She hadn't expected Jared to be so anxious to hear about his brother. Maybe the two of them had been closer than she realized. She felt bad that she hadn't made the offer sooner. No one knew better than Kinsey the importance of family.

"Beth and I lived in Virginia. Clark came to Lynchburg to work," Kinsey said.

"He was building a factory and warehouses," Jared said.

"Beth and I were at the hardware store." Kinsey didn't mention that she and her stepsister both worked there, or that they shared a tiny room in the run-down boardinghouse next door. "Clark came in and ordered materials for the buildings. That's how the three of us met. He was taken with Beth right away, and she with him, of course."

A fine gentleman, Clark Mason had been. Well-dressed, handsome, obviously a man of position. And far beyond the hopes of two simple farm girls like Kinsey and her stepsister.

"Clark asked if he could call on Beth, if he could take her out to supper but she refused, at first," Kinsey said, her heart aching at the memory of Beth crying at the hopelessness of the situation. Nothing decent to wear, shoes worn thin, mended stockings. Simply not being *good enough* for the likes of Clark Mason.

"But Clark convinced her," Jared said. Not a question, but a statement. He knew his brother well.

Kinsey smiled at the rare courage Beth had displayed the afternoon Clark had asked her out once more and she'd told him the truth of her circumstances. She and Kinsey on their own in the city, orphaned, the few relatives still alive left behind on the patch of dirt that passed for a farm. Beth working two jobs and Kinsey three to eat and keep a roof over their heads, both determined to make something of themselves, though not really knowing how.

"Your brother was a genuinely kind and caring man," Kinsey said. "Completely and totally in love with Beth. Unconcerned about anything but their feelings for each other. They married after only two months."

"Clark wrote to the family, after it was done," Jared said. "He sounded happy."

"I wish you could have seen them together," Kinsey said, her words carrying the wistful bliss she remembered from that time. "Clark bought a lovely home for them. He insisted that I live there, too. He knew how close Beth and I were. He was kind and generous."

The home had been more than lovely, it had been grand, on the best street in town. The finest home Beth or Kinsey had ever been in, let alone lived in. Clark had let Beth furnish the house any way she chose, insisting that she buy freely and only the best. She and Kinsey had devoted hours to the task, treasuring every minute.

"I used to hear them sometimes," Kinsey said softly. "Laughing together at something private, something secret, that only the two of them knew or understood. It was as if, at times, they could read each other's thoughts. They were devoted to one another."

"So if your stepsister was so much in love with Clark, why didn't she come home with him after he was killed? Meet the family?" Jared asked. "No one ever met her but my mother."

"Yes, your mother. Amelia." Kinsey's fond recollections of Beth and Clark vanished, replaced by a haunting, ugly memory. For a moment, she considered telling Jared the whole truth, not just a portion of it. But, again, she couldn't bring herself to do it.

"The accident at the construction site that killed Clark might as well have killed Beth, too,"

Kinsey said. "She was distraught, completely overwhelmed by grief."

"That's it?" Jared demanded. "That's the reason she shipped my brother home in a pine box, like he was nothing?"

"It was wrong of her to do that," Kinsey said, and she'd told Beth as much at the time. But there were other things for Beth to worry about, namely the birth of the child she was carrying, and keeping the baby away from the Masons. After what had happened with Amelia, Kinsey didn't really blame her.

Jared seemed somewhat placated that Kinsey agreed with him, then asked, "So why did she run away? Why did she keep the baby a secret?"

Because she knew that the Masons would take the child from her, just as they were now trying to take him from Kinsey.

"She was afraid," Kinsey said.

"Of what?" Jared demanded.

"Everything."

The simple answer didn't suit Jared. She could tell by his deepening frown. But it was all Kinsey intended to explain. Beth had been afraid right from the first moment she'd met Clark. Afraid she wouldn't be good enough, afraid he'd see that one day, afraid he'd leave her. Then she'd been afraid for her unborn child. Kinsey didn't blame her for any of it.

"That's what I want to explain," she said, drawing in a breath and finally getting down to the real reason she'd come to Jared tonight. "After Beth and I left Lynchburg we traveled south, finally staying in South Carolina. We had distant relatives in Charleston and they let us live with them for a while, until Sam was born. You know the details, of course, from the Pinkerton report."

"Beth died shortly after Sam was born," Jared said.

Kinsey nodded, forcing back the flood of emotion that accompanied the memory. Beth's joy at seeing Sam, well and healthy, before being overtaken by the fever that finally claimed her life.

"She begged me to take care of Sam," Kinsey said. "Beth knew she was dying and she couldn't bear the thought of her child being turned over to the Mason family, to strangers. I swore to her I wouldn't let that happen, that I would take care of Sam."

"Did you swear that you'd pass yourself off as his mother?" Jared asked.

His words stung, but Kinsey knew she deserved them—to Jared's way of thinking, anyway.

"It didn't start out that way," she told him. "We traveled from town to town, trying to find a place that seemed like home, and people just assumed that I was a widow and that Sam was my child. I let them believe it."

"And it was a good way to hide."

Kinsey supposed she deserved that harsh criticism, too, because it was true.

"Look, all I want you to understand is that I took Sam because his mother wanted me to," Kinsey said. "Beth and I were as close as sisters. Her family took me in when my parents died, gave me their name when I was nine years old. I would have done anything for Beth."

"So why are you telling me this now? Do you think this will make me throw my hands up and walk away? Forget that boy is my brother's son?"

"I have Sam with his mother's blessing. I love him. That's more than you can say," Kinsey told him.

"I don't have to say anything," Jared replied. "The boy is family. A blood relative. He belongs with us."

"He belongs with me," Kinsey told him, her

anger rising. "You'll see for yourself, now that you're here."

"You're damn right I'll be watching what goes on."

He sounded smug and arrogant. Fear filtered through Kinsey's growing anger.

"Good," she told him. "You're living here now. You can keep watch on everything Sam and I do."

"I sure as hell will."

"I just hope you can manage it without sleeping."

Jared's brows drew together. "What's that supposed to mean?"

"You can't keep watch day and night," Kinsey pointed out. "If I decided to leave Crystal Springs, I could be hours away while you slept, and you wouldn't even know it."

Jared glared at her but Kinsey didn't wait for a response. Instead she gave him a sweet smile.

"Sleep well," she bade, and slipped out of his room.

Chapter Ten

He looked terrible.

Kinsey pressed her lips together at the sight of Jared coming into the kitchen the next morning. Red, swollen eyes. Heavy lids. Unshaven. Bone-tired.

Yet he somehow managed to look tall and sturdy, taking up what little space was left in the kitchen as the women went about getting breakfast prepared.

Kinsey wished she hadn't noticed. And she certainly wished the realization hadn't caused a whispering sensation to flutter through her. She couldn't afford any such feelings—whatever they were—about Jared Mason.

Last night she'd tried once again to reason with him, to convince him to leave Crystal Springs once and for all. She'd told him the truth and that hadn't been enough.

If the truth wouldn't send him on his way, she needed something more. Lying awake last night, thinking of him upstairs in the room right above hers, Kinsey knew she had to try something—anything—else.

Kinsey stirred the pot of oatmeal. "Did you sleep well in your room?" she asked, managing to sound sincere and pleasant, and loud enough that both Lily and Nell heard her.

Jared cut his gaze to her. Kinsey was sure the look he gave her had intimidated a great number of high-powered businessmen on the east coast, but she just stared right back.

"I slept fine," Jared said, the words coming out in a deep grumble.

"I don't think so," Kinsey declared, then said to Nell, "Mr. Mason needs a different room."

Awareness brightened his face. He knew what she was doing.

"I don't need a different room," he said.

"Nell," she went on. "Mr. Mason should be moved to one of the nicer rooms—say, one at the front of the house."

"Well, of course," Nell agreed, as she took a stack of plates from the cupboard. "We'll move you—"

"I'm fine," he declared with enough force that should have ended the discussion.

"I don't think he slept well," Kinsey went on. "Just look at him."

Lily, kneading the biscuit dough, and Nell both paused in their work to stare.

"You do look tired," Lily agreed.

"He looks as if he was awake all night," Kinsey said. "Is that true, Mr. Mason? Were you up all night, walking the floors, staring out the window, perhaps? Watching for…something?"

She already knew the answer to her question, of course. After she'd threatened to run off with Sam during the night, how could he have slept a wink?

"I'm not tired and I don't need another room," Jared declared.

"Maybe you should take a little nap this afternoon?" Kinsey suggested.

"An hour or two—what could you miss in that time?"

He knew exactly what he might miss, and exactly what Kinsey was suggesting, but he didn't say anything.

"Have you tried Nell's coffee?" Kinsey asked, gesturing to the pot on the stove.

His gaze lurched to the bubbling blue-speckled pot and he licked his lips.

"Nell makes the best coffee in town." Kinsey fetched a cup from the cupboard, poured, then looked straight at him and sipped it herself.

Jared's mouth opened, but no words came out.

"Delicious," Kinsey declared. She held up the pot and made a little pouty face. "Goodness, that was the last of it. Too bad. Nell will make more in a while. Maybe."

Jared pushed his fingers through his hair and glared at her.

"Mama!" Sam came into the kitchen wearing his nightshirt and juggling an armload of clothes, his eyes wide, his face eager. "Can I go now, Mama? Can I?"

Kinsey wiped her hands on her apron and knelt in front of him. "Anxious to get started, are you?"

Sam nodded quickly. "Am I 'posed to wear these?" he asked, gathering the shirt and trousers close to him.

"Big day?" Nell asked, moving past them to the stove.

"I get to go take care of horses today," Sam announced, bouncing on his toes.

"Since today is Saturday, Mack Gleason next

door is taking his boys to the livery stable with him to help out," Kinsey explained. "He said Sam could go with them."

"And I can stay all day," Sam declared.

Nell smiled. "My goodness, what a treat that is."

Sam pushed his bundle of clothing at Kinsey. "I gots to get ready, Mama."

She folded his small shirt and trousers, trying to avoid any more wrinkles, and rose. "Have some breakfast first, honey."

"But Mama—"

"Don't worry. Mr. Gleason and the boys won't leave without you," she said. "I promise."

Sam climbed into a chair at the table and Kinsey noticed that now Jared was seated there as well. The similarities—and differences—of the two of them struck her.

She considered Sam a big boy, so heavy now she could barely lift him, destined to be tall, like his father. But seeing him now, side by side with Jared, brought a new dimension to her thought.

Jared, with his straight shoulders. Wide chest. Long arms and legs. Big hands. His features were sharp, angular, strong. Beside him sat Sam, soft, round, still babylike in so many ways.

The future flashed in front of her. This—

Jared—is what Sam would look like one day. The imagined years rolled backward at the same instant and Kinsey knew that, in Sam, she witnessed Jared's childhood. Her heart fluttered at this glimpse into the past.

Jared yawned and stretched, spreading out his long arms and expanding his chest, bringing Kinsey's thoughts firmly into the here and now, and causing her heart to flutter once more in an entirely different way.

"Goodness..." Kinsey muttered under her breath and turned back to the stove, busying herself with breakfast.

By the time the three women had served the eggs, bacon, oatmeal, fried potatoes and hot biscuits, Sam had finished his meal. Kinsey went with him into their bedroom and helped him get washed and dressed.

Sam raced back into the kitchen, Kinsey following, as he called a goodbye to Nell and Lily seated at the table.

"Have fun today," Nell said.

"Take good care of those horses," Lily said.

"I will!" Sam spared them a quick wave and ran outside.

Kinsey got the last of the oatmeal cookies from the pastry chest, wrapped them in a linen towel, and followed. The morning air was cool and fresh, the sky filled with sun-drenched white, billowy clouds promising fine weather for the day Sam had looked forward to all week.

She was pleased to have found herself living next door to the Gleason family. Mack owned the livery stable and made a good living for his wife and sons. He and Dora were generous folks, frequently including Sam in the activities they planned for their boys.

Spending the day at the livery stable ranked high for Sam and the Gleason boys. They filled the morning feeding and grooming the horses, oiling the tack and cleaning the stalls before having the picnic lunch Dora packed. Afternoons were spent in the loft, playing in the hay, climbing in the rafters, chasing mice and doing other things that boys loved to do and that Kinsey still couldn't understand.

She spotted Mack outside his back door, his four young sons gathered around him.

"Good morning," she said in greeting and handed the bundle of cookies to Mack.

He tipped his hat at Kinsey. "Dora's got the house to herself today since I'm taking the boys. Maybe you can stop over so she doesn't get lonely."

Kinsey couldn't imagine Dora getting lonely but rather treasuring the peace and quiet of having the house to herself for a change.

"I'll stop by if I get a chance, but Saturdays are a busy day for us," she said, nodding toward the boardinghouse. "Cleaning day, plus getting ready for services tomorrow."

Mack nodded again, then clapped his hands together loudly. "Let's go, boys!"

Kinsey hurried to catch Sam's hand as he swarmed past with the other boys.

"You be a good boy today," she said, as she straightened the collar of his shirt. "And do what Mr. Gleason tells you to do."

"I will, Mama."

She got him to stand still long enough to plant a kiss on his cheek, then he raced away to catch up with the other boys. Kinsey got to her feet, watching him go, feeling that little tug at her heart every time Sam left her. School, church, with trusted friends—it didn't matter. She always fought the urge to race after him, gather him in her arms, cradle him against her, keep him safe and protected.

"Good day, Mrs. Templeton," Jared said as he walked by, following Sam and the Gleasons.

A little tremor stirred within her. She glanced back at the boardinghouse. She hadn't heard him come outside.

"Where are you going?" she asked.

Jared smiled and her blood ran cold. That was the same smile she'd given him in the kitchen just moments ago.

He gestured toward the road. "Thought I'd head on over to the livery with the Gleasons… and Sam."

She gasped. "No, you are not."

"Actually, I am." Jared nodded slowly. "Does that worry you?"

"Of course it does, and you know it. I told you I don't want you around Sam. I don't want you close to him."

"You're worried I might run off with Sam? I can see your problem. I'll be right there with the boy at the stables where they rent horses. Why, if a person wanted to, he could ride all the way to Cold Creek in an afternoon. The stagecoach comes through there real often, not to mention the trains. And from there…"

Panic gripped Kinsey's heart. "Don't you dare—"

"Let's just say this is my way of getting to

know what sort of life you and the boy lead. Isn't that what you wanted me to do?"

"I never meant for you to—"

"You're welcome to come down to the livery, check on things." Jared shook his head. "But you can't do that, can you. You've got to stay here *all day*. You're working. You've got cleaning to do. And you've got to get things ready for services tomorrow. Right?"

Kinsey didn't know how he'd learned this. He must have overheard Nell and Lily talking in the kitchen this morning.

"You gave your word," Kinsey told him. "You promised you'd stay in town. That you wouldn't—"

"Calm down," Jared said, though his words were anything but reassuring. He smiled then, driving her anxiety skyward again. "I'm just going to be down at the livery with him for the day. It's not like you'll be up worrying—*all night*."

Kinsey fumed as she watched Jared go, his long legs quickly taking him closer to Sam.

How could he do this? How could he suggest that he might run away with Sam? What kind of person would do that?

Someone just like herself, Kinsey realized.

And the fact that this is exactly what she'd done to him last night brought her no peace whatsoever.

Chapter Eleven

She looked terrible.

Kinsey knew it. She didn't need to consult a mirror for confirmation.

Late-afternoon shadows—finally—crept across the yard from the Gleasons' house, signaling the time Mack usually came home from the livery stable and ending this long, hellish day. Kinsey stood by the kitchen window gazing out as Nell and Lily worked behind her.

She'd worried herself frantic since this morning when Jared had left intending to spend the day with Sam and the Gleasons at the livery. Was he simply trying to get back at her for doing the same to him last night?

Or would he actually take Sam?

Kinsey hadn't left it to chance. All day, between the cleaning, cooking and baking, she'd slipped out of the boardinghouse, run—actually run—through the alleys to the livery stable at the other end of town, and watched from the corner of the bank building until she'd spied Sam, safe and sound, playing with the Gleason boys. Then, another dash back to the boardinghouse, working double time to make up for her absence.

Kinsey had lost count of how many times she'd made the hurried trip today. But she felt every minute and every step in her aching bones.

"So what do you think, Kinsey?" Nell called.

She turned, realizing that she hadn't been listening to the conversation. Neither Nell or Lily had seemed to notice her unexplained absences today, her odd behavior, or the fact that she'd ignored their gossip as they cooked.

Nell spoke again. "I'll bet there will be an announcement at services tomorrow about Miss Patterson and the new church. Reverend Battenfield has to do *something*. Things can't go on like this much longer."

"I'm afraid Miss Patterson is never going to give her approval to a new church," Lily said. "We'll be at her mercy forever. Just like poor Sarah is. I don't know how that sweet girl manages with an aunt like Bess Patterson. Miss

Patterson wants to control everything in this town and everything in Sarah's life."

"You wouldn't be referring to young Caleb Burk, now would you?" Nell asked. She lowered her voice. "I saw the two of them talking outside of Herb Foster's feed and grain store the other day. He's quite taken with her."

"Not that it matters—to Bess Patterson, anyway," Lily said. "She's made up her mind about Caleb. And that will mean nothing but heartache for those two young people. They should realize that and accept it."

"Unfortunately, you can't pick who you fall in love with," Kinsey said, checking the chickens in the oven. "It just happens."

Lily burst out crying. She clamped the hem of her apron to her mouth and rushed outside.

"Oh, dear…" Kinsey shared a look with Nell, then sighed. "I shouldn't have mentioned people being in love, not with things the way they are with her and Isaac."

"Lily's feelings are very tender these days," Nell agreed. "Go on outside and see about her."

Kinsey found Lily on the porch steps. She sat down beside her and waited until her tears slowed to sniffles, then patted her hand.

"Isaac loves you," Kinsey said.

Lily gulped. "I wish he didn't. I wish he'd just stop."

"He can't. And you know he won't."

"Oh, that man is so stubborn," Lily said, her emotions teetering between anger and hurt now.

A little wave of guilt swept through Kinsey as she realized that she'd been so caught up in her own problems, she hadn't asked Lily about her meeting with Isaac last night. But maybe Lily wouldn't have been ready to discuss it until now, given how high her emotions still ran.

"How did it go between the two of you last night?" she asked.

Lily fished a handkerchief from her skirt pocket and wiped her nose. "Isaac said we'll have whatever sort of marriage I want, if I'll just come back home."

"He misses you. I'm sure your house is very empty without you there," Kinsey said. She'd long admired the house Isaac and Lily lived in on one of the town's best side streets. Not large, nothing fancy, but Lily had made it into a warm, welcoming home for the two of them.

"But I can't go back," Lily said, worrying her

handkerchief between her fingers. "I can't be a real wife to him. I can't take a chance—"

"I know," Kinsey said, and she did know full well that returning to Isaac, risking another pregnancy and the chance of losing another baby, would be too much for Lily to bear.

"A few weeks ago I wrote a letter to my cousin in Baltimore." Lily glanced down at her handkerchief, then at Kinsey. "I asked if I could come live with her."

"And leave Crystal Springs—and Isaac—for good?"

Lily nodded. "I should hear back from her soon."

"But would you? Leave, I mean, if she says it's all right with her?"

Lily sighed tiredly. "I'm just so unhappy here. And Isaac is unhappy. And…well, I don't know what to do."

"Did you tell Isaac?"

"Last night."

So much for her attempt at reconciling their marriage, Kinsey thought.

"I'd better get back inside and help Nell," Lily said, rising from the step.

Kinsey rose, too, but, hearing voices from the

road, didn't follow Lily inside. The tension that had gripped her all day eased at the sight of Sam and the Gleason boys hiking homeward, Jared and Mack following in their wake. She walked to meet them.

"Did you boys have fun?" she asked.

They all started talking at once, big smiles on their smudged faces. From the snippets Kinsey could make out, she determined the boys had a wonderful time tending the horses, had found a new litter of kittens in the loft and they'd started a bug collection.

"See?" Eddie, who was the same age as Sam, thrust a glass jar at Kinsey proudly displaying the four-and eight-legged critters climbing over a handful of straw stuffed inside.

"Oh, my, that's quite a collection." Kinsey managed a smile and forced herself not to reel back. Having a son meant that bugs, spiders, worms and the like were apt to be presented to her at any given moment, something Kinsey still could not always face without wincing.

"Come on, boys, lets get inside, get cleaned up," Mack said. He turned to Jared. "Appreciate your help today."

"Sure thing," he replied.

"Bye, Uncle Jared," the Gleason boys called,

their voices tumbling over top of each other as they headed home.

"Did you have a good time?" Kinsey asked Sam.

His eyes widened and he nodded his head so hard his bangs floated up and down.

"Go on inside and get washed up," Kinsey said. "You can tell me all about it at supper."

Sam scooted around her and into the house, leaving Kinsey and Jared alone in the yard.

He looked even more tired than this morning when he'd stumbled in for breakfast, she thought. But at the moment she took no pleasure in it, not considering how bone-tired she was herself.

"See?" Jared said. "I brought him back."

"I hope that means you'll sleep well tonight— *all night*." Kinsey threw the words at him, whipped around and headed for the house.

"And I hope you get lots of work done on Monday," Jared called, "while Sam's *in school* all day."

She rounded on him. "I've had enough of your threats."

"And I've had enough of yours."

"Then leave town. Go. Now," Kinsey told him.

Jared took a step closer. "Not until I get what I came here for."

"That will never happen." Kinsey glared into his face. "So you'd better get used to being up all night, watching to make sure I don't run off with him."

Jared leaned down. "And you'd better get used to running back and forth to the schoolhouse all day."

They glared at each other. Kinsey felt heat roll off of him, her own heart beating faster. Desperation, anger, fear and frustration all warred within her. Jared's expression, mirroring her same feelings, was taut with determination.

The hopelessness of their situation swept over Kinsey but she dug deep searching for strength, refusing to give up or give in to this man.

"Truce," he said.

Kinsey blinked up at him, unsure if she'd heard correctly.

"Truce," Jared said again. He backed away, gesturing a surrender with his hands.

Her heart lurched. "You're—you're leaving?"

His gaze hit her sharply. "No. But we can't keep going like this."

He sounded calm and reasonable, but it only served to put Kinsey on guard again.

"I can't stay up all night, watching out the window," Jared said. "And you can't spend your day trying to keep up on your work while you run all over town checking on Sam."

It made sense, of course. Yet Kinsey wasn't ready to believe him, to go along with his idea.

"How do I know you'll keep your word?" she asked.

"You still don't trust me, do you?"

"No."

"Well, I don't trust you either—completely. Not yet, anyway."

"So where does that leave us?" she asked.

Jared didn't hesitate. "Bring your Bible out here. I'll swear on it. Will you?"

"I'll do better than that," Kinsey said. "Bring Sam out here. I'll swear on his life."

A little smile curled the corner of Jared's mouth. "If you ever have kids of your own, Kinsey, you're going to be one hell of a mama."

Her cheeks flushed and yet she was proud—and pleased—that Jared noticed and understood her commitment to Sam.

"Have we got a deal?" Jared asked.

Kinsey studied him for a moment. In the fading light she could see the weariness around his eyes. His clothes were dusty. She guessed that helping out at the livery today, along with his lack of sleep, had taken their toll.

A body as big and strong as his must be truly exhausted to show these signs, she caught herself thinking.

An unexpected heat rolled through Kinsey. She jerked her gaze from him.

"So, how about it?" he asked.

She drew in a breath and looked up at him. "Do I have your word?"

"I promise I'll stay in town."

"You don't have to promise me that," Kinsey said. "You can leave anytime you'd like—as long as you don't take Sam with you."

Jared shifted from foot to foot, holding back what might have been a grin, or was perhaps an effort to keep control of his patience. He wasn't, she suspected, used to having his word questioned. And, surely, no one had ever asked him to leave before.

"I won't run off with Sam," Jared said, quietly, solemnly. "I swear."

Kinsey studied him, trying to read his expression, his tone, wondering if she could believe him. This decision was probably the biggest she'd made in her life. Yet she had so little to go on.

She hardly knew Jared Mason. He'd come into her life, disrupted everything, threatened to take from her the most precious part of her heart.

But she had let him kiss her. The memory zinged through Kinsey, rekindling the heat that she'd tried to keep under control. The thoughts raced on, making her aware that she hadn't simply allowed his kisses, she'd encouraged them.

Kinsey gave herself a shake, chasing away the thought.

"I don't know if I can trust you," she said.

Jared angled his head. "I'd just like to point out that you're the one who ran off with the boy in the first place."

He was right, of course. If anyone had reason to doubt a promise of this magnitude, it was Jared.

"All right, then," Kinsey said, drawing in a breath. "I won't leave Crystal Springs with Sam, if you won't kidnap him and take him back east with you."

"I'm agreeable with that."

A fleeting threat of worry wound through Kinsey. She narrowed her eyes at him. "But I'll tell you right now, Jared Mason, if you go back on your word, if you steal Sam away from me, I'll hunt you down. I'll take him back. And you'll be very sorry you ever laid eyes on me."

"I consider myself warned," Jared said, then offered his hand. "Do we have a deal?"

Kinsey hesitated another moment, then put her hand in his. Heat rushed through her palm and up her arm. His long fingers curled around hers, a snug, warm fit.

"Yes, we have a deal," she said.

Yet he didn't turn loose of her hand. He held on and leaned down until their faces were inches apart.

"I didn't come here to hurt you, Kinsey," Jared said softly. "I'd like to think you didn't mean to hurt my family when you took Sam away from us."

She gazed up at him. "I was just doing what I thought was best."

"And so am I."

"Where does that leave us?" Kinsey asked.

"Damn if I know."

Chapter Twelve

"You be a good boy, Sam," Kinsey said, kneeling in front of her son. "Do what Miss Lily says."

"Okay, Mama," he promised.

"Don't worry. We'll be fine," Lily said.

Kinsey gave Sam a hug and kiss. He'd already washed up for the night and had on his nightshirt. After all the fun he'd had with the Gleason boys today at the livery stable, she didn't expect him to be awake much longer.

"Thanks, Lily." She rose. "I'll be back as soon as I can."

"Where are you going?" Jared asked.

As he had the night before, Jared had remained in the kitchen eating an extra dessert while the women cleaned the supper dishes and all the other boarders gathered in the parlor or on the front porch, or headed up to their rooms.

"Saturday night," Kinsey said, taking her wrap

from the hook beside the door. "I have dishes to wash at the White Dove Café."

She went outside, the night air cool but refreshing, helping to chase the sleepiness from her head. The day had been long, very long, and she was more tired than usual.

Halfway across the yard she heard the door slap shut and footsteps in the grass behind her. Jared appeared at her side.

"Thought I'd walk you into town," he said.

"I'm perfectly capable of walking by myself," she pointed out. "I've done it dozens of times and nothing has happened."

"I don't know," Jared mused. "Seems I recall that last Saturday night a man you didn't even know kissed you in the alley."

Kinsey gasped, her cheeks heated. "That—that was different."

"Are you saying you didn't mind it?" he asked.

"No—yes—no. I mean..."

Jared chuckled softly and Kinsey glanced up to see the little smile on his face. He was teasing her...and enjoying it.

"So what happened with the sheriff and his wife last night?" Jared asked, as they started walking side by side.

Relieved by the change of subject, Kinsey related to him what Lily had told her.

"She's thinking of heading back east to live with her cousin?" Jared shook his head. "Running away never solved anything."

Kinsey wondered if there was an underlying meaning to his words directed at her, but didn't say anything.

"I can only imagine how upset Isaac must be," she said. "Maybe I should have stayed out of their affairs."

"You did the right thing."

She glanced up at him. "Do you think so?"

"Can't give up just because things get hard."

Even if he hadn't said it with such conviction, Kinsey would have known those were Jared's true feelings. After all, he'd been an important part of a thriving east coast business, he'd overseen what must have been many difficult construction projects. And, of course, he'd come the thousands of miles to Crystal Springs to get his nephew.

They reached the edge of town and walked down the boardwalk toward the White Dove Café. Storefronts were dark but lights showed in the windows of the jailhouse. Music and laughter drifted out the doors of the Wild Cat Saloon.

Jared walked with her down the alley to the rear of the restaurant. The back door stood open. Rich aromas from the kitchen wafted outside along with voices and the clang of pots and pans.

Kinsey hesitated. "Our truce. You're serious, aren't you? You gave your word and—"

"I didn't walk you over here just to make sure this is where you were going," Jared told her. "And no, I won't go back to the boardinghouse and take Sam."

She supposed she should have been embarrassed for asking. They'd agreed on the truce. They'd each given their word. And it was the best thing for both of them. They couldn't continue the way they were going.

"Look," Jared said. "I know you've got reason not to trust me yet. All I can say is that you knew Clark, what sort of man he was, what sort of family he came from."

She studied him in the faint light, then said, "I'd better get to work."

Jared glanced inside the kitchen. Boiling pots and sizzling skillets on the cookstove. Women squeezing past each other, dishing up food and balancing trays. A big washtub and dozens of dirty dishes stacked next to it.

The place looked hot, the work hard. Kinsey

was surely as tired as he, and Jared sure as hell wouldn't want to spend the next few hours washing that mountain of dishes.

"Do you have to do this tonight?" he asked.

"I need the money. Regardless of what you think, I do have a plan for the future." Kinsey nodded through the door. "Besides, I see that Dixie's here tonight. All I'll have to do is wash."

Jared looked past her and spotted the young woman who'd served his supper to him the first time he'd eaten here. He remembered her well.

Kinsey went into the kitchen and everyone greeted her as she put on an apron and stepped up to the washtub. Her smile seemed to light up the place.

It seemed to light up a little spot in Jared's chest, too, he realized. He knew Kinsey was tired—he sure as hell was—but there she was washing dishes, talking and laughing.

For an instant, he wanted to go inside, too, to hear what she was saying. He backed away, the notion making him uncomfortable, and headed for Main Street.

On the boardwalk he eyed the saloon down the block, thinking he'd like to go in but wondering if he should. Given the newly developed problem with his wife, Sheriff Vaughn probably wasn't in the best of moods. Half the town might end up in a jail cell before the night was over.

But Jared headed over anyway. Pushing through the bat-wing doors he made his way to the bar and ordered a beer. The place was noisy, smoky and crowded. A little while later, a man eased up next to him.

"Glad to see you're still in town," he said.

Jared studied him a minute. Caleb Burk, he recalled. The man he'd met at the jailhouse who'd borrowed his technical journals.

"I'll be here for a while," Jared said.

"Looking to start a new building project?" Caleb asked. "I figured that's why you're here, right?"

"Sure," Jared said and sipped his beer.

It was as good a story as any, he decided. And it wasn't outside the realm of possibility. Jared, like all the Masons, frequently traveled to different places on the lookout for a new opportunity.

"Crystal Springs is prime for more businesses," Caleb said, signaling the bartender for a beer. "With the train stopping here twice a week now, things should boom. Did you see the new train station? Glad to have it, but, damn, it should have been a lot bigger."

"You think so?" Jared asked.

"It's the first thing new folks see when they arrive in Crystal Springs. Should have been bigger, grander, something that made people want to stay here, if you ask me."

"Sounds like you know what you're talking about."

Caleb looked embarrassed, then shook his head. "As I mentioned, I was a surveyor and an engineer in the army. Got a taste for building things."

"So what are you doing in Crystal Springs?"

"I had to come back and take over my pa's general store after he passed on. MacAvoy. I'm sure you've seen it, right across the street from Hudson's Mercantile. Our store's named after my mama's side of the family since they staked him in the business." Caleb shook his head. "My mama's pretty headstrong."

Like all the women in this town, Jared thought.

"A business like that must keep you busy," Jared said. "Thinking of expanding—"

Jared's attention strayed to Sheriff Vaughn as he pushed through the bat-wing doors. He carried a sawed-off shotgun, wore a pistol on each hip, and looked as if he actually hoped someone would cross him tonight.

It didn't take long for that to happen. Two cowboys, who seemed to have been drinking for a while, said something as Isaac walked in front of them. Jared couldn't hear the words, could only guess what they were by the sheriff's reaction. He backhanded one of them, relieved him of his pistol, then grabbed his collar and dragged him outside.

Conversation, noise and laughter continued in the saloon. Such instances were commonplace, apparently. But Jared kept an eye on the other cowboy. He lingered for a moment, then headed out the door.

Jared didn't like the look of things.

"I'll be back," he said to Caleb and followed the cowboy outside.

On the boardwalk, Jared saw Sheriff Vaughn pulling his prisoner, a little unsteady on his feet, toward the jail. No sign of the second cowboy. Jared headed toward the sheriff. Just ahead, between him and the sheriff, the cowboy darted out of the alley, a piece of wood the size of a fire log drawn back over his shoulder. He rushed toward the sheriff but Jared got to him first and tackled him from behind.

Jared went down on top of the cowboy, planting his knee in his back and pinning him to the ground. Sheriff Vaughn whirled around, dragging his prisoner with him, as Jared yanked the log from the cowboy's hand and threw it into the street.

Jared and Isaac stayed like that for a moment, staring at each other. Then footsteps pounded the boardwalk behind them and Caleb Burk showed up.

"Damn, Sheriff, this fella meant to kill you," Caleb said, gesturing to the man on the ground.

Jared rose. Caleb lent a hand pulling the cowboy to his feet and they all headed toward the jail. Isaac locked the two prisoners in different cells.

In the office again, he looked angry—mostly at himself—and maybe a little embarrassed that not only had the cowboy almost attacked him from behind, but that Jared was the one who'd saved him.

"Uh, look, Mason," Isaac said. "I, uh…"

"Forget it," Jared said, waving away his words.

"I'll stay here while you finish your rounds," Caleb said. He rummaged through the desk drawer and pulled out a badge as he said to Jared, "I help out as deputy, time to time."

"I figured you'd be paying a call on Sarah

Patterson tonight," Isaac said. "Or, at least, trying to."

"I tried, all right. That aunt of hers would have nothing to do with it." Caleb turned to Jared. "Miss Bess Patterson's got no use for men like me who served time in the army. Soldiers are coarse and common, she says. Not good enough for her niece."

"And what does Sarah think?" Jared asked.

Caleb smiled. "Sarah's the finest woman I've ever met. Pretty, smart, funny. I think she'd let me court her if that aunt of hers wouldn't—sorry, Sheriff. I shouldn't have said anything, what with your problem with your own wife."

Isaac winced, then headed toward the door. "I'll be out on rounds."

Jared followed him outside and expected the sheriff to go about his business. Instead, he stopped next to Jared.

"I appreciate what you did," Isaac said softly. "Especially after…"

"After you locked me up for no reason?" Jared asked.

"I had a reason," he pointed out. "A damn good reason."

At that moment Jared almost admired Isaac's

determination to win back his wife—even if it had cost Jared four days in jail.

"I understand things took a turn for the worse," Jared said.

Isaac looked hard at him for an instant, unhappy surely that his personal life had become an open book, then just sighed heavily.

"Lily thinks she wants to move back east." Isaac shook his head. "I've got to stop her… somehow."

"She's not gone yet," Jared said. "Looks like that should give you an advantage."

"Yeah, you'd think…," he agreed, then nodded across the street in the direction of the White Dove Café. "What's going on with you and your brother's wife?"

"The Pinkerton detective's report was wrong," Jared told him. "Kinsey is my brother's sister-in-law. She took the boy after his wife died."

Isaac was silent for a moment, seemingly taking it in, reshuffling the story he'd read in the Pinkerton report while Jared was in jail.

"Kinsey will never let that boy go," he finally said.

"She's not even blood kin," Jared said. "Kinsey's a stepsister to my brother's wife."

"Doesn't matter," Isaac said. "You'll never get that boy away from her."

Jared supposed the sheriff thought he knew what he was talking about, given how two babies—both dead—had driven his own wife out of their home.

A woman appeared in the darkened alley beside the White Dove. Jared's heart lurched, thinking it was Kinsey. But when she stepped up onto the boardwalk and the light caught her face, he realized it was Dixie, the serving girl from the restaurant.

She spied Jared and Isaac quickly, then darted across the street. A few feet from them, her gait changed to a saunter, slow and measured, her face showing a knowing smile.

"Why, good evening, Sheriff, Mr. Mason," she greeted them, stepping up between them on the boardwalk.

Jared didn't know how she knew his name, except that the town was still small enough that gossip spread quickly. Yet Dixie, it seemed to Jared, was the sort of woman who'd make sure she found out such things.

"Finished at the White Dove already?" Isaac asked. "The place looks pretty busy tonight."

"I finished up early," Dixie said. Then she favored them with another smile and latched on to Isaac's arm. "And lucky for me, finding Crystal Spring's finest sheriff waiting right here to walk me home."

Isaac shifted, trying to distance himself from Dixie, but she moved closer.

"It's frightening being on the streets alone at night," Dixie declared.

She slid her palm up his arm. "But I'll feel good...real good...if you see me home."

"All right, then, let's go." Isaac pulled his arm from her grasp, then barked, "Mason. Come on."

Dixie talked the whole way home, nearly each thought she expressed seeming to require her touching Isaac's arm. When they reached the house she lived in on the edge of town, she hesitated on the porch.

"I know how tough things have been for you, Isaac, what with your wife leaving you, and all, how that can make a man feel...lonely," Dixie said. She sidled a little closer. "So if you ever need someone to talk to or...anything...just let me know."

"Good night, Miss Dixie," Isaac said, stepping away quickly and heading back toward Main Street.

Jared fell in step next to him, Isaac grumbling under his breath.

"That girl's folks are fine, Christian people. I don't know how the hell she..."

His words faded away, but Jared was sure he knew exactly what Isaac meant.

Back on Main Street, Isaac headed off alone, rattling shop doors, peering into dark alleys. Jared glanced at the saloon and considered going back inside but didn't. He walked the streets, studying the buildings, the architecture of the town, and found himself returning again and again to the White Dove Café. Standing across the street from the restaurant, he finally saw the last patron leave, the door close, the shades descend and the windows go dark.

He watched the alley, shifting from foot to foot, waiting until he spotted a ripple in the darkness, a figure moving toward the street.

Kinsey. He felt his every muscle flex, relax, tighten again. His breath quickened. He crossed the street into the alley, and waited in the spot where, just a few days ago, he'd kissed her for the first time.

Kinsey stopped when she saw him in the shadows, then came forward slowly.

She'd wondered if she'd find him waiting for

her tonight. The thought of Jared lurking in the alley—the alley where he'd kissed her—had roamed through her mind all night. And if she did find him there, would he kiss her again. Did she want him to?

"Thought I'd walk you home," Jared said.

"I doubt a strange man will want to kiss me again," she told him.

"Then what about a man you already know?"

Jared moved closer, drawing her nearer with the heat his body gave off. A male energy that seemed to consume her.

"Does that mean you want to kiss me?" Kinsey asked.

"Do you want me to?"

"Well, no, of course I don't," she insisted, her words sounding less than convincing, even to her own ears.

Jared ran his finger down her cheek. "Didn't you like it when I kissed you before?"

She pressed her lips together primly. "I really don't recall."

Jared grinned. "Then I'll have to make a better impression on you next time."

Kinsey moved ahead of him out of the alley, and within a step or two he was beside her. Tall, strong, long striding steps that he shortened to keep pace with her.

"Business slow at the restaurant tonight?" Jared asked.

"Hardly," Kinsey said. "And it didn't help that Dixie came down with a headache and left early."

The boardinghouse was dark and silent when they entered the kitchen. A solitary lamp burned beside the door, left lighted each night as a courtesy for the boarders. Jared followed her to the hallway at the rear of the house and they stopped outside her bedroom door. Inside, the lantern she left burning for Sam glowed softly.

"Thank you for walking me home," she whispered, and turned to go inside.

"Kinsey?"

She turned back, gazing up at him expectantly.

"One more thing," Jared told her.

Then he stepped closer and eased her against him, covering her mouth with a dizzying kiss. Hot and moist, his lips moved over hers. His palm crept up her back into the hair at her nape. He cradled her there as his tongue slipped inside her mouth.

Kinsey gasped, startled by the intimacy. Jared moaned softly and eased closer, bringing her full against him. His heat, his strength, the sheer maleness of him sapped her strength. She swayed against him and opened her mouth further. He deepened their kiss for a long moment, then pulled away.

His hot breath puffed against her face. A lingering heat consumed her. Slowly, he backed away.

"Good night," he whispered, then turned and went up the stairs to his room.

Kinsey stood rooted to the spot, too stunned to move, watching the staircase as if he might come back and kiss her again.

Kiss her again?

Kinsey's thoughts whirled. What if he did? What if he *didn't?* What if—

A board squeaked and a shadow moved through the kitchen. Kinsey gasped, the haze of Jared's kiss fleeing before the possibility of losing her job.

Had someone—a boarder—been lurking in the kitchen and seen them kissing?

Good gracious, what was she doing?

Jared himself was a boarder. Nell wouldn't tolerate such conduct from Kinsey, or any of her employees. The reputation of a boardinghouse was important—perhaps more important to its success than the accommodations themselves.

Nell couldn't afford a scandal. And Kinsey couldn't afford to lose her job.

Kinsey dashed into her room and closed the door quietly behind her.

Chapter Thirteen

The rubble that had been the Crystal Springs church, the shade trees and the benches underneath looked inviting as Kinsey arrived for services. Sam dashed across the yard toward a group of his friends. Kinsey kept an eye on him as she joined several women gathered in a small circle and exchanged pleasantries.

Yet her gaze didn't stay on Sam but skipped through the gathering, searching out and finally landing on Jared as he stood across the yard talking to Caleb Burk.

Kinsey wasn't sure he'd be at church this morning. She hadn't seen him at the boardinghouse. As usual, she ran late, leaving long after everyone else had departed.

How handsome he looked, Kinsey thought, her heart lurching in a way that had become familiar. Serious, too. His brows were drawn together slightly as he spoke with Caleb. She wondered what they were talking about. Maybe if she wandered over she could—

"—was in jail."

Kinsey's attention snapped back to the conversation of the women gathered around her.

"Jail?" Emma Foster gasped. "Mr. Mason was in jail?"

Hannah Nelson, who ran the hotel, nodded. "Sheriff Vaughn came over to pick up Mr. Mason's belongings. Told me about it himself."

All the women turned toward Jared, concern in their expressions.

"I heard it was a mistake," Maggie Hudson said. "Mr. Mason is actually a businessman from back east."

Emma Foster shook her head. "I don't know…"

"The sheriff seemed very sure when he came to the hotel," Hannah Nelson declared.

Guilt stabbed Kinsey's heart. She'd arranged for Jared's jail time on trumped-up charges. Word had gotten around town and some of the women were concerned.

She gazed across the churchyard at Jared. Only Caleb Burk stood with him, talking. A week ago when Jared had come to services, she'd seen him surrounded by a number of men in town.

Everyone had been warm and welcoming. Now, it seemed, most of the townsfolk were reluctant to approach him.

Kinsey gulped, trying to force down her guilt. Of course, that wasn't the end of the world. Folks would learn the truth. Word would get out that Jared's incarceration had been a mistake. People would warm up to him again, become friendly once more, make him welcome in Crystal Springs.

Eventually.

A chill swept over Kinsey. How long would that take? Days? Weeks? And how long could anyone live in a place where they were looked upon with suspicion? Made to feel uncomfortable?

Kinsey had moved from town to town for much of her life. She knew how it felt to be an outsider. To never belong. Certainly, Jared wasn't used to it. With his large family and the political and social connections he'd bragged about, Kinsey doubted there had ever been a time when Jared had faced the uncertainty of acceptance.

And if it became too unbearable for Jared, what if he broke the fragile truce the two of them had forged? What if he left Crystal Springs?

And took Sam with him.

Kinsey gasped softly. Good gracious, what had she done? What had she set in motion?

The chatter of the women around her faded as they headed toward the rows of benches beneath the trees. Kinsey realized Reverend Battenfield had taken his place and was ready to start the service.

"I'm going to need your help this afternoon," Nell whispered, appearing next to Kinsey. "I know it's your day off, but the reverend just asked me if he could hold a meeting at the boardinghouse."

"A meeting?"

Nell leaned in a little. "He says it's about getting the new church built."

"Miss Patterson has agreed to—"

"Shh." Nell glanced around. "Bess Patterson doesn't know about the meeting. Can you give me a hand with the refreshments?"

"Of course."

"And don't tell anyone," Nell whispered.

Sam raced up to Kinsey, breathing hard, perspiration dotting his nose. She took his hand and the two of them moved to their usual spot on the benches as the rest of the congregation found seats. Kinsey spotted Jared. He sat alone at the end of the last bench. No one sat close.

People moved past him. A few nodded. Fewer still spoke.

Kinsey drew in a breath as she sat down on the bench and settled Sam next to her.

Jared might very well find living in Crystal Springs unbearable. He might leave, despite the promise he'd made to stay. And if he did, he'd surely take Sam with him.

Since first realizing who Jared was, Kinsey had tried everything to get him to leave.

Now she had to find a way to get him to stay.

Jared settled into one of the straight-back dining chairs that had been brought into the parlor, and dug into another piece of pie. His third, so far.

From his seat at the back of the room, he took in the meeting that had been going on for some time now. Reverend Battenfield was there, along with the town's mayor and a number of businessmen. Jared wasn't sure exactly what the meeting was about. He wasn't really listening. Something to do with a new church and some old battleax named Patterson.

Sheriff Vaughn was also in attendance, though Jared suspected he was more interested in seeing Lily than taking part in the discussion going on.

Jared didn't blame the sheriff. Lily was a good-looking woman, capable, with a good head on her shoulders. Any man would be lucky to have her for his wife. Despite the problems the two of them faced at the moment, in Jared's opinion, Isaac Vaughn would be a fool to let her get away.

Slouching a little lower in his chair, Jared shoved another bite of pie in his mouth. A cool breeze wafted through the open windows and the voices droned on. A nice Sunday afternoon, he decided.

Of course, maybe it wasn't so nice for Kinsey, Nell and Lily who'd had to hurry back from church and prepare refreshments for the group. They made it look effortless, though, moving around the room with trays, pouring coffee and lemonade, keeping fresh slices of pies and cookies on the sideboard in the dining room. Some women had that way about them. Making things look comforting and inviting.

Jared's gaze settled on Kinsey as she moved around the room, refilling lemonade glasses. A pretty woman, no doubt about it. He couldn't help but notice the way her skirt swayed when she walked. Or the little swirl when she turned that offered a glimpse of her ankles. She had on a bibbed apron that drew attention to her bosom.

And a fine bosom it was, Jared decided as he pushed another bite of pie into his mouth. Round and firm. Probably just the right size to fit his hand. Soft and—

"—Mr. Mason."

The whole room turned to stare at him.

What the hell was going on?

Kinsey, standing at the front of the room, gestured toward him.

"Mr. Mason is the perfect man for the job," she declared.

Jared gulped down the bite of pie. What job?

Everyone continued to stare.

"He has political connections," Kinsey said, "and social position. Important friends in high places."

Jared sat up straighter in the chair. What the devil was she talking about?

"His family in New York owns a very large construction company," Kinsey said. "Mr. Mason has personally overseen the design and construction of factories, warehouses, large buildings of all sorts."

"I've seen his technical journals and talked to him about it," Caleb said. "He knows construction, all right."

Isaac Vaughn stood up. "And as for that business about him being in jail, that was a mistake. He's in the clear."

Jared put his plate aside. "What's going on—"

"Well, then," Reverend Battenfield said, "I guess that settles it."

Heads nodded around the room.

"It sure does," Mayor Fisher agreed.

"Settles what?" Jared asked. "I—"

"Let's have a prayer," the reverend said.

"But—"

Jared fell silent as heads bowed and Reverend Battenfield led the prayer thanking the good Lord for His blessing and asking Him to give the town—and Jared—the strength they would all need in the coming weeks.

"Amen," echoed around the room. Then everyone filed past Jared, shaking hands and offering thanks and assistance.

By the time the last man left the parlor, he figured out what he'd been volunteered for while he was whiling away the Sunday afternoon eating pie and thinking about Kinsey's bosom.

He found her in the kitchen with Nell and Lily, washing dishes.

"Here he is, our town hero," Nell declared. "I know you can charm Miss Patterson into building our new church right away."

"Charm her?" Lily scoffed. "You'd better give that woman a piece of your mind right off. Tell her how things are going to be done."

"Don't make her mad," Nell insisted. "We need that new church, and the sooner the better."

"Miss Patterson has been coddled too long," Lily said.

"Well, either way," Nell conceded, "you've got your work cut out for you."

"Seems so," Jared said. He edged closer to Kinsey who was washing the dishes. "Can I talk to you outside?"

She wouldn't look up at him. "I'm busy."

"Oh, run on," Nell declared. "I can finish up here."

"Well, all right." Kinsey dried her hands and rolled down her sleeves, then went outside with Jared.

They walked toward the rear of the yard. Sam and the Gleason boys played nearby. The sun cast long shadows and the air was cool. Jared gave her a hard look and Kinsey knew he was angry with her.

"I thought we had a deal," Jared said.

She glared right back. "Don't raise your voice at me."

She could see that her admonishment didn't suit him but she didn't care.

"That's what this is all about, isn't it?" he asked, his voice level now. "You volunteered me to head up building this new church so I won't leave town?"

"Yes. Partly."

"I called the truce. It was my idea. I gave you my word. And you still don't believe me?"

"How dare I not? Is that what you mean?" Her own anger was growing now. "With your political connections and your social position, I should simply turn my future over to you, no questions asked?"

"I only want what's best for the boy."

"And growing up as a Mason is your idea of what's best?"

"What's wrong with it?"

"Growing up to be pompous and arrogant?"

He looked surprised. "Is that what you think of me?"

"Sweet-talking someone really goes against your grain. You'd much rather just roll over everyone to get your way," Kinsey said.

"But keeping you in Crystal Springs, working on the church is only part of the reason I suggested you take over the project."

His brows drew together, suspicious now. She couldn't really blame him. She had, after all, had him locked up in jail.

"I want people to like you," Kinsey said.

"I don't give a damn whether people like me or not," Jared told her, and she was absolutely sure that was true.

"See? That's exactly what I'm talking about," Kinsey told him.

"Hell, if that Miss Patterson is holding up the church construction, I'll donate the money myself."

"No, you can't do that," Kinsey said. "Then you'll be no better than Miss Patterson. The town will just tolerate you because of your money. Must I remind you that you have no political or social connections in this town? Nobody knows you. And, believe me, it's very difficult to live in a place where you have no friends, where you don't belong."

Jared's face softened a little. "That's happened to you?"

Kinsey hesitated a moment, the memories still painful after all these years. "My parents died when I was a child. I had no other family. The Templetons took me in, gave me a home, told me I was part of their family but—"

"But you knew you weren't."

Kinsey nodded. "It was the same during the years after Beth died and Sam and I were traveling, searching for a place to live. I never felt like I had a home until we got here to Crystal Springs."

"If you come to New York with Sam and me, you'll be part of our family," Jared said softly. "My brother, my father and mother, they'll—"

"No." Kinsey whirled away, unable to listen to another word, and headed for the house.

Jared didn't go after her, though it took everything he had stay put.

What had Kinsey been through? What sort of life had she endured?

He knew the facts, some from the Pinkerton report, some from the things she'd told him. But hard facts didn't reveal the things she'd surely suffered through. The loss of her parents. Trying to fit into the Templeton family. Seeing her stepsister happily married, yet not having those things for herself. Then losing Clark, who'd been kind and accepting, and Beth, the last of her family.

No wonder she clung to Sam the way she did.

Jared watched as Kinsey disappeared into the

house, then looked at Clark's son playing with the Gleason boys.

Jared didn't blame Kinsey for the way she felt or the way she acted. He understood it.

He understood, too, that if he was ever going to take Sam back to New York with him, first he'd have to get Kinsey to trust him.

Chapter Fourteen

Midmorning was a time Kinsey enjoyed, most days. Breakfast served and the kitchen cleaned, Sam sent off to school, nothing expected of her for several hours when supper preparation began. She had even more time to herself, now that she no longer trekked into town to watch the arrival of passengers on the stagecoach and trains.

Seated on the bench beside the woodshed, Kinsey closed her eyes, relishing the cool breeze, the glorious sunshine beaming through the thick branches of the oak tree. The solitude was welcome, and she was grateful for a few minutes alone to—

Kinsey's eyes sprang open and she saw Jared walking toward her. How had she known? She hadn't heard the door slam, his footsteps were but a whisper in the grass. Had she somehow sensed his approach?

Was that possible?

Good gracious, she couldn't even enjoy a quiet moment outdoors without that man intruding somehow, making her heart lurch and her stomach feel funny.

He stood over her for a moment, then dropped onto the bench beside her. Kinsey couldn't help but notice how good he smelled. Soap and cotton, and something musky.

"I came to ask you a favor," Jared said. "Would you mind if I walk Sam home from school today?"

"I told you I don't want you around Sam."

Jared grinned. "But seeing as how I'm on my way to being so well thought of in town, thanks to you volunteering me to build the new church, I figured you might change your mind."

"I did that for your own good, and for the good of the town," she told him.

"That would be mighty generous of you," Jared conceded. "But I think there's more to it. I think you volunteered me to build the church to ease your own guilt for having me thrown into jail."

Kinsey squirmed a little but kept her chin up. "Is that what you think?"

"It is. And I also think you hope that by getting me involved in what's going on in town, I'll start seeing the good side of this place and be more likely to leave Sam here with you."

"You think that, too, huh?"

"I do."

Kinsey shifted uncomfortably on the bench. Of course, everything he'd said was true. She'd thought all those things, considered all those possibilities, and come to those conclusions exactly as he'd speculated.

She wouldn't admit it, though.

"Would you like to know what I think?" she asked.

"What's that?"

"You *think* too much," Kinsey declared. "You have too much time on your hands. You should get busy working on those church plans."

Jared waved away her concern. "Designing a church isn't a big deal."

"You haven't met Miss Patterson yet," she warned.

"I'm not worried," he told her.

"You should at least take a look at the materials you have to work with."

Jared frowned. "Materials have already been bought? Before a plan was developed and decided on?"

"Miss Patterson ordered everything right away," Kinsey said. "Of course, no one suspected it would be so difficult to get her to agree to what the church would look like."

"I'd better have a look at what was ordered." Jared was quiet for a moment, then said, "Don't worry. I won't go by the school. Not until you say it's all right."

"I don't want Sam to be confused about things," Kinsey said. "I don't want him to wonder who you are. He already calls you 'uncle' which, I'm sure, was your idea."

"I am his uncle," Jared pointed out.

"I don't want him getting attached to you. What happens when you leave? He'll miss you. Wonder where you've gone. Why you left. I don't want him to be hurt."

"I understand." Jared nodded. "But the truth is, this might be my only chance to spend time with the boy. I want him to remember me. When Sam grows up he'll ask about his pa, about his family. He might even come to New York."

Kinsey gasped. Jared was right, of course, and the notion frightened her.

"I'd never thought that far ahead," she said.

"You've got your hands full just getting through

the day with him," Jared said. "It's hard raising him alone, working like you do. The future seems a long way off."

Jared rose. "I'm going to track down my building materials, see what I've got to work with for the church. Would you come with me?"

"Yes, I'd like that," Kinsey said, surprised not only by his invitation but her ready acceptance. She hesitated a moment. "But not because I want to make sure you don't go by the school and see Sam."

His brows bobbed upward. "The thought never occurred to me."

"Really?"

"Well, maybe it did cross my mind," Jared said. "But only for a second."

"I guess I'm going to have to keep a close eye on you." Kinsey rose from the bench and shrugged. "No matter. I'm used to dealing with children."

Jared gave her a half grin and gestured with his hand. "After you, Mrs. Templeton."

They slipped inside the boardinghouse just long enough for Kinsey to get her bonnet and handbag, and Jared to fetch his hat, then headed toward town.

"So where're these building materials?" he asked as they walked.

"Half is at the MacAvoy General Store and half is at Hudson's Mercantile," Kinsey explained. "Miss Patterson felt she had to give the business to both the stores."

"A little healthy competition going on there?"

"I don't know how healthy it is," Kinsey told him. "Dabney Hudson and Ida Burk don't get along. I'm afraid Mr. Hudson is going to have a stroke one day, he's so riled up all the time. I wonder how his daughter manages to work there with him. She has the patience of a saint."

Main Street was busy with shoppers and folks going about their business as Kinsey and Jared stepped up onto the boardwalk. Wagons and carriages filled the dusty road. Horses were tied to hitching posts.

Caleb Burk, wearing a shop apron and sweeping up, smiled when they approached.

"Figured you'd be by today," Caleb said, pausing in his sweeping.

"Come to check out the building supplies for the church, have you?" Ida Burk asked, appearing in the doorway. She was a tiny, gray-haired woman, wearing a crisp apron. "You'll find the best items here at MacAvoy's. Top quality goods. Not like…some places."

Ida gave a dismissive wave across the street toward Hudson's Mercantile, then disappeared into the store.

Caleb looked a little embarrassed as he set the broom aside. "It's in the back storeroom. I'll show you."

Kinsey and Jared followed Caleb into the store, the neat shelves filled with every sort of item imaginable.

"I've got some ideas for the church," Ida announced from behind the counter. "Now here's what I think you should do."

Kinsey drifted to the display of fabrics near the front window. Bolts of colorful cloth were stacked on shelves along with boxes of buttons and threads. She ran her hand along the fabrics, feeling the textures, assessing the subtle hues, the different patterns.

Beautiful, all of them. Each could be made into a special garment. The black, a sturdy pair of men's trousers. The gold brocade, a fine-looking vest. And the yellow. What a lovely dress it would make for a spring afternoon outing.

Kinsey pressed her lips together, studying the

fabrics. Pink would be pretty, too, of course. And with a little extra yardage she could fashion a matching handbag. Oh, but the blue. Blue was her favorite color. Or the lavender. She could—

Heat wafted over her and her spine tingled in a familiar way. Kinsey glanced back and saw Jared standing next to her.

How did he keep doing that?

"I was just looking at fabric," Kinsey said, suddenly uncomfortable that he'd caught her daydreaming. "For Sam. He's growing like a weed now."

Jared nodded toward the fabric and frowned. "You're going to make my nephew a shirt out of that frilly purple stuff?"

Kinsey gasped, realizing her hand still rested on the lavender eyelet fabric. "No, I…I—"

"Mr. Mason?" Ida hurried down the aisle toward them. "I thought of something else you ought to put in the church."

Kinsey marveled at the patience Jared exhibited as Ida gave a detailed description of her idea for the church.

"Thank you, Mrs. Burk," he said, as she wound down, then added quickly, "Good day," and headed toward the door.

Caleb was on the boardwalk again, sweeping. "Appreciate the help," he said, as they walked past.

"Sure thing," Jared said.

"What was that about?" Kinsey asked, as they paused at the edge of the boardwalk.

To her surprise, Jared closed his hand around her elbow. Heat ran up her arm, warming her instantly. He held her as he watched two wagons amble down the street, then escorted her safely to the other side.

"Caleb bought the place next door to his store," Jared explained.

"I didn't know," Kinsey said, glancing back over her shoulder. The small building had housed a restaurant which hadn't fared well in Crystal Springs. The owners had moved out a few weeks ago.

"Caleb wants to expand the store into the new building," Jared said. "Asked if I could give him a hand with the plans."

"Oh, dear. I wonder if Mr. Hudson knows?"

Kinsey wondered, too, why so many people on the street seemed to be staring at her and Jared. Was it because of the gossip about Jared's jail time? Or because, for the first time ever, Kinsey was escorted through town on the arm of a handsome man?

"Don't believe a word that woman says!"

Dabney Hudson rushed toward them, gesturing across the street toward the MacAvoy General Store. His cheeks were red and his balding head damp with perspiration.

"I know what that woman, that Ida Burk, was saying. Well, I can imagine. Word for word." Dabney stuck out his hand and introduced himself to Jared. "Don't believe it, not for a minute."

"Papa, please," Maggie Hudson pleaded, coming out of Hudson's Mercantile after him.

Dabney ignored his daughter. "Right here at Hudson's Mercantile is where you'll find the best quality products. No question about it. I ordered the finest—the *finest*—building supplies for the church."

"Papa, calm down. You know what the doctor—"

"Come on here, Mr. Mason," Dabney said, gesturing toward the alley that ran beside the mercantile. "I'll show you my warehouse. You've seen nothing finer anywhere on the east coast—I guarantee it!"

Kinsey's heart went out to Maggie as she watched her father and Jared head down the alley together. Maggie was only a few years younger than Kinsey and, everyone agreed, one of the prettiest women in Crystal Springs. One of the kindest, too, though she preferred to stay in the background during church and social functions.

Maggie had a lot to live down.

"We got in a new shipment of fabric yesterday. I held some of it back, some of the prettiest bolts," Maggie said. "Would you like to see it?"

Maggie knew how Kinsey loved the different fabrics and always told her when a new shipment had arrived. Not that Kinsey could often afford the luxury of a new dress.

Hudson's Mercantile was as neat and clean as their competition across the street. The shelves were carefully arranged with a full array of items needed by the townsfolk, and the ranchers and miners who managed monthly trips to Crystal Springs.

"Papa thinks it's a waste of shelf space to carry such fine fabrics," Maggie said as they slipped through the curtain behind the counter into the storage room. "But just look at this."

She moved a crate aside, then lifted the lid off a larger one revealing the bolts of fabric.

"Oh, my…" Kinsey gasped softly as she and Maggie pulled the bolts from the packing crate.

Satin, velvet, lace. A rainbow of colors. Rich blues, deep greens and garnets. Light shades of purple, pink, yellow and blue.

Kinsey's mind raced, taking in the hues and textures. She could imagine Lily in the green, Nell wearing the garnet. Maggie, of course, with her dark hair, blue eyes and milky skin, would look perfect in any of the colors. In Kinsey's mind she saw every woman in town wearing just the right color, style and cut.

"Oh, the dresses I could make…" she said, running her hand along the fabric.

"This blue would be beautiful on you, Kinsey. I can put this aside for you," Maggie offered. "Papa won't know."

"I really shouldn't…"

"I'll save it for a few days, until you decide," Maggie said.

An ache of longing filled Kinsey. Oh, to own a spectacular gown again. To hear the rustle and feel the fine fabric against her skin. To slip into silk stockings, dainty shoes.

Her mind sped back to that one special night in Richmond. At the hotel where Clark had taken Beth and insisted Kinsey come, too. He'd spared no expense in buying their clothing, allowing his wife and sister-in-law to indulge their every fantasy, every whim. The evening had started out as a fairy tale. But then…

As always when Kinsey thought of that night,

she wondered how differently things might have turned out.

Surely, she wouldn't be in Crystal Springs.

And Clark might still be alive.

Chapter Fifteen

Dabney Hudson's voice suddenly blared from the back of the storeroom, jarring Kinsey from her troubling thoughts of the past. Kinsey and Maggie quickly pushed the bolts of fabric inside the crate and closed the lid.

"She's up to something!" Dabney declared, shaking his fist in the direction of MacAvoy's. "Something's up. I can feel it. That Ida Burk is plotting to ruin me."

"Papa," Maggie admonished. "That's simply not true. Ida and Caleb Burk are good people."

"She's always undercutting my prices. Trying to steal my customers. Did you see her price on tomatoes?" Dabney demanded. "A whole bushel sitting right outside her door. Two cents—*two cents*—lower than my price. She's trying to put me out of business, I tell you."

"Thanks for the list of building supplies," Jared

said, patting his shirt pocket. He hooked Kinsey's elbow and headed toward the front of the store.

"Before you go," Dabney called, following them, "I've got a great idea for the church. Two steeples, front and back. Three bells in each. Nothing like it anywhere."

Jared nodded thoughtfully. "I'll keep that in mind."

Kinsey said a quick goodbye to Maggie and left the store with Jared. She always had mixed feelings about coming to Hudson's. Maggie was a treasure, but that father of hers was always a trial. Most everyone wondered where Maggie found the patience to deal with the man.

Not that she had a choice, really.

"Looks like the entire town is more than anxious to help with the new church," Kinsey said, as they headed down the boardwalk together.

"Yeah. I'm getting lots of help, all right." Jared paused and looked around. "I'm hungry. How about something to eat?"

Kinsey hesitated, not sure what to do. How strange to be invited out to a meal. She couldn't remember the last time that had happened.

"Being seen in your company will elevate the town's opinion of me," Jared said. "That's what you want, isn't it?"

Kinsey smiled. "In the interest in keeping my son, then yes, I suppose I should have lunch with you."

They walked to the White Dove Café. Along the way Kinsey pointed out Sheriff Vaughn's house down a side street, the home where Mayor Fisher and his family lived and several other landmarks in town.

It was odd taking a seat at a table in the restaurant where Kinsey spent so much time working. For an instant, she wanted to head back into the kitchen, fetch the coffee pot herself.

But Mrs. Townsend greeted them with a smile as they took a table near the window and she filled their coffee cups.

"Busy today," Kinsey commented, glancing around.

"Very. But no Dixie, of course." Mrs. Townsend's troubled expression bloomed into a pleasant smile once more. "Mr. Mason, I heard you'd taken on the church project. We're all praying for you."

"Thank you," Jared said. "How about bringing us the chicken special?"

"Sure thing," Mrs. Townsend said. "Oh, and by the way, I have an idea for the church that I'm sure you'll love."

"Can't wait to hear it," Jared said.

She smiled sweetly and disappeared into the kitchen.

"Does this happen whenever you start a new project?" Kinsey asked. "Everyone has an idea they want to share?"

"World's full of ideas," Jared said. "Developing that idea into something substantial is the interesting part."

"You enjoy your work?"

Jared smiled a special smile. Kinsey had noticed the same look on Clark's face when he was busy working in his study or when she and Beth visited him at a construction site. True joy and fulfillment.

Jared sipped his coffee. "I've got a project waiting for me when I get back home. I'll be heading up to Maine for a few months."

"That's what all your brothers do, isn't it?" Kinsey asked. "Move around, oversee projects?"

"Have to go where the work is."

"I guess Clark's decision to stay in Virginia caused a bit of a rift in the family," Kinsey said.

Jared frowned. "What are you talking about?"

"Oh, I thought you knew," she said, feeling a little guilty for speaking out of turn, though she supposed it didn't matter now. "Clark and Beth discussed it. He decided that with Sam on the way, he wanted to stay in one place. In Virginia. He wanted to have a permanent home."

Jared looked thoughtful. "Clark decided to do that?"

"I got the feeling that having a family of his own changed things for him," Kinsey said. "I suppose being married, with a child on the way, could do that."

"Maybe…"

"You don't agree?" she asked.

"A man's got to do what's best for himself and for his family. He's got to build a business, keep it running."

"Even if that doesn't suit his wife?"

Jared dismissed her words with a wave of his hand. "Truth is, I'll be lucky if I find a wife who even notices I'm gone for months at a time."

"Sounds as if you don't have very high standards for a wife."

"Do you mean falling in love, being crazy about the woman I marry, expecting her to feel the same about me?"

"That's the way it usually works," Kinsey pointed out.

"All I'm looking for is a woman I can tolerate. One I can live with. That's it."

Mrs. Townsend came in from the kitchen and placed hot plates of chicken, potatoes and vegetables on their table, along with a basket of fresh bread.

"Stained glass windows," she said. "For the church. I saw them in a picture once. I think our church should have dozens of those beautiful windows. Why, we can use them instead of walls. Doesn't that sound delightful?"

"Yes, ma'am," Jared said. "I'll keep it in mind."

Mrs. Townsend smiled and headed back into the kitchen.

Jared dug into his meal and nodded through the window in the direction of Hudson's Mercantile.

"So what were you and Hudson's daughter hiding in those crates?"

"Nothing," Kinsey insisted, then cringed hearing the childish tone in her voice. She glanced up at Jared's raised eyebrows and knowing smirk, and knew that was the exact look she'd given Sam on more than one occasion.

"Fabric," she admitted, then smiled remembering the color and feel of the cloth. "The blue satin was beautiful. I can picture it made into a grand dress. Maggie orders the most lovely fabrics, when she can do it without her father knowing it."

"Hudson's got something against women having nice clothes?" Jared asked.

"He prefers simpler fashions. Thinks they're more appropriate for women," Kinsey said. "You see, some time back, there was an…incident… with Maggie's mother."

"And another man?"

"If it had been simply another man…" Kinsey's voice trailed off. "Well, if that's all it was, things might be easier for Maggie."

Jared nodded and Kinsey was glad she didn't have to go into more detail. They ate in silence for a moment, then Jared spoke again.

"The other night you said you had a plan for your future. What is it?"

Kinsey remembered mentioning to him that she had a plan when he'd asked her not to work last Saturday night washing dishes here at this very restaurant. He hadn't mentioned it since and she'd thought her comment had passed unnoticed. Apparently, it hadn't.

Not much, it seemed, got past Jared.

Kinsey stalled for a moment, sampling the vegetables and potatoes on her plate. The truth was she'd considered many plans but hadn't settled on anything yet. Not that she could afford to act on a plan, at the moment.

"I intend to start my own business," she finally said, because that was the one thing she'd always dreamed of doing.

"What sort of business?" Jared asked, breaking off a chunk of the bread.

"Anything but a restaurant," Kinsey told him.

"Washed enough dishes already?" Jared asked.

"Enough to last a lifetime," she said.

Jared nodded. "The town's growing. There must be a number of businesses that are needed."

Kinsey smiled, as old memories surfaced. "Beth and I used to dream about owning our own dress shop. Making the most beautiful gowns imaginable."

"I haven't seen a place like that in town," Jared said.

"Mrs. Hartwood had a dress shop but closed it after she had a baby," Kinsey said. "She never sews for anyone now."

"Why don't you open a shop?"

There were so many reasons, Kinsey hardly knew where to start. She'd need a store, fabric, thread, buttons, patterns, dress forms. She'd have to make up some dresses to display in her shop windows, to show what she was capable of, to lure customers in.

But the two things she'd need most were the

same things that always seemed to be in shortest supply: time and money.

How would she support Sam and herself? How would she give her son the attention he deserved? *And* open a business?

Kinsey drew in a breath, shifting the idea to the recesses of her mind. "I might open a dress shop one day."

Jared didn't say anything else and Kinsey was glad. He ordered pie for them and they ate it while he talked about some of his building projects.

"I guess I'd better get back to the boardinghouse," Kinsey said, glancing out the window and seeing that the afternoon had passed quickly.

Jared paid their tab and they walked outside together. He settled his hat on his head and looked down at her.

"Thanks for eating with me," he said. "I've had a lot of meals alone. It's nice to have company."

Kinsey smiled. "I enjoyed it," she said, and she truly meant it.

Spending this time with Jared had been more peaceful than she'd thought possible. He'd been a thorn in her side since he'd arrived in Crystal Springs. It surprised her to see this different side of him.

"School will be dismissed soon," Kinsey said. "We can walk over and get Sam, if you'd like."

Jared looked down at her, a mixture of surprise and suspicion on his face, as if he were reluctant to believe this bit of good fortune.

"You're sure?" he asked.

No, she wasn't sure. Maybe it would prove a mistake. But the truth was that, as Jared had said, he was Sam's uncle. He was family. And that counted for a great deal in Kinsey's mind.

"I'm sure," she said, then couldn't resist a teasing smile. "There's usually quite a few other mamas there after school. Maybe you can pick up some more ideas on building the church?"

Jared chuckled and rolled his eyes, and they headed down the boardwalk toward the schoolhouse at the edge of town.

"Mrs. Templeton! Mrs. Templeton!"

Nathan Gannon, the senior express agent, rushed out of the stage depot as they walked past, waving an envelope.

"Glad I caught you. Saved me a trip," he said, adjusting his sleeve garters and straightening his visor. "Would you pass this along to Mrs. Vaughn? It just came for her."

"Certainly," Kinsey said.

"Appreciate it," Nathan said. Then he leaned

back a little and peered up at Jared. "Mr. Mason, is it? Glad to hear you've taken over building the church. Listen, I've got some ideas for you."

"Write them down, will you? I'll pick them up later."

"Sure thing." Nathan hustled back into the depot.

Kinsey stared down at the envelope in her hand and felt a little chill. Jared looked over her shoulder.

"Is that from...?" he asked.

"Baltimore," Kinsey said, seeing the return address in the corner. "It must be from Lily's cousin."

"Damn," he whispered.

Kinsey heaved a troubled breath. "I guess she'll find out tonight whether she's leaving Crystal Springs."

Chapter Sixteen

Nell's husband, who'd built the boardinghouse on a grand scale, had included a study for himself. No one ever used it. The door stayed closed and locked, off-limits to the residents. In fact, Kinsey hadn't thought much about the room until Nell mentioned it as the supper dishes were finished up.

"Mr. Mason," Nell announced, producing the key from her skirt pocket. "For you."

As was his custom, Jared ate in the kitchen, rather than in the dining room with the rest of the residents. He looked up from his cup of coffee.

"You'll need a comfortable place to work on the church plans," Nell said. "The study will be perfect."

Kinsey exchanged a look with Lily as she carried the last stack of dried dishes to the cupboard. Neither of them had been inside the study, but both followed behind Nell as she led the way out of the kitchen along with Jared and Sam.

At the back corner of the house, Nell unlocked the door and stepped inside, lighting the lanterns on the wall. The spacious room came alive displaying floor-to-ceiling bookshelves on two walls, a massive mahogany desk, leather settee and chairs and a thick rug on the floor.

"Oh, my…," Lily sighed.

"This is beautiful," Kinsey agreed, never imagining such a lovely room was hidden away behind the locked door. Sam peeked out from around her skirt, his eyes wide. "Don't touch anything," she whispered.

"My husband, God rest his soul, ordered all the furniture, the books, everything from back east," Nell said. "He never got to use this room, but I know he'd be happy that it's being put to good use, to plan the town's new church."

"Thank you, Nell," Jared said, accepting the key that she passed to him.

Nell gave the room another quick gaze, then, seemingly lost in recollections of her husband, hurried away.

"This is nicer than your room upstairs," Kinsey said quietly to Jared.

"Bigger, too," he said.

"How are the plans coming?" Lily asked.

"I'll have something to show to Miss Patterson in a few days," Jared said.

"The sooner the better," Lily said.

"Mama, can we read that book?" Sam asked, pointing to a tall, wide book on one of the upper shelves.

Kinsey hurried over. "Please, Sam, don't touch anything. These books belong to Nell, not us."

"But, Mama, I want to see the big red one," Sam said, stretching upward. "Please?"

"All right," Kinsey said. "But just a quick look."

She held out her arms to pick him up, but Jared stopped her.

"Can I do that?" he asked.

His offer surprised her, but she nodded.

"Come up here, partner," Jared said.

Effortlessly, he lifted Sam and held him close to the bookcase. Kinsey marveled at the strength Jared displayed, easily holding Sam in one arm. She could barely pick Sam up anymore.

"This is a book of maps," Jared said, reading the spine.

Kinsey joined them. "Maps of the whole world. My goodness, Sam, you picked a good book to read."

His eyes widened. "Can we read it? Can we?"

"I'll ask Miss Nell," Jared promised. "If she—"

A sniffle interrupted Jared, and Kinsey turned to see Lily hurrying from the room. She'd often thought how it must hurt Lily to see Sam every day, watching him grow up and knowing she didn't—and probably would never—have a child of her own.

"Go see about her," Jared said softly.

Kinsey wanted to go, yet she hesitated.

Jared must have read her thoughts. "I'll take care of Sam. We'll stay right here in the study. I swear."

Kinsey looked back and forth between the two of them and saw sincerity on Jared's face, puzzlement on Sam's. The boy didn't understand what was going on and Kinsey intended to keep it that way.

"I'll just be a minute," Kinsey said, and hurried out of the study.

She checked the kitchen, looked outside, then made the long climb up the stairs to the third floor where Lily had a room across the hall from Nell's. She knocked softly on the door, then opened it and stepped in when she heard Lily's soft crying.

The room was small, but Lily had turned it into a home, as she did with everything she touched.

A warm quilt on the bed, ruffled curtains on the windows, a colorful rug, fresh flowers on the bureau.

Lily stood by the window, sniffling into a handkerchief.

"I'm sorry," she said. "I don't know what came over me downstairs just now. I was looking at the way Jared held little Sam and for a minute I—I imagined…"

Lily cried harder now. Kinsey put her arm around her shoulders, offering what little comfort she could. No doubt, in Lily's mind, she had seen Isaac and one of their children, rather than Jared and Sam.

How many times must Lily have envisioned such a sight?

How many times might Isaac have done the same thing? she wondered.

"Let me get Isaac," Kinsey said softly. "That husband of yours has got some very big shoulders for you to cry on."

Lily sobbed harder and shook her head. "No, no…I can't do that."

"Isaac could probably use some comforting, too," Kinsey said.

Her eyes widened, as if she hadn't thought of that. But, still, she shook her head.

"No…" she said, her voice a raw whisper.

For an instant, Kinsey felt anger toward Lily. She had the one thing any woman would dearly love to have: a good husband. One who loved her, cherished her, provided for her and would do anything she asked. Yet Lily was so hurt she couldn't see those things. She couldn't appreciate them.

Kinsey pushed aside her anger, recalling what Lily had been through with the deaths of both her babies. Kinsey wasn't sure how she'd feel under those same circumstances. She hoped she wouldn't turn away from her husband, as Lily had, but who knew for sure until confronted with the situation.

Lily wiped her nose and eyes and drew in a breath, as if willing her emotions into submission.

"That letter you brought me from the express office this afternoon," she said. "It was from my cousin in Baltimore."

"What did she say?"

"I can come live with her…if I want to."

Kinsey's heart sank. She'd hoped Lily's cousin would turn her down, refuse her request to come live with her, leaving Lily no choice but to stay in Crystal Springs and work out her problems with Isaac.

"What are you going to do?" Kinsey asked.

Lily turned her tear-streaked face to Kinsey. "I don't know. I just don't know what to do."

When Kinsey returned to the study she found Jared seated in the leather chair behind the desk and Sam on his lap. They were both leaning over a big book, a map of the world spread out on its pages.

How handsome the two of them looked, Kinsey thought. And so much alike. Dark heads bowed forward, little frowns of concentration on their faces. Jared spoke softly and pointed while Sam nodded.

Then she realized what the two of them were looking at.

"Did Nell give her permission to look at that book?" she asked, walking to the desk.

Both their heads came up at the same time, eyes wide now. They glanced at each other.

"Uncle Jared said it was all right," Sam said.

Jared cut his gaze to the boy, then back to Kinsey. "I figured she wouldn't care."

Kinsey gave her sternest look to Sam. "But we don't take things without asking, do we, Sam?"

"No, ma'am," he said quietly.

"Maybe you should remind Uncle Jared of that next time," Kinsey said, giving Jared a disapproving look. "Come on, Sam, time for bed."

"'Night, Uncle Jared." Sam slipped off his lap and hurried out of the room.

"It was just a book," Jared said. "Nell wouldn't have cared."

"Probably not," Kinsey said. "But Sam needs to mind his manners. He needs to do what's right. You can't be a bad example."

"A bad example?" Jared got to his feet. "I wasn't a bad—"

He stopped then and looked the tiniest bit contrite. "All right. Fine."

Kinsey got Sam tucked into bed, enduring more than the usual questions from him. Sam had an inquisitive mind, sometimes asking things that Kinsey never considered. But by the time she kissed his cheek and turned the lantern down low, Sam was already asleep.

Slipping out of their room, Kinsey headed for the study. As she approached, she saw lantern light still shining inside. Only then did she wonder why she'd been drawn back to this room.

She knew why immediately upon entering and finding Jared on the settee, leafing through a book. The lantern beside him cast golden light over his features. How handsome he was.

Kinsey felt a little silly returning to the study so quickly, as if she had a right to be there. But Jared seemed to sense her presence and looked up right away. Was that a hint of a smile on his face? Or something else"

He got to his feet and just stared at her. Maybe he was a little surprised to see her. Kinsey couldn't be sure.

The one thing she was sure of was that the hour was late and all the other boardinghouse residents had retired for the evening. She knew she should go too. It wasn't proper for her to be here, alone with Jared.

"How's Lily?" Jared asked.

Kinsey ventured farther into the room, telling herself that she would stay for only a moment.

"She'd stopped crying when I left her room," Kinsey said.

Jared walked closer. "And that letter from her cousin in Baltimore?"

"An invitation to come live there." Kinsey's shoulders slumped, hearing her own words spoken aloud.

"Damn..." Jared mumbled.

She nodded. "I tried talking to her, tried to get

her to let me fetch Isaac, but she wouldn't have any part of it—or him."

"So is she leaving?"

"She doesn't know yet. I don't know how she can make that decision without consulting Isaac. That's no way to treat a husband," Kinsey declared, then realized what she'd said. "I suppose I should keep my opinion to myself. I've never had a husband and I never will."

Jared caught her gaze. "You don't like the idea of being married?"

"Having a husband would present certain… problems," Kinsey said, feeling her cheeks grow warm.

"Such as?"

For a man who so often seemed to read her thoughts, Jared apparently had no idea what she was referring to. Or maybe he was simply teasing her again.

Honestly, this man seemed to test her patience in so many ways.

"Any man who agreed to marry me would have certain *expectations*," Kinsey said, bobbing her brows as if that might further explain her concerns. "Everyone in the world—except for you— thinks that I was married, that I'd given birth to a child."

"*Oh.*" Jared nodded. Then his gaze dipped, covering the length of her, bringing a deeper heat to her cheeks.

"I can never marry," Kinsey said, pushing through her discomfort. "How would I ever explain?"

"You might just tell the truth?" Jared suggested, then gave her a small grin. "I say that because I'm trying to set a good example."

Kinsey smiled, though she didn't want to, then dismissed their conversation with the wave of her hand.

"It doesn't matter, anyway. I have no plans to marry anytime soon," she said.

"Hard for me to believe there's not a man in this town somewhere who's not shown an interest in you," Jared said, his gaze seeming to see straight through her.

When she'd arrived in Crystal Springs, she'd had her share of attention from the single men in town. But she'd been so busy with Sam, with finding a job and a place to live that she'd paid little attention. She'd discouraged the few men who had persisted in their attempts to court her until they finally directed their romantic overtures elsewhere.

"You're expecting to fall head over heels in love with someone, right?" Jared asked.

Kinsey couldn't deny his words. "I admit, I have high expectations, after seeing how happy Clark and Beth were."

Jared eased closer. "Two people in love. I wonder what that feels like?"

Kinsey gazed up at him, feeling the heat of his body. "Yes," she whispered. "I wonder what it feels like."

"Maybe something like this?"

Jared closed his arms around her and drew her to him. Kinsey went willingly, feeling her soft curves fall against his hard angles. He gazed into her eyes for a few seconds. Then his arm circled her waist and he pulled her up, kissing her on the mouth.

He blended their lips together and looped his other arm around her, closing her in a tight circle. Warmth spread through Kinsey as his mouth moved over hers. She lifted herself onto her toes and draped her arms around his neck, feeling the need to hold on as he deepened their kiss.

Jared groaned low in his throat causing Kinsey to whimper in response. Heat rolled off of him as he angled closer and ran his hand up her spine.

He dug his fingers into the hair at her nape, weakening her knees.

He pulled away then, his mouth still hovering near hers, his hot breath puffing against her lips. Kinsey didn't let go either, simply hung in his embrace, unsteady on her feet. She didn't know how he remained standing.

Jared eased back a little and gazed into her eyes. The intense heat from his body cooled a little with the distance between them. Kinsey craved it and moved closer once more.

"Is this what it feels like to be in love?" she whispered, gazing up into his eyes.

"Is—what?" He looked confused, the only time she'd ever seen that expression on his face. "I, uh, I'm not thinking so clearly…right now."

Passion, heat—something—swelled inside Kinsey with the knowledge of what she'd done to him. This highly intelligent man, capable and competent, suddenly rendered mindless after their kiss. She'd done that to him…and it seemed all right with him.

Jared strummed his finger down her cheek and lowered his head again. Kinsey's heart thudded harder in her chest, expecting another kiss.

His head jerked up. He swung her behind him

and stepped forward toward the door. She held on to his arm.

"I thought I saw something," Jared said, then shook his head. "I guess it was…nothing."

Kinsey gasped. Had someone come to the doorway, seen the two of them kissing—*again*?

She would lose her job.

Glancing up at Jared, another emotion rushed through her mind, replacing the fear: it might be worth it.

Chapter Seventeen

How the hell was he going to design a church when his head was filled with sinful thoughts?

Jared looked up from the plans spread out on the desk in front of him and glanced at the door. Footsteps? Had he heard someone approach? Was it Kinsey?

He waited for a few seconds. No light, delicate scent tantalized his nose. No rustling of skirts and petticoats.

No Kinsey.

Grumbling under his breath, Jared turned back to the plans he'd been working on for several days now. He'd looked over the designs the townsfolk had come up with, the crude drawings that Miss Patterson had rejected. He'd considered all the wild, crazy ideas the people of Crystal Springs had bombarded him with since he'd taken on this project. And still, he hadn't finalized a plan of his own. How could he with all the distractions?

Thoughts of Kinsey, mainly. Her scent wafting through the study, somehow reaching him from all corners of the house. Thinking he heard the swish of her skirts and all those petticoats underneath. His head bobbing up and down from the plans to the door, expecting to see her standing there.

She'd been into the study a few times, letting him know meals were ready, asking if he needed anything, or bringing him another cup of coffee. Each time the mere appearance of her had set him back another hour or two as he tried to refocus his thoughts on the church plans.

So it was Kinsey's fault that his work wasn't done, Jared decided. Kinsey kept interrupting him.

And when she *didn't,* he found himself wishing that she *would.*

He never should have kissed her, Jared decided as he twirled a pencil between his fingers and stared off at nothing. Never should have held her in his arms, felt her soft breasts against his chest, buried his nose in the sweet hollow of her neck, splayed his fingers—

"Hellfire…" Jared pushed to his feet, fighting off another wave of wanting, and looked down in disgust at the church plans on the desk.

What the hell was wrong with him? He'd designed buildings much more complex in half the time. And he didn't have eternity to devote to this project. He had a job waiting for him in Maine, one that he couldn't put off. He needed to get the church plan finished so he could leave this town as soon as the situation with Clark's boy was resolved.

He had responsibilities, commitments and plans that couldn't wait. And here he was befuddled by a one-room church.

Or maybe it wasn't the church that befuddled him.

Kinsey drifted back into Jared's mind. Her smile, her scent…all those petticoats…

"Damn." Jared tossed the pencil aside and stalked out of the study.

Kinsey whirled as Jared strode into the kitchen, she and Lily exchanging a troubled look as he headed toward the back door without a word.

"How're the plans—"

"I'm chopping wood," he barked as he kept going.

"But, Jared, we have plenty of—"

The door slammed shut as he disappeared outside.

Kinsey and Lily both peered after him.

"He looks a little...worked up," Lily offered.

"I suppose sitting at a desk for hours can wear on a person," Kinsey said.

Lily gave her a knowing look. "I don't think boredom is his problem."

"Oh?" Kinsey thought for a moment, then her cheeks flushed. *"Oh!"*

Lily took a stack of plates from the cupboard and headed for the dining room.

Kinsey hurried back to the sideboard and concentrated on peeling potatoes for supper. Good gracious, what a turn her life had taken since Jared Mason arrived. Here she was thinking all sorts of *thoughts* about him—of all people.

Determinedly, she focused on the potatoes, slicing away the peelings. Midafternoon. Sam would be home from school soon. Supper had to be prepared. Dozens of things to do.

Yet how could she concentrate with the ringing of the axe intruding on her every thought?

Kinsey glanced out the window. At the woodshed, Jared raised the axe high over his head and slammed it down, splitting a log in half with one powerful swing. He'd rolled back his sleeves and she could see the hard muscles in his forearms. Flexing, straining. He was sweating already. Dampness darkened the back of his shirt.

Her heart beat a little faster as she watched. She remembered going to the construction site in Lynchburg with Beth to visit Clark, seeing him climb the skeletal building frame, quick as a cat, strong as a panther. Kinsey imagined Jared doing the same. Those long legs and big shoulders. Muscular arms. The same arms that had held her close, pulled her against him with such tenderness as he'd pressed his mouth to hers and—Jared suddenly dropped the axe and turned. Kinsey gasped as she saw Sam and the Gleason boys running toward him.

She'd been so caught up watching Jared she hadn't noticed her own son, let alone the four friends with him. What had happened to her?

Kinsey gave herself a mental shake and glanced around. Luckily, Lily hadn't returned to the kitchen to notice her blatant ogling. She hurried to the sideboard and the potatoes that waited, forcing herself to concentrate on the task.

Playful screams and wild laughter interrupted her again. Kinsey went back to the window and saw Sam and all the Gleason boys piled up together on the ground. What sort of wrestling match were they having? Kinsey wondered.

Then amid the tangle of arms and legs, she spotted Jared. At the very bottom of the stack, he lay flat on the ground, all the boys atop him struggling to hold him down. They seemed to be succeeding, too, Kinsey realized. She smiled at the joy the boys were having, tumbling over each other, wrestling, squirming, laughing, all working together against Jared.

Then she took pity on him. Should she go outside and intervene? Make the boys let him go? He was a big, strong man but there were five of the boys and maybe—

A guttural growl like a grizzly bear sounded and Jared surged to his feet, bringing all the boys up with him. They screamed and hung on, dangling from his back, his shoulders, his arms, his legs.

Kinsey's heart lurched. Such strength…

And such care, she realized a moment later. The boys seemed to cling to him for their lives but, actually, Jared held the two smallest to keep them from falling. He could have easily shaken off even the older boys, but didn't.

Kinsey had never roughhoused with Sam the

way Jared did. First of all, she couldn't have lifted him, and really, she'd never considered doing it. Yet Sam seemed to love it. He giggled and wrestled and squealed with delight.

A little knot tugged at Kinsey's stomach. She'd never seen Sam look happier...ever.

"Sam? Sam!"

Kinsey shaded her eyes against the final rays of the disappearing sun, searching the yard for Sam. He'd gone outside after supper to play with the Gleason boys. Now there was no sign of any of them.

She headed out the door but Nell called to her from across the room.

"Sam's inside," she said, gesturing through the house. "I saw him a while ago with Mr. Mason."

How unlike Sam, Kinsey thought as she walked toward the study. Playing outside with his friends was his favorite past time. She wondered for a moment if he wasn't feeling well.

She found him in the study perched on a stack of books in a dining room chair pulled up to the desk. Jared sat beside him. Both of them were busy working.

Kinsey smiled when she saw the two of them

together, her heart warming as it seemed to so often now.

"What are you two up to?" she asked, coming into the room. Both their heads came up at the same time.

"Making a picture, Mama," Sam said, waving the paper he was working on.

She eased between the two of them and looked down at Sam's picture, a drawing of a tree. It always amazed her that, at so young a age, the boy already showed his father's artistic gift.

"Very nice," Kinsey said, touching the top of his head. She turned to Jared. "And what are you making?"

"It's a church, Mama," Sam told her. "Only it doesn't look like a church. But that's okay, huh, Uncle Jared?"

"It will look like a church when it gets built," Jared said.

Kinsey looked over his shoulder at the straight lines, the sharp angles he'd drawn, the carefully printed numbers and words he'd included. She'd seen Clark do this sort of thing and always marveled at how, not only had he drawn it, but also understood it.

"Is this what you'll show Miss Patterson?" Kinsey asked.

"No. This," Jared said, pulling a smaller drawing from another stack of paper. This one was a pencil rendering of the church.

"It's beautiful," Kinsey said. "I don't see how Miss Patterson can not like it."

"I'll finish up the last of it tonight, and show it to her tomorrow," Jared said, sounding confident that his work would please her.

"Evening," Caleb Burk called, coming into the room.

They all exchanged greetings.

"I appreciate your help on this," Caleb said, setting the satchel he carried on the desk.

"I understand you're adding on to the store," Kinsey said.

"It's the right thing for the business," Caleb said, then shook his head sorrowfully. "But the Lord only knows what Dabney Hudson will do when he finds out."

Everyone nodded in agreement.

"Come along, Sam, let's go," Kinsey said.

"No, Mama," he pleaded.

"These men have work to do," she said.

"I don't want to go, Mama." He turned to Jared. "Can I stay, Uncle Jared? Can I?"

He shrugged. "Sure. You can—"

Kinsey threw Jared a look that silenced him instantly and even caused Caleb to draw in a quick breath.

"Mama…said…*no*," Kinsey said.

All three of them shuffled uncomfortably, before Jared spoke up.

"You need to do what your mama said," he told Sam. "She's the boss. She knows what's best."

Sam pressed his lips together, but didn't protest.

"Of course," Jared said, "maybe if you ask her really, really nice, she'll change her mind."

Sam's eyes widened. "Can I stay, Mama? Please? Please? I'll be good. I promise. Please?"

"It's all right if he stays," Jared offered.

Kinsey relented. "All right, Sam, you can stay for a while longer," she said and was rewarded with the big smile she loved to see.

"I'll get some coffee," she offered.

"I'll give you a hand," Jared said.

They walked into the kitchen together. Jared fetched cups, saucers and a tray from the cupboard while Kinsey got the coffee pot warming on the stove. She filled the cups.

"Sam's a good boy," Jared said. "He'd have made Clark a proud papa."

Tears sprang in Kinsey's eyes. "It breaks my heart to think what Clark and Beth missed out on with him."

Jared eased his arm around her shoulders and pulled her close. He rested his cheek atop her head. His strength flowed into her, somehow fortifying her against the thoughts of Sam's parents that often troubled her.

"The boy's lucky to have you for his mama," Jared said softly.

A tear rolled down Kinsey's cheek and she looked up at him. "I love Sam so much, Jared."

"I know," he said. "I can see that."

He snuggled her close again and they stood in the embrace for a while. How nice it felt, Kinsey thought, to have someone who knew the truth of Sam's past, who understood what she'd been through, who shared her feelings.

She sniffed and looked up at Jared again. "Sam's really taken to you."

"That makes me a lucky man," he said.

Jared touched her cheek with his thumb, blotting the tear that hung there. Then he leaned down and planted a soft kiss on the spot.

It was the sweetest kiss Kinsey had ever received—or could ever imagine. None of the heat or intensity of the other kisses Jared had given her. Just kindness in this one. Caring and tenderness.

Jared lingered a moment, then picked up the tray and left the kitchen. Kinsey watched him go, feeling a little bit of her go along with him. For an instant, she thought she might cry again.

The door to the side porch opened and Lily came inside. Kinsey wondered if perhaps Lily had seen her and Jared in the kitchen together. But Lily seemed deep in thought, not really seeing Kinsey there at all.

Halfway across the kitchen, she stopped and turned back to Kinsey.

"I've made my decision about going to Baltimore," she said, looking even more troubled now. "I'm going."

"Oh, Lily…"

"I've made up my mind," she said. "It's for the best. I just can't live here anymore with all the… memories."

"What about your friends? All the people who care about you?" Kinsey asked. "What about Isaac?"

"I—I don't know…" Tears swelled in Lily's eyes but she gulped them down.

"You *are* going to tell him, aren't you? You can't just leave without a word," Kinsey said, afraid that Lily might do just that.

"I'll tell him." Lily swiped a tear from the corner of her eye. "Somehow…"

Kinsey's heart ached as Lily hurried from the room, up the back steps toward the third floor. She envisioned Lily crying herself to sleep tonight and decided that she'd go up later and check on her.

Maybe she would get Lily to change her mind. Make her see that running away didn't solve anything.

Yet wasn't that exactly what she had done? She'd run away with Sam. Even if it was with Beth's blessing and for all the right reasons; perhaps she should have stayed and confronted the Mason family. Nothing had been resolved by her actions those years ago. She'd just postponed the inevitable. Jared was here. He'd found them and was determined to take Sam away—

"Oh, gracious…" Kinsey whispered the words in the silent kitchen as a reality she'd never expected sliced through her.

Jared might very well take Sam away from her.

And that would mean Jared would leave, too.

Chapter Eighteen

Nell took the last platter of scrambled eggs into the dining room for the boardinghouse residents as Lily put some on the smaller table in the kitchen. From the cookstove where Kinsey stood frying bacon, she glanced back into her bedroom and saw Sam buttoning his shirt.

"Come on, honey," she called. "Breakfast is almost ready."

"We've got a hungry bunch this morning," Nell said, coming back from the dining room.

Lily pulled another pan of biscuits from the oven. "Maybe this will satisfy them," she said.

Kinsey put the strips of sizzling bacon onto a platter and took it to the kitchen table, expecting to see Sam already seated there.

"Sam?" She turned and looked back toward their bedroom, then said to Lily, "I'll be right back."

She made a quick search of the bedroom but

didn't find him. How unlike Sam, she thought, standing in the back hallway. She hadn't seen him go outside so there was only one direction he could have gone.

Kinsey climbed the stairway and heard Sam's voice coming from down the hall.

From Jared's room.

Kinsey hesitated. The door stood open but it was highly inappropriate for her to enter the room, even if she'd already done so once before—and been soundly kissed in the process.

How did she keep ending up in these awkward situations with Jared?

Yet it wasn't right for Sam to be in Jared's room. Upon hiring Kinsey for the job, Nell had made it clear that Sam wasn't to disturb the residents. Kinsey agreed completely. The folks who boarded with Nell paid good money to live there and should be afforded privacy and a quiet atmosphere. Sam's behavior had never been a problem.

Until now.

Kinsey glanced back down the staircase. What if Nell came looking for her? Would she fire her if Sam disturbed one of her residents?

Of course, she was sure Jared wouldn't complain, but Kinsey couldn't take the chance. She simply could not lose her job.

"Sam? Come out here." She hurried to the door. And froze.

Jared stood at the washstand naked from the waist up. Half his face was covered with white foamy soap, the other shaved clean. He held a straight razor in his hand. A white towel was thrown over one bare shoulder.

Dark hair covered his chest and washboard belly, then disappeared into the waist band of his trousers. Beads of water clung in the crinkly hair, glistening in the morning sunlight.

"Morning," Jared said, his voice low and mellow.

"G-good…morning," Kinsey said, realizing that she'd stopped breathing for a moment. She drew in a breath but couldn't take her eyes off of him. She'd never seen a man's bare chest before.

At least, none that looked like Jared's.

Straight shoulders, bulging arms, a wide chest, a tight belly with hair that seemed to arrow straight down to his—

"Look, Mama, Uncle Jared's shaving," Sam said.

Only then did she notice Sam sitting on the

bureau next to the washstand holding a shave mug in his hand.

"I'm getting some help this morning," Jared said, gesturing to Sam.

If Jared was embarrassed at being caught without his shirt, he gave no indication. Instead he looked relaxed and content—with Sam's presence and her own.

"See, Mama? That's a razor and that thing right there is to keep it sharp," Sam said, pointing. "Come here, Mama. Look. Look at what Uncle Jared's doing."

If she looked any longer, she might melt into a puddle on the floor.

"Come along, Sam. You don't want to be late for school," Kinsey said, forcing herself into motion.

"But, Mama..."

"Do what your mama says." Jared dropped the razor into the washbasin and lifted Sam to the floor. He patted his back and sent him on his way.

"Go eat your breakfast," Kinsey said as Sam scooted past. She knew she should follow, but then Jared walked toward her and she couldn't seem to budge from the spot.

He towered over her, his closeness somehow

stealing her breath once more. He smelled of soap. The side of his face he'd already shaved looked dewy and soft.

What would it be like to touch it? Kinsey's hand suddenly ached with the need to press her palm against his cheek.

And, maybe, against his chest, too. Certainly his shoulders, the flexing muscles of his arms. Or rake her fingers through the sprinkling of coarse hair that swirled around his—

"There's something not right about this situation," Jared said.

Kinsey's cheeks flamed. Had he read her thoughts? Was her expression so obvious?

Then she realized that Jared was gazing down the hallway toward the staircase.

"That boy's five years old," he said, "and he's never seen a man shave before?"

Well, it was an impressive sight, Kinsey thought, not to be missed.

Then she realized that Jared meant something else entirely.

"Who's going to teach Sam to shave when he gets old enough?" Jared asked. "Have you thought about that?"

He hadn't said the words unkindly or with any sort of accusation, but with concern and worry.

"I never thought about it," Kinsey admitted. "He's only five, as you pointed out."

Jared let the words hang there for a minute, then nodded. "I guess you'll get it figured out."

She'd have to, wouldn't she?

"Breakfast is ready," she told him, then hurried back down the staircase and into the kitchen. She found Sam already at the table with Nell and Lily.

Kinsey smiled at his sweet face, his soft cheeks and chin. Sam shaving one day? It didn't seem possible.

Yet in that same instant, in her mind, she saw him swaddled in a blanket, sucking his thumb while she rocked him to sleep. Five years. Gone.

How had that happened?

And maybe she really should be concerned about how quickly the time would come when Sam needed a man to teach him to shave.

"I have a good feeling about today," Nell said, as she sat at the kitchen table across from Kinsey shelling peas. "I'm just sure Bess Patterson is going to love Mr. Mason's plan for the church."

"I hope you're right," Kinsey said, glancing out the window. Jared had left just after their noon meal, plans tucked inside his satchel, ready to present them to Miss Patterson. She expected him back any time now.

Nell leaned forward a little and, judging by the tilt of her head, Kinsey could see that she'd moved on to another subject entirely.

"Have you spoken with Lily about her…situation?" Nell asked in a low voice.

Kinsey was sure that Nell knew all about Lily's plan to leave Crystal Springs. And by tonight, the entire town would know it, too.

Lily had spent the morning in her room composing a letter to Isaac, advising him of her decision. She'd asked one of the residents to drop it by the sheriff's office on their way into town. Kinsey felt certain Isaac hadn't gotten it yet.

"I told her she should have talked to Isaac in person," Kinsey said, shaking her head.

"She couldn't face him," Nell said reasonably. "I understand that. You know he'll be upset. And I don't blame him, of course."

Kinsey could imagine Isaac Vaughn's reaction to learning from a letter that his wife was leaving town for good. *Upset* couldn't begin to describe his reaction.

"I was by Hudson's Mercantile earlier today," Nell said, changing their topic of conversation yet again. "Dabney showed me the most beautiful fabrics. They'd just come in."

"Oh?" Kinsey was reminded that Maggie had promised to save the blue satin fabric for her until she decided whether or not she could afford it.

"I was thinking I might treat myself to—"

Nell stopped, her attention drawn out the window. "Why, there comes Mr. Mason now. And he looks…oh, dear…"

Kinsey looked out the window at Jared heading toward the house. Obviously, from his expression, his meeting with Miss Patterson hadn't gone well.

Coming inside, Jared hung his hat on the hook beside the door and gave both Nell and Kinsey a courteous nod, then continued on toward the study.

Nell and Kinsey shared a troubled look.

"Maybe you should take him something to eat," Nell suggested.

It couldn't hurt, Kinsey decided.

She poured lemonade, got oatmeal cookies from the pie safe and went to the study. She found Jared slumped in the chair behind the desk, gazing up at the ceiling. He looked weary and annoyed.

Bess Patterson had that effect on most everyone.

"I'm guessing it didn't go well?" Kinsey asked, placing the tray on the desk.

Jared sat stewing for another moment, then sat up in the chair.

"Crystal Springs is never going to get a new church."

"You're—you're quitting?" she asked, surprised.

Jared shook his head. "It won't matter *who* comes up with a design for the church or what the building will look like. That Patterson woman won't like anything."

Kinsey placed the glass of lemonade in front of him. "She's a bit of a trial."

"I've seen this before in clients. Miss Patterson can't tell me what she wants because she doesn't know herself." Jared gulped down half the lemonade, then popped a whole cookie in his mouth. "No matter what you show her, she's not going to like it. The town ought to buy those building supplies from her, and go ahead with the project on their own."

"I don't know if that's possible," Kinsey said. "As soon as Reverend Battenfield got here he started a building fund. But I doubt there's enough money in it to cover everything that's already been purchased. Besides, giving Miss

Patterson back her money and telling her it's not wanted would be highly insulting."

Jared seemed to consider her words as he helped himself to another cookie.

"Maybe if you came up with another design?" Kinsey suggested. "Surely Miss Patterson gave you some idea of what she was looking for."

"She gave me fifteen ideas. That's the problem. She can't settle on anything." Jared downed two more cookies and finished the lemonade. "I'll give it another try. Caleb is coming over tonight. Maybe he can think of something."

Jared pushed up from the chair and stretched his neck left, then right, as if shaking off the church, Miss Patterson and their problems.

"I want to take Sam fishing today when school's out," Jared said. "If you're agreeable."

The notion startled Kinsey. "I don't know if Sam would like to fish."

"The boy's never been fishing?" he asked, with more than a hint of accusation in his voice.

"Well, no. But I take him down to the creek," she told him. "We picnic and he wades in the water."

"That's not fishing, Kinsey. That's playing," Jared said. "MacAvoy's has fishing poles. I checked on them just now while I was in town. I can get Sam when school's out."

Just this morning she'd wondered who would teach Sam to shave. He would grow up one day and need to learn. She figured she could find someone when the time came. Mack Gleason next door, or Reverend Battenfield would both surely be willing to help out. And the truth was, Kinsey herself could show him, if all else failed.

But what about fishing? All boys, all men liked it. It was an essential part of their lives.

Could she teach Sam to fish?

Kinsey's stomach rolled at the thought. She might be able to handle a razor and strop, and whip up some soapy lather in a mug, but she simply could not abide the thought of digging worms, baiting a hook or touching a scaly, slimy fish. Better Jared handle this.

"I think Sam would enjoy that," Kinsey said.

"I'll have him back before supper," Jared promised.

Kinsey touched his arm as he headed for the door, a wave of worry passing over her.

"You have to watch him carefully," she said.

"I will."

"No. You don't understand." She tightened her grip on his arm. "You're not used to taking care of a child. You have to keep Sam close. You have to keep an eye on him all the time. The woods, the water…"

Jared looked down at her. "I won't let anything happen to him. I swear."

"You'll make him stay next to you, every minute?"

"If you'd feel better, you can come with us." Jared grinned. "You can bait the hooks."

Kinsey winced. "No, thanks."

He touched his finger to her cheek, then tilted her face up to his. "That's my brother's son. I'll take care of him."

Jared gave her a confident nod and walked to the door. He stopped and turned back.

"And remember, I offered to take care of you, too, if you'd let me," he said, then left.

Chapter Nineteen

Jared would take care of her?

The notion wouldn't quit swirling through Kinsey's mind as she prepared supper alongside Nell and Lily.

Of course, he was referring to the offer he'd made when he'd first arrived in Crystal Springs, expecting to take Sam back to New York with him immediately.

Pay for her education, stake her in a business, give her a place to live. Anything she wanted, he'd said.

He'd even suggested she live at the Mason home along with the rest of the family. Kinsey cringed at the thought. She would never—ever—agree to that.

Jared had made those generous offers as an incentive to get her to agree to giving Sam to the Masons. Hopefully, also, he'd had a concern for

Sam's welfare and knew that Kinsey's presence would insure a smooth transition to life in their New York household.

Kinsey sprinkled brown sugar and cinnamon on the pan of sweet potatoes and slid it into the oven. Her heart warmed a little recalling Jared's gentle words and even gentler touch when he'd made the offer again earlier this afternoon in the study. It didn't sound like a bargaining chip, as it had when he'd first come to Crystal Springs. It had sounded—

Kinsey stopped her thoughts, refusing to consider Jared, his offer or his motives any further. She simply would not allow herself to think of them.

Yet why did they continue to creep into her thoughts? Because, deep in her heart, the notion sounded appealing. Could that be it?

Pushing away the thought, Kinsey realized that both Nell and Lily had been unusually quiet through supper preparation, just as she had been. All three of the women seemed lost in thoughts of their own.

Yet for Lily, Kinsey imagined, the time that slipped past was more a waiting game. Since she'd sent Isaac the letter this morning telling him of her decision to leave, she still hadn't heard from him. Kinsey couldn't believe that Isaac would simply step aside and let Lily head back east without a word.

"Here come your fishermen," Nell said, grinning broadly as she gazed out the kitchen window.

Jared headed toward the house, two fishing poles in his hand. Sam was cuddled in his other arm, draped against Jared's shoulder, fast asleep.

What a pleasing sight, Kinsey decided, as she opened the door for them. Jared propped the fishing poles on the back porch and came inside.

Sam's arms hung limp at his sides, his eyes were closed tight, his mouth open.

"Looks like you wore him out," Kinsey said quietly.

Jared gave her a wry grin. "I'm not sure who wore out who."

He did look a little tired, Kinsey thought.

"I'd better put him to bed," she said.

Kinsey reached for Sam but Jared moved ahead of her and carried him to their bedroom off the kitchen. She got him settled under the covers for the night, then stepped back to look at him.

Something about watching Sam sleep brought

her peace and contentment as nothing else in her life ever had.

She glanced up to see Jared standing next to her.

"Do you think he'll sleep all night?" he asked.

"Probably," she said, then gave him a teasing smile because she'd seen him come home empty handed. "So, are we having fish for supper?"

He smiled, then nodded toward Sam. "He hasn't quite caught on to the idea that fishing is supposed to be quiet."

Kinsey envisioned Sam splashing through the creek, scaring off any fish that swam close.

"Will ham do for supper?" she asked Jared.

"Just let me go get cleaned up. I'll be back in a—"

"Lily!"

Kinsey and Jared both turned as Isaac bellowed his wife's name from outside the boardinghouse. Then the back door jerked open and Isaac stormed into the kitchen, a piece of paper clutched in his fist.

Jared hurried toward him, ready for anything, but Isaac stopped just inside the door, his gaze boring into Lily standing beside the stove. Absolute fury rolled off him.

An unease ripped through Kinsey at the anger on Isaac's face, but Lily simply stood in front of him, confident that she was in no physical danger from her husband.

"You are not leaving!" Isaac shouted, pointing his finger at her. "Do you hear me? You're not going *anywhere!* And you're sure as hell not going to *Baltimore!*"

"Isaac—" Lily began.

"You are my wife! We took vows before God! Have you forgotten that?" he demanded. "I've had enough of this nonsense! You're my wife and I want you home! With me! And you are not—*not*—going to Baltimore!"

Isaac stormed out of the kitchen, slamming the door behind him.

Lily burst into tears and ran upstairs.

The evening hours at the boardinghouse proved quieter but no happier. Kinsey and Nell both went up to check on Lily after Isaac's departure. All she did was cry so they left her alone.

"Maybe one of you should go talk to Isaac," Kinsey suggested to Jared and Caleb who were working in the study.

They both looked up at her as if she'd lost her mind.

"He could probably use someone to talk to," Kinsey told them.

"Yeah, probably," Jared conceded.

"I'll stop by his place on my way home," Caleb offered.

"And I'll go tomorrow morning," Jared said.

"I guess nobody is having much luck with the ladies in this town," Caleb said, shaking his head. "I went by Miss Patterson's house today and flat out asked her if I could court Sarah. I told her how I was adding on to the store, expanding the place, running a sound business. Didn't make any difference to her. She turned me down cold. Again."

It seemed that while Bess Patterson couldn't make a decision on the design of the church, she had no trouble determining that, in her opinion, Caleb wasn't good enough to court her niece.

"Wish I knew how to get in her good graces," Caleb said.

"That woman is impossible to please," Jared grumbled. "I swear, she wouldn't be happy if we built her a chapel all to herself."

"And named it 'The Church of Bess Patterson,'" Caleb added.

"With a fellowship hall thrown in for good measure," Kinsey added.

Jared jumped, startling Kinsey. His gaze met Caleb's and he nodded.

"You might be on to something," Caleb said, his eyes bright.

"You sure might be." Jared rifled through the papers on his desk and pulled out the church plans. Caleb leaned closer. "What if we built a separate fellowship hall? Right here on the back of the church?"

"We'll use her money for the hall, and name it after her," Caleb said.

"That way the town could decide on the design of the church, get it built, and let Miss Patterson figure out what she wants in her fellowship hall."

"Can you design a hall she'll like?" Caleb asked.

"I sure as hell can." Jared got a fresh piece of paper and started drawing.

"Let's put a sign on it with her name in big letters,"
Caleb said.

"Good idea," Jared agreed.

"If we use Miss Patterson's money to build the

fellowship hall, what will we use for the church?" Kinsey asked.

"I'll make sure the cost of the hall doesn't use up all her donated money. And I'll talk to Reverend Battenfield about how much he's got in the building fund," Jared said. He looked up at Kinsey, then Caleb. "You two might have just saved the church."

"Mama…"

Sam appeared in the doorway in his nightshirt, hair mussed, a pout on his lips, rubbing his eyes with his fists. Kinsey had seen that sleepy look many times.

"Come on, honey. Back to bed for you."

"No…"

But Sam didn't protest when she lifted him onto her shoulder. Instead, he laid his head down and closed his eyes again.

"Good night," she said softly to Jared and Caleb, and carried Sam out of the room.

Jared watched them go thinking that he wished he could be with Kinsey putting Sam to bed, rather than here working on the church plans. Even though he felt they were on to something with the fellowship hall, the notion of designing the building held no appeal at the moment.

"Do you want to call it quits for the night?" Caleb asked.

Yes, he wanted to. But where could he go? What could he do? He certainly couldn't follow the tug of his heart which urged him to go into Kinsey's bedroom and watch her put Sam to bed again.

"Let's keep at this for a while," Jared said, turning his attention back to the plans for the fellowship hall.

It took only a short while for Jared and Caleb to come up with the details and for Jared to sketch it out.

"If Reverend Battenfield likes the idea, I'll do a complete plan," Jared said. "Can you come with me tomorrow?"

"Sure," Caleb said with a wide smile. He rose from the desk. "Good night."

Jared blew out the lantern and left the study. He considered following Caleb out the front door. Some fresh air and a walk would feel good right now.

But instead he was drawn to the kitchen. Kinsey's bedroom door was pulled up but not shut tight. He saw lantern light shining around the edges, heard Kinsey's voice and the squeak of the rocker. Apparently, she was having trouble getting Sam back to sleep.

He thought about going inside, seeing if he could do something to help, then came to his senses.

Kinsey had been taking care of the boy for five years, and taking care of herself for longer than that. She knew what to do. She didn't need him.

The idea caused Jared's stomach to sour a little. He headed upstairs to his room. He lit the lantern and pulled open the windows. As before, he heard Kinsey's voice drifting up to him. She was reading to Sam again, the rocker squeaking rhythmically.

When he'd first heard the sound it had annoyed him. Now he'd come to listen for it.

Jared pulled off his vest and shirt and braced his hands against the windowsill. Moonlight threw shadows across the yard and the trees beyond.

He'd had his hands full today taking Sam fishing. Lord, that boy was full of energy. Jared remembered when he and his brothers had been the same way. Running, playing, shouting, fighting. They must have driven his mother to her wits' end, at times. No wonder she'd spent most of her time disciplining them. Jared and his brothers had learned to mind their mother—or else.

He couldn't imagine Kinsey doing anything more harsh than speaking to Sam in a stern voice. She had a way about her of making him behave, simple as that.

Maybe it would be different if Kinsey had five sons, as Jared's mother had.

Kinsey…pregnant…her belly round and full with a child.

Jared shifted, feeling the tension building in his body. He wanted her. He'd wanted her since the day he arrived on the stagecoach and caught sight of her across the street. Something about her had drawn him, even then. He'd kissed her, not knowing who she was. And she'd kissed him back. God, how she'd kissed him back.

Jared straightened away from the window and popped open a few of the buttons on his long johns, letting the cool air blow over his chest. It didn't help.

He tried thinking about the church project, and even the mental image of Bess Patterson didn't dim the desire for Kinsey that had claimed him.

He thought about the project waiting for him in Maine. About the follow-up telegram he needed to send to his father, extending his stay here in

Crystal Springs. About the work that awaited him back home.

Then Kinsey floated into his mind again, heating up his want for her even more. Should he go downstairs? If he listened at the window until he heard the rocker stop squeaking, he'd know she'd put Sam to bed. If he waited a few minutes, she'd change into her night clothes. He could go to her room, knock quietly. She'd answer, of course, and then he'd—

Do what? Jared struggled to fight off the rush of heat pumping through him. He knew what he wanted to do. Coax her up to his room again and—

He bit off a curse, one aimed at himself. What the hell was he thinking? That's not the reason he'd come to Crystal Springs.

Shame edged into his heart, cooling his desire for Kinsey, his want to indulge himself.

What would Clark think of the way he was acting, the things he was doing? Would he approve?

Jared doubted it.

Not after what he'd done to Clark.

Chapter Twenty

The boardinghouse was quiet in the afternoon. Usually, Kinsey enjoyed this time, but today the silence did nothing to soothe her.

She sat in her room, leafing through the Bloomingdale Brothers catalog Maggie had loaned her. It was last year's edition but the most current one available in Crystal Springs.

Even the illustrations of the beautiful dresses didn't lift Kinsey's spirits. Not at those prices. Most were over twenty dollars. Even the cheapest—four dollars—would stretch her budget beyond the breaking point.

Yet she couldn't help but imagine herself wearing what the catalog described as its "elegant reception costume" of watered silk. But priced at forty-two dollars, that wouldn't be possible. The blue silk fabric Maggie had shown her in

Hudson's back room came to mind, and Kinsey wondered if she could duplicate the dress herself.

Not that she had the time to attempt it, Kinsey thought, let alone money to squander on fabric. She had more pressing problems to attend to. Such as helping Lily. Surely there was something she could do.

Lily had come down to prepare breakfast this morning and Kinsey's heart had gone out to her. Her eyes were swollen and red. She looked as if she hadn't slept all night. Small wonder, given Isaac's outburst last evening, his demand that she abandon her plan to move to Baltimore and return home immediately. Nell had told her to go back upstairs and rest, but Lily had refused. By the time they'd washed and put away the last of the breakfast dishes, Lily was in tears again and on her way back up to her room.

Kinsey flipped farther into the Bloomingdale's catalog to the page displaying the ladies' jerseys. Made of wool or cashmere, the blouses boasted embroidery, braided or beaded trim. Those wouldn't take long to sew, she decided. She could replicate them easily.

If she had the time, of course.

Maybe she'd take the catalog up to Lily in a bit,

see if she'd like to look at it. It might get her mind off her problems, even for a short while.

Jared crept into Kinsey's thoughts now. He'd been quiet this morning at breakfast too. Unusual for him. She wondered if he was unsettled about approaching Reverend Battenfield with his idea for the fellowship hall today. She doubted it. Goodness knows, Jared had presented his designs to some of the wealthiest, most successful businessmen on the east coast.

But the way he kept looking at her.... Kinsey closed the catalog for a moment, remembering the phantom warmth that had come over her each time she looked up and caught Jared staring at her. He seemed to feel it, too, a warmth—*a something*—because his cheeks seemed to flush, as if he had a fever. Finally, he got up abruptly from the table, fetched his satchel and left.

Kinsey fanned herself with a few pages of the catalog. Gracious, it had gotten warm sitting here by the window.

She noticed then that she'd opened the catalog to the page of boys' clothing. The suits were handsome. Sam would look like a perfect little gentleman in one. How she wished she could order one for him. Right out of the catalog. One she didn't make herself or accept as a hand-me-down from someone else. One made in a modern factory and shipped by train all the way across the country, just for Sam.

She looked over the selection featured on the page. A jersey suit, lined with silk in navy blue for three dollars. Another that featured a sailor collar, trimmed in blue braid, "one of the most stylish suits of the season," the catalog description read. Or "The Webster Suit," plaited back and front, with a belt, in gray or brown. A notice at the bottom of the page stated that a pocket dictionary, "handsomely bound in cloth will be presented to every purchaser of the Webster Suit."

She closed her eyes for a moment. Oh, how she wished she could get that for Sam.

The men's suits were featured on the next page. The first illustration was of a "full dress evening or wedding suit," made of black broadcloth and lined with satin or serge. There was the Prince Albert suit, the four-button cutaway, seersucker suits, linen suits, alpaca and linen dusters. Fabrics offered were English mohair, imported worsteds, cashmere and flannel.

She imagined Jared wearing each of the featured suits. A little smile played on her lips thinking how handsome he would look.

Or looked. Back in New York. Where he dressed in such fine clothing every day.

How many suits did Jared own? she wondered. Any from the Bloomingdale Brothers catalogue? Probably not. Surely his suits came from somewhere far nicer and were much more expensive. He had a whole closet of them, she was sure.

Kinsey flipped through the catalog. Wrappers, linen dusters, shawls. A scandalous bathing suit that exposed ankles and forearms. There were aprons and night robes, hosiery and gloves.

What must it be like to actually visit the Bloomingdale Brothers store? Kinsey flipped to the front of the catalog and saw the impressive five-story building pictured on the cover. Inside, a note stated that it was located on 3rd Avenue and 59th Street, in New York City.

Jared's home. The home of his family. Did they visit the store? she wondered. How exciting it must be to stroll among the aisles filled with such lovely merchandise. How would one ever make a choice from so many items?

Kinsey knew she'd never find out.

Or could she?

Everything she saw and wanted—for herself and for Sam—could be theirs. Jared and the Mason family could easily afford any of it—all of it. Clark had been generous. Jared would be too, she knew.

She'd seen the way Jared helped with Sam. He'd filled the fatherly role lacking in Sam's life. A boy needed someone to show him how to be a man. Kinsey could never do that.

Kinsey glanced at the catalog once more. She wouldn't have to sit and dream anymore—and Sam would have everything he needed, including a proper male influence in his life.

All she had to do was take Jared up on his offer. Move to New York.

With Sam.

"How'd it go?" Caleb asked, stepping out of the MacAvoy General Store as Jared approached.

He'd wanted Caleb to accompany him on his visit to the reverend today to present the plans for the new church and their idea for the fellowship hall to be built in Miss Patterson's honor. Caleb had helped come up with both, and Jared figured it only right that he should be there.

But the store had been busy this morning, too busy for Caleb to leave, so Jared had gone alone. Now Caleb looked anxious to hear how the meeting went.

"Let's take a look at your addition," Jared said,

nodding toward the building next door where Caleb intended to expand the store. He didn't want to talk about the church plans here on the street and take a chance of being overheard. Not yet, anyway.

Caleb glanced back inside the general store and hesitated for a moment, then went next door. The place was empty. The former owner had taken everything, leaving nothing but dust and cobwebs.

"Good news," Jared said, not wanting to make Caleb wait. "Reverend Battenfield thought the idea of the fellowship hall was a good one."

"Hot damn..."

"He wanted to talk it over with the mayor first, so we went over to his house."

"That wife of his didn't cook for you, did she?" Caleb asked with concern.

"Afraid so," Jared said, and touched his belly. "But the mayor's all for the idea of the hall. He wanted to take it up with a couple of other men in town, just to be sure. We did that and everybody's in agreement."

"They all liked the idea?"

"Everybody," Jared said. "And I told them it was your idea. Yours and Kinsey's."

A proud smile bloomed on Caleb's face for a moment, then he grew serious again.

"What about the money to build both?" he asked.

"It's taken care of."

His eyebrows raised. "Reverend Battenfield had enough in the building fund?"

Jared glanced away. "All the finances are in order."

"When can we get started?"

Jared explained that the reverend and the mayor planned to pay a call on Miss Patterson this evening and give her the "good news."

"I'm ordering the extra building supplies," he said. "Half from you. Half from Hudson's."

"That's fair," Caleb conceded. "We can get them here soon. Won't create much of a delay."

"So, when are you starting on this place?" Jared asked, gesturing around them. He'd gone over Caleb's plan for the expansion of the general store and been in here with him a few times to take measurements. Caleb didn't really need the help. He'd done a good job on his own. Apparently, he'd received excellent training during his service in the army.

"Starting today. I'm doing the work myself," Caleb said. He shook his head. "To tell you the truth, I don't really like shopkeeping. I have to help my ma with the store, but I'm going to enjoy building this addition."

"No crew to help you?"

"Think I'll need one?"

Jared turned a practiced gaze to the ceiling beams. "Yeah, you'll need some help," he said.

"Is that an offer?"

The notion took Jared by surprise. He hadn't actually worked at a construction site in years. His days of feeling the weight of a hammer and the pull of a saw were long behind him, replaced by giving instructions to the job foreman, overseeing the budget, and solving the daily problems that arose with suppliers, clients and crews.

"Sure," Jared said, pleased by the thought. "Sure, I'll work with you."

Caleb smiled and offered his hand. "I appreciate it."

Kinsey looked at the ears of corn on the sideboard waiting to be shucked for tonight's supper. Dozens of them. And who would do that chore but Nell, Lily...and her.

Visions of the Bloomingdale Brothers store in New York lingered in her mind. Kinsey imagined pulling up in front of it in a grand carriage, a servant helping her to the ground, sweeping through the entrance and spending the day picking out anything and everything she wanted.

It made for a pleasing daydream. But it would never be a reality, for her, anyway.

She looked at the corn again. Jared's mother surely never shucked corn. Cooks performed the task. Amelia Mason had no need to do it herself.

Kinsey chided herself for her unkind thoughts. She'd only met the woman once, and actually, she hadn't met her at all, just overheard her words. So perhaps she shouldn't judge the woman. But Kinsey couldn't help it. After all, wasn't the true mark of a person indicated by the way they conducted themselves when they didn't know someone was watching or listening?

Lily stepped into the kitchen, shooing away the unhappy memory and bringing Kinsey's thoughts back to the present, thankfully. Amelia Mason had played too big a role in her life already.

Her friend looked tired, her eyes still red and swollen. Seemed she'd been crying again.

"Can I get you some coffee?" Kinsey asked.

Lily glanced back over her shoulder. "Is Nell here?" she asked quietly.

"She went into town. But I can go find her

for you," Kinsey said, thinking Lily wanted to discuss her leaving with Nell.

"No," Lily said, still looking troubled. She leaned in a little and lowered her voice. "I need to talk to you."

A wave of alarm shuddered through Kinsey. She'd thought she understood Lily's feeling, but now, suddenly, she wasn't so sure.

Lily glanced around once more, then said, "I saw you kissing Jared."

Kinsey gasped and her cheeks flamed. So her instincts had been right. Someone had seen them together. Yet knowing that person was Lily made it no less embarrassing.

"Well, I—we—that is—"

"I didn't mean to spy. I just happened to see you two together," Lily said. "Jared is a very nice man, and you've been married before so I'm sure you know what you're doing, where it could… lead."

"Well…"

"Seeing you two kissing made me think of Isaac and me."

For the first time in a very long while, Kinsey saw a hint of a smile on Lily's face.

"I remembered how good things used to be with him…before," Lily said. "And after last night when he was so angry that I was leaving, it made me think that maybe he really does still love me, despite…everything."

"Oh, Lily, I'm sure Isaac still loves you."

"And I still love him. I always have. That's never been the problem."

"What are you going to do?" Kinsey asked, unable to keep the hopeful tone from her voice.

"I've decided to stay in Crystal Springs. Give Isaac and me another chance."

"Oh, Lily, that's wonderful." Kinsey threw her arms around her and they shared a hug.

"I'm going to the jail tonight after supper and tell him what I've decided," Lily said.

"Tonight? No, don't wait. Go now."

Lily shook her head. "But we'll have to start supper soon and I can't—"

"Go!" Kinsey pulled her to the back door.

Lily paused and smiled. "I really feel like this is the right thing to do."

"Of course it is." Kinsey had never been so happy for anyone in her life.

"If I don't come back home tonight, don't worry," Lily said with a grin.

Kinsey's cheeks flamed again. "Just go."

Lily hurried out the door toward town.

* * *

Dabney Hudson paced the boardwalk in front of his mercantile eyeing Jared sharply as he left MacAvoy's and crossed the street. Jared braced himself.

"That Ida Burk is up to something," Dabney insisted, hurrying along beside Jared, shaking his finger at the MacAvoy General Store. "She is, isn't she. I know she is. Something going on. That woman is trying to ruin my business. Ruin it, I tell you."

Jared wasn't about to break the news that Caleb was expanding the store. Dabney would figure it out for himself soon enough when construction began. Jared hoped he was nowhere close when that happened.

"Stealing my customers, that's what she's doing," Dabney declared as he followed Jared into the store.

"Papa, please," Maggie admonished from behind the counter. She gave Jared an apologetic smile. "Good afternoon, Mr. Mason."

He tipped his hat, thinking that Kinsey was right. This young woman had the patience of a saint, putting up with her father the way she did.

Dabney swung around and glared out the door

again. "Good God, that Burk woman just lowered her price on apples!"

His cheeks turned bright red as he set his jaw and stalked outside.

Maggie looked embarrassed but put on a brave face as she came from behind the counter.

"What can we do for you?" she asked.

"I need a few things." Jared pulled from his shirt pocket the list of building supplies he'd prepared after he left Mayor Fisher and Reverend Battenfield a short while ago, and presented it to Maggie.

Her eyes widened. "My goodness. What's this all about?"

"Just some additional supplies for the new church," Jared said. He'd promised the mayor and reverend that he'd keep quiet about the details of the planned fellowship hall until after the announcement during services on Sunday.

Maggie raised an eyebrow but didn't ask any more questions. "I'll send a wagon up to the lumber mill tomorrow and have everything ready in a day or so."

Dabney bustled back into the store and snatched the list from Maggie's hand.

"More materials for the church, right? I reckon MacAvoy's got part of this order, too?" he demanded.

"Half," Jared said. "MacAvoy's got half."

"Huh." Dabney stalked off to the stockroom.

An uncomfortable moment passed with Jared remembering the story Kinsey had told her about Maggie's mother. She'd run off with another man. After spending just a few minutes with Dabney, Jared couldn't really blame the woman, yet resented that she'd gone and left Maggie in this intolerable situation with her father.

"Would you tell Kinsey I'm still saving that fabric for her?" Maggie said. "The blue silk."

Jared recalled that Kinsey had mentioned the fabric when they'd had lunch together.

"I can't hold it back much longer," Maggie said. She shook her head and looked embarrassed again. "Papa saw it in the crate and told a couple of other women about it. I'm sure someone will snap it up quickly."

"I'll do that." Jared tipped his hat and left the store.

He was anxious to get back to the boarding-house, get to work finalizing the plans for the hall. He was hungry, too, more than ready for the good meal he knew would soon be prepared by Kinsey, Nell and Lily.

But that wasn't the only reason, he realized. He wanted to tell Kinsey about how his day had gone. He knew she'd be excited about the news and want to hear all the details.

But Jared's pace slowed when he spied the jail-house. Much as he disliked the place, he knew he should stop in, see how Isaac was holding up. After last night, he figured it was the decent thing to do.

When Jared stepped inside, he found Herb Foster reared back in the chair, leafing through the Wanted posters.

"Sheriff's gone home for a spell." Herb shook his head. "Isaac's not doing so good."

Jared didn't blame him. The news that Lily was leaving town had been too much for him, judging from last night's scene in the kitchen of the boardinghouse.

"I'm keeping an eye on things here. Something wrong?" Herb asked. "Sheriff said to come get him if anything was going on. He lives just down the street and around the corner."

Jared remembered Kinsey pointing out the Vaughn home when they'd been in town together.

"I'll catch up with Isaac later," Jared said.

Herb nodded and turned back to the Wanted posters.

Jared was almost relieved that Isaac wasn't at the jail. He found himself angry at the situation between the sheriff and his wife. He was glad Isaac had put his foot down and forbidden Lily to leave town. He wasn't sure, though, if it would do any good.

His stomach rumbled again, reminding Jared that he was hungry, so he headed toward the boardinghouse. To his surprise, he saw Lily heading in his direction on the other side of the street. Her strides were long, her expression determined.

Watching her for a moment, Jared saw her disappear into the sheriff's office. Seemed as if another confrontation between the couple was imminent.

Jared continued on his way and cast a glance at Isaac's house as he passed the side street. To his surprise, he saw Isaac standing in the open doorway, talking to Dixie on the front porch.

"Hmm…" Jared murmured.

Why would Dixie be at Isaac's place?

Chapter Twenty-One

"Uncle Jared!"

Sam's greeting drifted all the way into the kitchen, causing Kinsey to look out the window and see Jared striding toward the boardinghouse. Sam, who'd been playing with the Gleason boys, ran to meet him. Jared lifted him high into the air, gave him a little toss, then pulled him close. Sam screamed with delight and threw both arms around Jared's neck.

Kinsey smiled, pleased beyond reason by the sight. The two of them had spent a great deal of time together, doing everything from wrestling in the backyard to sitting side by side in the study, drawing plans and pictures. Jared seemed at ease with Sam, and Sam reveled in everything Jared did.

Yet despite the happiness Kinsey experienced, it was an odd feeling for her. She'd never had anyone to share Sam with, other than friends such as Nell, Lily and the Gleasons. Somehow, with Jared, it was different.

Perhaps because he was, truly, Sam's family. Since she was nine years old and her parents had died, Kinsey couldn't imagine anything more dear than a family of her own.

The back door opened and Jared walked inside still carrying Sam.

"We're hungry, Mama," Sam declared. "Huh, Uncle Jared?"

"Starving," he agreed, giving the boy a little bounce. "I'll bet your mama's got something good for us to eat tonight."

"Cookies? Can we have cookies for supper?" Sam asked, his eyes wide.

Jared shook his head. "Mamas never serve cookies for supper."

Sam leaned closer to him. "Sometimes if you promise to be good, she'll let you do stuff like that."

His brow bobbed and he gave Kinsey a probing look. "Is that so? Well, then, I promise to be good."

"Me, too," Sam swore.

Kinsey couldn't hold back her smile, thoroughly

captivated by the two of them. "You can have cookies—but not until after supper."

"But, Mama," Sam complained.

"We've got to do what your mama says. She's the boss around here." Jared put him down. "Run on outside, partner. I've got to talk to your mama for a while."

"Are you coming out, Uncle Jared? Are you?"

"I'll be out in a while," he said. "Run on, now."

Sam dashed out the back door leaving Jared and Kinsey alone in the kitchen.

He looked around the room at the supper preparations underway and frowned.

"You're not cooking by yourself, are you?" he asked. "I saw Lily in town just now. Where is Nell?"

"Nell will be here any minute, and as for Lily—"

Hysterical screams sounded outside. Kinsey and Jared rushed to the door and saw Lily running toward the boardinghouse, sobbing, her skirt gathered in her hand and loose strands of her hair blowing in the breeze.

"What the—" Jared began.

Then Isaac appeared behind her, running hard after her. He caught up and reached for her arm. Lily spun away.

"Lily, it's not what you think—"

"I'm leaving!" she screamed, still sobbing.

"Lily, please, you know that woman doesn't mean—"

"I hate you!"

She clamped her hand over her mouth, yet was unable to stifle her sobs, and ran into the boardinghouse. She stopped when she saw Kinsey.

"I—I went to the house to—to tell him that I wasn't leaving," Lily cried. "And—and Dixie was there."

Kinsey gasped. "Dixie?"

"I—I thought we could get over our problems, and—and all the while Isaac was carrying on with *her!*"

Another wave of sobs overcame Lily and she ran toward the back stairway and pounded up the steps to her room.

Kinsey shook her head. "Isaac and Dixie? I can't believe it."

"Lily believes it. And that's all that matters," Jared said.

Kinsey moved through the evening, feeling the weight of everything going on around her. Nell helped get supper ready, then went upstairs to talk to Lily, but to no avail. Lily would probably cry herself to sleep again tonight, Kinsey thought.

Jared had gone outside and talked to Isaac for a while. Watching from the window Kinsey had seen the emotion on Isaac's face. He was completely beside himself, thinking that he'd lost Lily for good.

Jared had reported back that, according to Isaac, Dixie had come by the house but he'd wanted nothing to do with her and sent her on her way. Just his bad luck that Lily had appeared at that moment, too.

Dixie was a woman of questionable virtue and reputation. Everyone in town knew it. Unsavory gossip always swirled about her. Yet Kinsey couldn't help but wonder if, given the state of their marriage, Isaac hadn't given in and done the unthinkable.

Staring out her bedroom window at the darkness, a mantle seemed to settle over Kinsey, its weight dragging her down. She glanced at Sam on his bed, sleeping soundly, finally. She'd just gotten him to sleep. Somehow he sensed the upset in the house and was fussy, clinging to Kinsey, not wanting to go to bed. It had taken more than the usual number of stories before he dozed off on her lap tonight.

Even the sight of Sam sleeping peacefully failed to warm Kinsey's heart.

So many things in the lives of those she cared about seemed hopeless tonight. Lily and Isaac's marriage was over. Nell's husband had died. Caleb couldn't court the woman he loved.

Clark and Beth came to mind, as they had so often since Jared arrived. Kinsey felt their loss, still, for herself but also for Sam. And as she'd done before, she considered what Clark's death had done to the Mason family.

Kinsey's thoughts meandered on, spiraling downward. She would never have a husband of her own, or a family beyond Sam. Never have another child, one that would truly be her very own.

Jared slipped into her thoughts and her heartache deepened. His eventual marriage was doomed even before it began. What had he said of his expectation of a wife? A woman he could tolerate? One he could live with?

The sadness of all the lost loves, all the destroyed lives, all the grand futures that would never be, seemed too much to bear. Tears pooled in her eyes but Kinsey forced herself to choke them back.

Who was there to hold her? To wipe her tears? To assure her that everything would be all right?

No one.

She sniffed and left the bedroom. The house was quiet. The residents had all gone upstairs to their rooms. For a moment Kinsey considered checking on Lily, but doubted she could offer her much hope in her current state.

Kinsey found herself standing in the doorway of the study. Jared sat at the desk, the lantern glowing beside him as he concentrated on something in front of him, and her heart ached anew.

He looked up, sensing her, somehow. But instead of his usual welcoming smile, Jared frowned and came to his feet.

"What's wrong?" he asked, rounding the desk.

How had he known? she wondered, then decided that from the look on her face, her emotional state couldn't have been too difficult to recognize.

Yet who was she to disturb him? She was no one to him. And he had been nothing but trouble since he arrived in Crystal Springs. Still, her instinct had been to go to him.

"Nothing," Kinsey said, glancing away.

Jared came closer and touched her chin, lifting her face. He tilted his head, silently questioning her claim.

"Everything's wrong," she finally said, then pulled away and sniffed, fighting back another wave of tears.

"What happened?" he asked, concern in his voice. "Is Sam all right? Did something happen?"

"No, it's nothing like that." Kinsey swiped at her eyes. "It's just that everything seems so…so hopeless."

"Isaac and Lily, you mean?"

"I can't imagine how they'll save their marriage now."

Jared nodded. "They can work things out, still. If two people love each other, they can handle their problems—regardless."

"I hope you're right," Kinsey said, but in her heart, she doubted it.

Another rush of emotion threatened to overcome Kinsey so she gave herself a shake and gestured toward the desk.

"Are you working on the church plans?" she asked.

Jared nodded, though he didn't seem much interested in the project at the moment.

"We didn't get a chance to talk about it this

evening, but the reverend and the mayor both liked the idea of the fellowship hall. They said to go ahead with it." Jared touched his forehead, as if remembering something. "And I stopped by Hudson's Mercantile today. Maggie asked me to remind you about the fabric. That jackass father of hers found it and offered it to some of the other women in town, so if you want it, she says you should buy it right away."

"My fabric…" Kinsey gulped hard.

On top of all the other losses that seemed to bear down on her tonight, now the fabric she admired so much would be sold out from under her?

The fabric…something else she'd never have.

She recalled looking at the Bloomingdale Brothers catalog and fantasizing how she could visit the store herself and shop to her delight, if she moved to New York with Sam, as Jared wanted.

How foolish that notion had been. A silly day-dream. Because all of it was well beyond her reach. Everything.

Emotion swelled inside Kinsey and this time she couldn't force it down.

"I—I have to go." She managed to squeeze the

words through her tight throat, and hurried from the room.

Jared called after her but she kept going. She needed to cry. She had to cry.

Kinsey hurried through the kitchen and out the back door to her favorite spot on the bench beside the woodshed. She buried her face in her hands and sobbed.

She cried for Lily and Isaac, for Caleb and Sarah, for Clark and Beth. She cried for Sam, too, and for the fabric she would never be able to afford, for the dress shop she'd never own and the grand store she would never shop in. She cried for everything.

Kinsey had accepted all of these things in her life, up until recently. She'd understood her past, seen her future clearly and she'd been satisfied with all of it.

What was different now? What had changed? Jared.

The realization struck her hard, causing her to jerk upright and gasp aloud.

Then footsteps brushed the grass and she saw a figure coming toward her, silhouetted against the few lights burning in the boardinghouse.

No mistaking those shoulders.

Kinsey sniffed, her emotions whirling in a hundred different directions now.

Jared stood over her. "I'll go get you that fabric. Right now."

She blinked up at him. "What?"

"I'll go get it for you. Even if I have to break down the door and drag Hudson out of bed." He said it quickly, as if he hoped she wanted him to do just that.

Kinsey's heart swelled, bringing on another rush of emotion.

"Oh, Jared…" She burst into tears again.

"Wait. No. Don't cry again. I didn't mean to make you—no, stop."

He waved his hands frantically but that just made her cry harder. Then he glanced around, as if he might see someone who could help, and when no one materialized, Jared dropped onto the bench next to her.

"Come here," he said, his deep voice sounding gruff and soothing at the same time.

Jared pulled her against his shoulder and Kinsey went willingly, snuggling against his chest as he looped his arms around her, encasing her with warmth and strength. She sobbed for a few minutes, and even after her tears stopped, Jared held her. Kinsey had never been held this way before, with such tenderness, and she wasn't anxious to break the bond between them.

When she finally lifted her head and sat up, Jared pulled a white handkerchief from his hip pocket and offered it to her. She dabbed her eyes and wiped her nose, then pulled in a ragged breath.

"This isn't about the fabric, is it?" he asked.

"No."

"Damn…that would be a lot easier to handle."

Kinsey giggled softly, an unexpected release of her emotions.

"So many things seem hopeless, suddenly," she said, though, even to her own ears, that simple explanation seemed woefully inadequate for her outpouring of tears.

"Feeling bad for Lily and Isaac?" Jared asked.

"Yes, them," Kinsey said. "You, too."

"Me?"

She felt him tense, as if the very idea of someone worrying about him was so foreign he didn't understand it.

"Your plan for selecting a wife—well, it's just sad," Kinsey said. "And it doesn't sound to me as if you'll have much of a marriage."

"I'm just being practical."

She couldn't argue with that. "I suppose it will

suit you since your work takes you away from home for so long. But good gracious, Jared, what will you do if your wife wants to come with you?"

"I don't think that's going to happen," he told her.

"You wouldn't want that? A wife who's always around?"

"Sure. Under the right circumstances."

"And what would those circumstances be?" she asked.

Jared looked at her for a long moment, then laid his finger to her chin. A tingle raced through Kinsey.

How could he do that with a single touch?

All thoughts flew from her mind and she could think of nothing as he leaned closer. Her heart quickened as Jared closed his mouth over hers in a deep kiss.

Once more, he pulled her against him. Kinsey threw her arms around his neck as he trailed his hot lips down her cheek to the hollow at her throat. His hand caressed the hair at her neck. She leaned her head back, her breath quick, her heart racing. His strength, his touch seared her, binding her to him.

Jared lifted his hand to cup her breast. Kinsey

gasped. He moaned. The air heated around them. She grabbed his shirt and held on.

His lips claimed hers again with a new urgency. She felt his heart pounding against her hand. He shifted and laid her back on the bench, easing himself against her thigh. Kinsey's breath caught at the hard feel of him. She curled her leg around his.

She was lost. Lost in the moment, lost in his arms, in his kiss and in this discovery. And, Kinsey knew, in the haze of unexpected want and desire, right here, right now, was exactly where she wanted to be.

Jared lifted his head, ending their kiss, and gazed into her eyes. In the dim light she saw a hunger, a desire in him that she'd never witnessed before. It coursed through her, leaving a hot trail, making her want him, too.

"We…we should stop," Jared said, his breath coming in hot ragged puffs.

His expression didn't match his words and it troubled Kinsey. Had she done something wrong?

He levered himself off of her and sat up, then took her hands and pulled her up next to him on the bench. He looked at her then and Kinsey saw the ragged emotion, the longing, the potent energy. It seemed to radiate from him, engulfing her. She saw, too, the pain of self-control and restraint, and knew she hadn't done anything wrong.

Jared glanced around, at the Gleason house, at the rear of the boardinghouse, as if he'd suddenly remembered where he was and it put him on edge.

"We should go inside," he whispered.

A different sort of heat flushed Kinsey's cheeks, not because the neighbors or the boardinghouse residents might have seen them together, but because she didn't want to go inside. She wanted to stay here, under the starlit night sky, locked in Jared's arms, feeling his lips, his kisses.

But he rose from the bench and she stood next to him, her legs a little shaky. Jared entwined his fingers through hers as they walked inside. At the door to her bedroom he paused and gave her a long, lingering look. Kinsey felt herself rise onto her toes, expecting—wanting?—him to kiss her again.

But he backed away toward the staircase and just when she thought he'd disappear up the stairs, Jared rushed forward and locked her in his arms again. His lips covered hers with a hot, damp kiss. Kinsey held on, allowing him to slip inside her mouth, shifting her body to once more feel his want for her.

Jared groaned again, then broke away, resting his head against her forehead. Heat enveloped them. Neither moved.

As before, Jared came to his senses first. He touched his palm to her cheek and drew it away slowly, then bounded up the staircase, as if afraid that should he linger any longer, he might not leave at all.

Kinsey's heart banged into her throat and hung there as she stared at the empty staircase, wishing him to come back, overwhelmed by the temptation to run after him.

But why?

The only rational thought she'd had since running, in tears, to the bench by the woodshed, startled her.

Why? Why would she even consider following him upstairs?

But Kinsey knew the answer at once.

She'd fallen in love with Jared Mason.

Chapter Twenty-Two

Kinsey doubted that Nell's late husband had foreseen the activity his study would host, or that he could have predicted the role it would play in the building of Crystal Springs' new church.

Regardless, Nell had given her blessing to the use of the study, even after she'd seen the growing number of townsfolk who'd used it in the last week or so.

Kinsey sat at the table in the corner that, surely, Nell's husband had intended for card play, along with Emma Foster, Ida Burk and Nell, sewing the curtains for the new church and fellowship hall.

Crowded around the desk across the room were Jared, Caleb and a half-dozen other men, working on preparation for the construction of the buildings.

"So, suddenly, Bess Patterson is anxious to

get construction underway?" Ida commented, not bothering to hide the hint of disdain in her voice as she drew stitches through the royal blue fabric.

"Figures, doesn't it," Emma agreed.

"At least we're finally getting the church built," Nell said, pausing, needle in hand. She glanced over at the desk where the men worked. "And, of course, Bess Patterson would want her fellowship hall completed at the same time as the church."

"How else could we have a grand celebration in her honor?" Ida added.

Kinsey couldn't blame the women for their gossip. They weren't the only ones making the same comments. For all the problems Miss Patterson had caused by delaying the selection of a design for the church, she'd had no hesitation giving Jared her approval on his very first plan for the "Bess Patterson Fellowship Hall," a separate wing of the church.

After Reverend Battenfield made the announcement during Sunday services, the town had turned out in support for the new construction and the celebration to follow. Nell had offered the use of the boardinghouse's study and the men and women of Crystal Springs had showed up every evening, refreshments in hand, to plan and prepare for the one-day church-raising that would take place on Saturday. Sunday's service would be special, the reverend had promised. The dedication of the Bess Patterson Fellowship Hall would follow, along with an afternoon of food, music and fun.

Kinsey enjoyed the evenings, with so many people stopping by to lend a hand. Isaac came by most every night, claiming he wanted to see Lily and talk to her. Kinsey thought perhaps he just wanted to make sure Lily was still in town.

Lily had promised Nell that she would continue her employment at the boardinghouse until she found a replacement. She'd said she would stay, too, to help out with the church for as long as the town needed her.

Kinsey had talked to her, urged her to give Isaac another chance but Lily had been adamant. She was leaving for Baltimore as soon as her commitments in Crystal Springs were completed. Though Lily refused to speak to her husband now, he still came around each night, asking after her. He seemed to wither at every new rejection.

"I heard that Sarah Patterson was here last night," Ida said in a low voice, leaning forward slightly.

Kinsey and the other women glanced at Caleb

seated at the desk, all of them, surely, thinking the same.

"Perhaps now Bess Patterson will change her tune about Caleb," Emma speculated. "He's a nice young man and he and Sarah make a lovely couple."

"He's certainly shown himself to be an up-standing citizen with his work on the church," Nell agreed.

"As had Mr. Mason," Ida said.

Kinsey's stomach lurched and she glanced up to see all three of the other ladies watching her. Her cheeks warmed. Were her feelings for Jared that obvious?

Commotion from the other side of the room saved Kinsey from having to say anything—not that she knew what she'd say, anyway. The men rose from their chairs and conversation wound down. Apparently they were finished for the night.

The women put their sewing aside and tidied up the study.

"Looks as if all the window curtains will be finished in a day or so," Ida said, nodding toward the stack that had already been completed.

"We'll be ready by Saturday," Emma agreed.

Conversation carried the group out of the study

and onto the front porch of the boardinghouse. More ideas and thoughts were discussed, then finally, everyone left. Nell excused herself and headed up to her room, leaving Kinsey and Jared on the porch together.

He drew in a big breath and let it out slowly, feeling the tension across his back and shoulders.

"Tired?" Kinsey asked.

"Thinking too much lately," he said, rubbing tiny circles on his temples with his fingertips.

He'd worked on the plans and preparations for the church and fellowship hall almost nonstop for days. He was in charge of all aspects of the project and it suited him fine. He'd overseen construction of buildings far more complex than these.

Yet he took this project as seriously, shouldering the burden of responsibility, answering questions, making decisions, giving directions. Caleb was knowledgable, but even he turned to Jared for answers at times.

The cool evening breeze blew, rustling the trees in the front yard and causing the porch swing to creak a little. Kinsey remained at his side and she too seemed content with the silence between them.

Jared knew he'd spent too much time at that

desk in the study, too much time answering questions, making plans. He knew his limitations and it was long past time to stretch his legs, get some fresh air. He could do that right now, he reminded himself.

Any other night, he'd do just that. Head down to the saloon for a beer, maybe talk to a stranger about anything but construction projects.

But when Jared looked down at Kinsey next to him, he couldn't move. She held him here, somehow. She made him want to stay put.

Yet, at the same time, she caused a restlessness in him that he couldn't explain. A drive to do *something*. He didn't know what, exactly, but forces he didn't understand pulled at him.

Maybe it was Crystal Springs, he thought, shifting his gaze to the lights of Main Street in the distance. Folks here moved at their own pace, did things in their own time, in their own way. It bothered him, but he didn't know why.

Nor did he know why Kinsey was standing next to him, on a dark porch, the two of them alone together, and he hadn't already taken her into his arms and kissed her.

He wanted to. He wanted to do just that—and more.

It struck Jared odd that he'd never once looked

at the women in his social circle back in New York, the ones he'd sized up as a wife, and thought about them the way he thought of Kinsey. He'd never wanted one of those women the way he wanted her.

She was a decent woman, though. Not the kind to trifle with. It was tough, sometimes, to hold himself back. Especially after the way they'd kissed, held each other, touched each other. Seeing her with Sam, he had to remind himself that she had never been a married woman, never known a man or brought a child into the world.

He could restrain himself well enough when seeing her over the breakfast table or throughout the day when their paths crossed. Daylight hours, he was fine. But when Jared found himself awake in the dead of night, knowing she was in bed just a floor below him, his imagination running wild and his body straining, keeping pure thoughts in his head wasn't easy.

Kinsey in her night clothes. Her dark hair spread out across her white pillow—

"Uncle Jared?"

Sam's voice interrupted his thoughts, making him feel a little guilty. He turned to see the boy

standing in the doorway in his nightshirt, looking sleepy-eyed.

"What are you doing out of bed?" Kinsey
asked, going to him.

Sam darted past her to Jared. He scooped the
boy up and held him with one arm.

"Can we go fishing tomorrow, Uncle Jared?
Can we?" he asked.

"I can't go tomorrow. I'll be busy working on
the church pews."

"Please? Please, can we go?" Sam asked.

"Those pews are important. Most of the men
in town will be there working, too," Jared explained.

"But I want us to go fishing," Sam said.

"I can't, partner, because—"

"Sam," Kinsey said, touching him on the back.
"Uncle Jared said no."

Sam pressed his lips together and laid his head
on Jared's shoulder.

"You don't have to give him an explanation,"
Kinsey said quietly to Jared. "He's too young to
understand it. And, more importantly, he should
mind you when you tell him no."

Jared routinely dealt with highly successful
businessmen, cutthroat suppliers and hardened

workmen, but none of that had prepared him for dealing with a five-year-old boy.

"I'll take you fishing soon, Sam, I promise," Jared told him, then hastened to add, "if it's all right with your mama, of course."

Sam lifted his head. "Can we, Mama?"

"Sure," she said.

Jared looked down at the boy. "How about if you come by MacAvoy's store after school tomorrow? You can help out building the pews."

His eyes got bigger. "Can I, Mama?"

"That would be fine," she said. "Back to bed now."

Jared followed Kinsey's swaying skirt through the house and into their bedroom off the kitchen.

"Can you read me another story, Mama?" Sam asked.

"I suppose one more story won't hurt," Kinsey said, getting a book off the shelf.

She sat in the rocker and Jared put the boy on her lap. He left the room but couldn't help but stop in the doorway and turn back.

The sight of the two of them together in the rocker caused his heart to ache. Kinsey was a beautiful woman and, ever since he'd first laid eyes on her, his body had wanted her in the worst way. She'd proved smart, hardheaded, decisive and industrious.

Yet seeing her with Sam on her lap and hearing the sweet melody of her voice as she read to him, touched him like nothing else ever had.

Jared just wished to hell he knew what it meant.

Chapter Twenty-Three

"Bye, Mama!"

Sam pulled out of Kinsey's hand and dashed down the boardwalk and through the open door of the shop next to the MacAvoy General Store. Coming here, spending the afternoon with Jared was all Sam had talked about since she met him after school just now.

Inside the building that had once been a restaurant, Kinsey saw about a dozen men and as many boys, working on the church pews, the door and window frames, and the trestle tables that would fill Miss Patterson's fellowship hall. Jared had explained that crews would complete much of the interior work ahead of time so it would be ready to install on Saturday after the buildings were erected.

The pounding of hammers and the grinding of saws drifted out onto the boardwalk along with the sweet smell of sawdust. Kinsey leaned inside, keeping an eye on Sam as he hurried to Jared. Her heart lurched, as it usually did at the sight of him. Today he looked more handsome than ever, with his sleeves rolled back, beads of perspiration on his forehead and a sprinkling of sawdust on his trousers.

She watched as Jared caught sight of Sam, then immediately turned to see her standing in the doorway. He looked a little grim, but he took Sam to where the other young boys were gathered and put him to work hammering nails into a board.

Kinsey waited on the boardwalk until Jared came outside.

"Looks as if you've got plenty of help today," she said.

"Yeah, I guess you could call it that," Jared said and drew in a heavy breath.

"It's different, isn't it?" she asked. "Working with the men in town rather than a construction crew."

"There's a lot more visiting than building going on," Jared told her.

Kinsey was sure that was true. She'd been into town earlier in the day and seen that the men came by, checked on progress, worked when they could, talked a while, then headed off to take care of their own businesses and families. Now that school was out, most all the boys in town were here, too.

"Surely there was a time in your life when you weren't rushing from project to project, from problem to problem. A time when you simply enjoyed what you were doing?" Kinsey asked.

Jared shrugged, as if he hadn't thought about it. Then he nodded inside. "I'll keep an eye on Sam and bring him home in time for supper. Don't worry. We'll be fine."

Kinsey's heart warmed, hearing Jared say those things, because she knew he meant them. He'd take care of Sam.

"I'm going over to Hudson's," Kinsey said. She gave Jared an encouraging smile. "Try to have fun."

Kinsey waited for a freight wagon to rumble down Main Street, then crossed. Stepping up on the boardwalk she couldn't help but look back— to check on Sam, she told herself. But it was Jared who took her gaze.

He stood in the doorway, watching her. Kinsey's skin warmed in response. Even from across the street she could feel the wonder of his touch.

How he'd changed since the first time they'd met. Jared had been her worst nightmare, her greatest fear. Now he'd become a constant in her life. He'd proved himself kind and caring. Gentle, with her and with Sam. She sensed that the two of them were among the very few who knew that side of Jared.

Beneath it all still lurked the heart of a predator. Tough, calculating, determined. Yet those qualities didn't scare her. She admired them, actually. They were part of the reason she'd fallen in love with him.

Kinsey felt her cheeks flush as she looked at Jared and her heart ached anew with the depth of emotion it held for him.

Was it love? she wondered, not for the first time. Kinsey had never loved a man before. She'd never experienced these feelings before. Yet what else could it be?

Not that it mattered, Kinsey told herself.

With one last look at Jared, she headed toward Hudson's Mercantile. He could play no part in her future, hers or Sam's. Even though she'd indulged in the daydream of living in New York, partaking of all the things Jared could provide, Kinsey knew she would never actually do any of those things.

Beth had tried it. And look what had happened.

Dabney Hudson paced back and forth across the entrance of his mercantile when Kinsey stepped inside. The store was empty of customers. Most everyone in town was across the street, next door to MacAvoy's.

"This is a plot to ruin my business," Dabney declared. He shook his fist. "That Ida Burk has those men over there, using that shop next door to lure them into her store."

"Actually, it was Caleb who suggested using the empty store," Kinsey pointed out.

She didn't add that he'd put off the construction of the general store expansion until the church work was completed. If Dabney Hudson didn't already know about Caleb's plans for the space, she wasn't going to be the one who told him.

"Ha!" Dabney declared, then stalked through the mercantile and out the back door.

"Sorry," Maggie said softly, coming out from behind the counter.

Kinsey waved her hand as if dismissing Dabney's foul mood, hoping it would ease Maggie's discomfort. Maggie carried the weight of her whole family on her shoulders, it seemed.

"I finished the church curtains you left for me," Maggie said.

"You're welcome to come to the boardinghouse and work on them," Kinsey offered, not for the first time. Maggie had refused the invitation before and Kinsey was sure she'd do so again, but she had to suggest it.

"No, no," Maggie said, shaking her head and glancing away. "I should work on them...here."

"If you change your mind..."

"I'll bring them to the church on Saturday," Maggie said.

"I told everyone who's come to the boardinghouse that you're helping with the sewing," Kinsey told her.

Maggie looked uncomfortable rather than grateful.

"We could really use your help with the cooking on Saturday," Kinsey said and gave her a smile. "We have to keep the men fed while they're working on the buildings, and we can use all the help we can get."

Maggie considered her words for a long moment, then said, "I'll help with the cooking, if you think it will be all right. If the others won't mind. I told Papa we should have donated all the materials for the church construction, but he wouldn't hear of it."

It surprised Kinsey to learn that Hudson's

Mercantile hadn't donated the construction materials. Not because Dabney was anything close to generous, but because she couldn't imagine that the townsfolk had contributed enough money to Reverend Battenfield's building fund to complete both the church and the fellowship hall, even after Miss Patterson's generous donation.

Kinsey moved on to another topic of conversation, hoping to relieve Maggie's discomfort.

"Could I see that blue fabric again?" she asked.

Maggie's cheeks flushed and she shook her head. "I'm sorry, Kinsey, but the fabric's been sold."

"Oh…"

Kinsey's heart sank a little. She'd known all along she couldn't afford the fabric, and that she didn't have the time to make herself a dress. But still…

She pulled herself up. "Well, I hope the woman who got it will enjoy it."

"I'm sure she will," Maggie said, and for the first time, managed a little smile.

Have fun, Kinsey had said.

Jared had let her words echo in his mind all afternoon. He'd tried to rein in the impatience at the slow pace of the work. He'd tried to relax and talk with the many, many men and women who stopped by the site to check on the progress, offer a suggestion or a bit of advice. He'd even tried to recall years long past, as a kid at his pa's lumber camp or an apprentice at his office, when he enjoyed the work, just for the work itself.

All afternoon he'd struggled to do those things, to take Kinsey's suggestion, to step back from the hectic pace he usually kept during a construction project.

Now, as shadows crept across the floor and some of the men drifted away for supper with their families, Jared realized that the tension he routinely lived with when he worked simply wasn't there. He found that he actually enjoyed stopping to talk with the mayor and the reverend when they'd come by, along with just about everyone else in town.

Of course, not as much was accomplished today as it could have been, but Jared knew they were still on schedule.

The men in Crystal Springs had often worked together on community projects before, he could see. They knew each other's strengths and weaknesses. They helped out without being asked. They jumped in, completing tasks without being directed to do so.

Even the boys were anxious to work. After school, the older ones had shown up and Jared had told them what needed doing. They got to it immediately.

The younger boys were just as anxious, though not as skilled.

Jared smiled as he looked at Sam, along with a half-dozen other young boys, hammering away on boards and blocks of wood in the corner, well away from the dangers of the actual construction. The work they performed didn't amount to much, just nailing together shelves—that would probably have to be re-done—but, young as they were, they knew they were part of the community, part of Crystal Springs.

Jared liked that feeling, too.

"Looks like we'll be ready for Friday night," Caleb said as he walked up.

Jared consulted the tablet in his hand that detailed all the interior work that had to be completed and hauled to the site on Friday night, and put in place for Saturday morning.

"Everything's on schedule," Jared agreed.

"The mayor's wife has all the women lined up to handle the meals on Saturday and the social on Sunday."

Jared frowned. "She's not cooking herself, is she?"

"No, thank God."

Jared's stomach rumbled, despite the thought of Mayor Fisher's wife's cooking. He was hungry and anxious to get home and eat. Most of the men must have felt the same because they came by for a final word with Jared, then headed out, some of them taking their sons with them.

Other men, too busy with their own businesses to help at the work site, came by to check on things and fetch their sons home for supper. The youngest boys who'd been nailing shelves with Sam, told Jared goodbye and promised to be back tomorrow to "help" again. Jared watched them go, something odd tugging inside him.

Finally, Caleb left, too, heading next door to the general store to check on things. Jared saw Sam still in the corner, banging nails into boards. He sat on his knees, holding the hammer in both hands, tongue between his teeth. He'd been at it all afternoon.

Jared's heart warmed unexpectedly. Sam, with five little years of life, trying so hard. Working. Striving. Taking part in what the men in town were accomplishing.

How proud Clark would have been.

Jared drew in a breath to force down his emotions and walked over.

"Time to go home," he said.

Sam kept his head down, kept hammering.

Jared knelt beside him. "Come on, Sam, let's go. The other boys have already gone."

Sam stopped then and looked up at him with a troubled expression. "Uncle Jared, when is my papa coming?"

Jared's heart nearly broke. He sank down into the dirt, staring at the earnest expression on Sam's face as he waited for Jared's answer.

What could he say? How could he explain? How could he ever make the boy understand?

"I don't know, Sam," Jared finally said. "I don't know."

But there was one thing Jared did know: no way in hell he was going to leave Crystal Springs and not take Clark's son with him.

Chapter Twenty-Four

Something was wrong.

Kinsey glanced back at Sam sleeping soundly in their room, and closed the door silently behind her. He'd been tired this evening, worn out from working at the construction site in town with the men and boys. He'd barely held his eyes open through supper. She hadn't even read him a story, just put him in bed and he'd fallen asleep immediately. He'd slept all evening, too, while she worked on the church curtains in the study with the other women who'd come by to finish up the project.

But that wasn't what troubled Kinsey. It was Jared.

He'd brought Sam home in time for supper, as promised, but he hadn't come into the boardinghouse. He hadn't eaten supper. He'd just sent Sam in, waited in the yard to make sure he went through the door, then turned and headed back toward town. None of the men working on the church plans had come over, but she hadn't expected them to. They'd completed everything the night before.

Now it was late. She and the other women had finished the last of the curtains and they'd gone on their way. The residents of the boardinghouse had retired for the night. Nell and Lily had both gone up to their rooms.

Jared was fine, of course. Kinsey knew he could take care of himself, even though he'd stopped wearing his gun a long time ago.

He was probably at the saloon, she decided as she walked through the kitchen. After working so hard for so long, he'd wanted a night to himself, to unwind, to relax, to think about something other than the church and fellowship hall that had become such a big part of his life here in Crystal Springs.

Or maybe he was visiting with Isaac. The two of them had become friends, and Jared seemed willing to console Isaac regarding Lily's impending move to Baltimore.

He could have stopped by MacAvoy's General Store and talked with Caleb. Kinsey considered this a strong possibility. The two of them were much alike, in their dispositions and in their love for building, so it seemed they always had something to discuss.

Kinsey sighed and looked out the kitchen window at the darkened yard. It was silly of her to worry about him. Jared was a grown man, capable and competent, and if he needed a night to himself, then so be it. Whether he was with Isaac or Caleb, or at the saloon, or—

She gasped as another possibility came to her.

That house just beyond the edge of town. The one far back from the road, hidden behind trees, nearly out of sight. Kinsey had heard whispered gossip about what went on there. Fallen women. Men who visited.

Had Jared gone there?

An unreasonable anger filled Kinsey along with a deeper sense of something else. Betrayal? Hurt?

Jealousy.

Yes, she was jealous. The thought of Jared with another woman, even one of those women, tore at her heart as nothing else ever had.

Yet she had no claim on Jared, she reminded herself. She never had. And he'd made no overtures toward her, beyond the kisses and intimacies they'd shared. Yet a fever rolled through her thinking that Jared might be in the arms of another woman.

From the parlor, she heard the clock strike the hour. He'd been unaccounted for quite some time now.

Had he been *there* all this time?

Good gracious, how long did these things take?

The back door burst open and Jared stalked into the kitchen. Kinsey's heart rose into her throat.

"I need to talk to you," he barked. "*Now.*"

He disappeared through the door to the main hallway, expecting her, apparently, to follow.

Stunned, Kinsey just stood there. What did a man look like after he'd done—that? Was there some telltale sign? A different expression?

From the whispered advice she'd gleaned over the years, Kinsey had thought men enjoyed—that. Jared looked to be anything but pleased.

Maybe it hadn't gone well. Was that possible?

And why had he insisted upon talking to her now?

Kinsey gave herself a shake and headed through the house.

She found Jared in the study, standing behind the desk. The light from the lantern glowed around him, doing nothing to soften his frown.

He still wore the work clothes she'd seen him in earlier today. Sleeves rolled back, collar open. A shadow of whispers covered his jaw.

A most sinful thought roared through Kinsey's mind: if the ladies at the house on the edge of town couldn't please him, then maybe she—

"I need to talk to you," Jared declared. He rounded the desk and closed the door with a thud.

Kinsey braced herself. She'd never seen him like this before. Not on that first day when he'd come for Sam, nor later when he'd discovered her true identity.

"What is it?" she asked, her mind reeling, her imagination conjuring up terrible thoughts.

"I can't leave Sam here."

The air around her seemed to chill, freezing her breath within her. An old familiar fear claimed her.

"But what about our agreement? You said—"

"I know what I said."

"You promised! You gave me your word!"

"I can't leave him!" Jared paced to the desk, then turned back. He drew in a breath, as if trying to calm himself. "I want you to come, too. I'll give you—"

"No…"

"—anything you want."

"No!"

"Listen to me!"

Jared planted himself in front of her, towering over her, but Kinsey wasn't frightened, wasn't intimidated. She pushed her chin up and glared at him.

"Please," Jared said softly, struggling to calm himself. "I don't want to deny him the only mama he's ever known. I'll give you anything, if you'll come."

"But Sam has a good life here," Kinsey declared.

Jared turned abruptly and paced to the other side of the room. Kinsey followed him.

"You can see that, surely," she insisted. "He's happy and he's healthy. He has friends and—"

Jared swung around, stopping her.

"You don't have to live with my family," he told her. "You can see Sam as often as you want. I'll build you your own house nearby."

"I don't want to live *nearby*."

"A big house. With servants."

"I don't want servants. I want Sam. I want my own life—here."

"I'll buy you a business. Anything you want."

"I—"

"Money. I'll give you—"

"Jared, stop this!" Kinsey gazed up at him, shaking her head. "Have you lost your mind? What's happened? What's changed that you're carrying on this way? Tell me."

He just looked at her, as if she'd startled him into hearing his own words. His shoulders sagged a little.

"I can't leave him. He's Clark's boy and I can't…"

Jared's words trailed off and he turned away, as if he couldn't face Kinsey any longer.

But she knew him well enough now to realize that something more was behind his words and his inability to look her in the eye.

She touched his arm and said softly, "There's something else going on in your mind, Jared. Something more than taking Sam to New York with you. Tell me what it is."

He glanced back at her but didn't say anything.

She tried again. "Explain it to me. Make me understand. And, maybe, I'll go along with what you want."

He turned to her then, caution and reluctance showing in his expression. He was afraid to believe her, of course, but there was something more. A bond, a very fragile bond, that had been slowly building between them. One that, she sensed, he wasn't sure would hold up under whatever was bothering him.

"Something happened today," she offered, hoping to spur him along.

A long moment passed before Jared spoke. "Today at the construction site when all the other fathers and sons were heading home, Sam asked when *his* papa was coming."

"Oh, dear…" Kinsey pressed her fingers to her lips, imagining the look on Sam's face at that moment. No wonder Jared was upset.

"He's never asked about his father before," Kinsey said, "but I knew he would, eventually."

"And what did you plan to tell him?" Jared asked.

"The truth, of course."

That didn't seem to satisfy Jared, only trouble him more.

"Sam will grow up. He'll ask questions about his papa, and I know you'll tell him what he wants to know," Jared said. "But that's all it will ever be. Questions and answers. Sam will never know what sort of man Clark was. How much he would have loved his son. How he could have treasured him."

Jared turned away once again. "I can't let that happen to Clark. I've done enough to him already."

A chill swept up Kinsey's spine and she was alarmed by what Jared *hadn't* said. Something had gone on between the brothers. That's what tore at Jared now. That was the cause behind his insistence on taking Sam back to New York, and probably the reason Jared had come to Crystal Springs in the first place, hell-bent on taking Sam home with him.

Kinsey had known Clark and now she knew Jared. Both spoke highly of the other. Both were good men. Yet, as with all siblings, there was a push and pull, a love and hate, a constant stretching of the bond that held them together.

From the look on Jared's face, Kinsey knew there was unfinished business between the brothers that haunted him still. Unfinished business that Jared felt could never be put to rest without taking Sam back to New York.

Kinsey touched his arm tenderly. "Tell me, Jared. Tell me what happened between you and Clark."

He glanced back at her and winced. "Clark died and I know it was my fault."

"Your fault? It couldn't possibly have been your fault. You were in Pennsylvania and—"

Jared held up his hand, stopping her. The weight of whatever was on his conscience seemed to make it difficult to stand straight. He turned to her with some effort.

"It was supposed to be me who handled the project in Virginia, not Clark," Jared said. "I started the work on it but then the Pennsylvania job came up. It was a bigger project, more complex, more prestigious."

"So you asked Clark to switch with you?"

Jared glanced away for a moment, then faced her again, as if he were confronting the unpleasant memories as well.

"I bullied him into it," Jared said. "He wanted the Pennsylvania project—it was supposed to be his. But I forced him to let me have it."

Two men, physically and mentally well matched, yet Jared was the dominant one. The strongest of all the Mason brothers, Kinsey had heard Clark say many times. Now, knowing both Jared and Clark, she could easily see how Clark would give in to his older brother, let him have his way.

"Clark had been deferring to you all his life,"

Kinsey said. "After all, you were the oldest. That's the way it is in families. He probably thought nothing about you taking the Pennsylvania project. He was strong, too. If he'd really wanted it, he would have fought you for it. But I never heard him mention it, certainly he never complained about it."

"Why would he? After the way things turned out for him?" Jared uttered a disgusted grunt. "When Clark wrote and said he'd gotten married, I couldn't believe it. He went on and on about what a wonderful wife he'd found, how much he loved her, how happy he was."

"But you weren't happy for your brother, were you?" Kinsey asked.

"I was envious…jealous…angry," Jared admitted. "I kept thinking that if I'd gone to Virginia, if I hadn't insisted Clark take that project, then maybe I'd be the one who found a good wife."

"Instead of one you could simply tolerate?" Kinsey asked.

Jared looked miserable. "I'm not proud of this. And I never told anyone what happened. I was too ashamed."

"Because then Clark was killed and, not only had you lost your brother, you felt guilty because you'd put him in that place, working on that project," Kinsey said. "Plus, you had to face your uncharitable thoughts about Clark's happiness with Beth."

Jared curled his hand into a fist. "That's why I've got to make it right, Kinsey. For Clark. I've got to take Sam back home to the family. See that he's raised right. Make sure he knows who is father was. Give him all the opportunities Clark would have given him."

"You'll only be appeasing your own conscience."

"No, I'll be giving the boy the birthright he's due," Jared said. "The only reason he's in the world is because I forced Clark to take that project. If I'd gone, like I was supposed to, things would have turned out far different."

"You don't know that."

"If it had been me in Virginia instead of Clark, do you think I would have married Beth?"

Kinsey shook her head, absolutely sure of her answer. "No. Never."

Jared nodded, as if she'd just made his point for him.

"All of this is my fault and I'm not going to dishonor my brother or let his son pay the price for what I've done any longer."

Kinsey gazed up at Jared, at his strong, determined face, and her stomach rolled into a tight knot.

She'd had no idea he felt this way, no clue that Jared considered himself responsible for Clark's death and, consequently, Sam's circumstances.

"After the church is built, I'm leaving Crystal Springs and taking Sam with me," Jared said. He shook his head sorrowfully. "I don't want to do this, Kinsey. I don't want to take him away from you. But I've got to."

Kinsey steeled her emotions. There was no way on earth she'd allow Jared to take Sam away from her.

Even if it meant doing something desperate to keep him.

Chapter Twenty-Five

The churchyard looked like the construction site that it was as evening shadows crawled across the materials assembled for tomorrow's church-raising.

Jared looked on with pride at how easily the project had come together. He'd set the priorities, figured out the schedule, divided up the workload. Finding volunteers was no problem here in Crystal Springs. Every man and boy in town, it seemed, was here working. Most of the women had shown up, too, bringing fresh drinking water, preparing food, watching the children and tending to minor injuries. They were as organized as the men.

Caleb walked over. "From the look of things, we'll get the church and fellowship hall built and outfitted tomorrow, as planned. Barring any unforeseen big problems."

"Problems always come up," Jared commented.

"I know." Caleb grinned. "That's the part of the job I like best."

Jared nodded, feeling the same as Caleb.

"I told everybody to be here before dawn tomorrow. We'll start work at first light." Caleb shook his head. "You know, I almost hate to see this project finished. I'll have to go back to shopkeeping all day."

Jared nodded. That didn't sound very appealing to him either.

"Maybe I can squeeze in a little time to work on other projects about town," Caleb said. "Some folks have asked about it since they've seen what we're doing here. Maybe you could do the same?"

"Maybe," Jared said.

He'd told no one but Kinsey that he intended to leave Crystal Springs as soon as this project was completed. He was sure she hadn't mentioned his plan to anyone.

Caleb nodded toward the trees. "Sheriff's coming this way. I saw him talking with his wife a while ago. I wonder how things are going?"

Isaac had been talking with Lily? Jared hadn't noticed. Every time he looked around, his gaze always seemed to fall on Kinsey.

She was still speaking to him, which surprised

him some. And she wasn't fighting him about taking Sam back to New York, which surprised him even more. She hadn't threatened to leave town, run away with the boy, hide him.

But neither had she given her blessing to him taking Sam back east. He couldn't imagine that she would willingly let the boy go.

Kinsey was planning something. He knew it. Jared had thought it over from every angle and couldn't figure it out. But he knew she was up to something. What was she planning?

Isaac ambled over. Every time Jared saw him, the sheriff seemed to look older, more worn out and despondent. Losing his wife had taken its toll. From the expression on his face, his talk with Lily hadn't brought good news.

The men exchanged a nod in greeting but nobody said anything. Finally, Isaac spoke.

"Lily says she's leaving town Monday morning." His words were barely audible, as if every ounce of life had been drained out of him.

"Damn," Caleb said softly. "Sorry to hear that, Sheriff. I thought she'd come to her senses by now."

"Yeah, me, too…"

"Are you just going to let her go?" Jared asked.

Isaac's gaze hardened. "I can't make her stay. God knows, I've tried."

"I guess Dixie showing up at your house didn't help anything," Caleb said.

Isaac grimaced. "I never laid a hand on that woman. I told Lily that. She'd know if I was lying."

Jared figured that was true. A husband and wife knew that sort of thing about each other. He thought of Kinsey again and his gaze roamed the gathering until he spotted her. She'd worked all day at the boardinghouse, she'd taken care of Sam and spent hours here helping at the church-yard. He knew she must be tired. She worked too hard. But still she looked beautiful.

So beautiful…

Kinsey lay in bed staring up at the ceiling, thinking of Jared in the room above her head. She'd heard his footsteps and followed his path around the room. From the door to the window, to the washstand, then to the bed. All had been silent up there for a while now.

She tried to estimate the time, but couldn't. Thoughts kept drifting in and out of her head, as they'd done for several days now. And all of them revolved on how she'd convince Jared to leave Sam here with her.

She was running out of time. Tomorrow he would be busy from dawn until into the night at the church. Sunday was Reverend Battenfield's service, then the social.

And after that, he intended to leave. With Sam. It was now or never.

Kinsey threw back the covers and got out of bed. She slipped on her robe as she checked Sam and made certain he was sleeping soundly, then left her room.

The boardinghouse was silent as she climbed the back staircase and stopped outside Jared's room. She glanced up and down the hallway and saw no one, then listened at the door. She heard nothing. Quietly, she opened it and slipped inside.

Faint moonlight beamed in through the open window bringing a slight breeze with it. Kinsey waited at the door, her heart racing at the thought of what she was about to do, how desperate she'd become.

Her eyes focused on the bed. Jared's bed. In the corner of the room, deep in the shadows she saw a jumble of covers. A wave of heat passed over her.

Did he sleep in a nightshirt? Back in New York he was considered a gentleman, and gentlemen slept in nightshirts, didn't they?

Somehow Kinsey couldn't picture it, couldn't imagine Jared's wide shoulders, his big arms hidden in a baggy nightshirt. So he slept in his long johns, probably. Yet it seemed too hot for that, she thought, even with the breeze blowing in through the window.

No nightshirt, no long johns. That only left—

Kinsey gasped in the silence, then pressed her lips together. Was he naked? Was she standing across the room ogling his bed and all the while he was naked amid those tangled sheets?

What was she thinking, coming here like this? She'd sworn she'd do anything to keep Sam, yet—

"Kinsey."

She jumped and swung around to see Jared sitting in the chair in the corner.

Wearing clothes.

Some clothes, anyway.

In the moonlight she saw that he had on trousers but no shirt; his feet were bare. He didn't rise from the chair, just sat there watching her.

Kinsey tugged at the knotted sash of her robe, desperate suddenly to do something with her hands. The motion seemed to draw Jared's attention. His gaze dipped to her middle, then rose slowly to her face again. Heat rushed through her and she became conscious of the press of fabric against her unbound breasts, her bare feet on the wooden floor, her hair trailing down her back.

Silence closed in on the room, somehow drawing Jared's presence nearer, though he hadn't moved from the chair. His gaze stayed on her. She heard his breathing quicken. She tingled in response.

"I'm here because of Sam," Kinsey said, her voice little more than a whisper.

Jared frowned but didn't say anything.

"I don't want you to take him so I've decided to—"

Jared sprang from the chair and was in front of her in two long strides. His nearness overwhelmed her. Heat rolled off of him, urging her to come closer.

He touched his palm to her cheek in a gentle caress and gazed into her eyes.

She gulped and tried again. "I've decided to tell you everything."

"You're here to talk?" he asked, drawing his hand away.

That he'd considered otherwise, startled her.

"Yes, of course," she said. Then it occurred to her exactly what he meant. "Did you think that I intended to—to—have my way with you in order to convince you to leave Sam here?"

Jared smiled. It was a smile that wound through her, touching every part of her.

"No," he said. "Maybe I was hoping, though."

She should have been insulted, but wasn't. Instead, Kinsey's flesh warmed and her heart beat a little faster.

What would it be like to give in to the desire that suddenly coursed through her? To turn herself over to him. To know him fully, completely?

His chest was bare, inches from her. She could reach out and touch him. Feel his hard muscles. Run her fingers through the curly hair. Was it coarse? Soft? She could find out right now.

Most of her life the very idea had been frightening and she imagined it a horrible, humiliating experience. But with Jared, she knew it wouldn't be. And that was because she loved him.

Her feelings for him, however, had no bearing on why she was here tonight.

Kinsey stepped back, hoping to break the invisible bond that held her near him. Cool air swirled between them.

"I came here to tell you everything," she said. "Everything about Clark's death."

Jared tensed and the warmth surrounding him suddenly chilled. He looked suspicious now. Maybe a little angry.

"I would never have told you this," Kinsey said. "But ever since you said that you believe you're responsible, in part, for Clark's death, I've known I had to tell you."

"You know something else? And you've never told me?" he demanded, his anger evident now. "Clark wasn't killed at the construction site? Working? It wasn't an accident?"

"No, no. That part is true. Just like Beth told your folks in the letter," she said quickly. "But there's more to it than that."

"Tell me. Tell me now."

Kinsey braced herself. She didn't like remembering what had happened that night, certainly didn't want to tell it—to anyone, but most especially Jared. Yet she couldn't go on letting him think he was at fault for Clark's death. And perhaps, just perhaps, it would convince Jared once and for all that Sam belonged here in Crystal Springs with her.

"When Clark and Beth had been married for a while, your mother sent word that she was coming for a visit, to meet her new daughter-in-law," Kinsey said.

"I know. I was in Pennsylvania, but Clark mentioned in a letter that she was coming to Richmond, and he and his wife were going there to see her," Jared said.

"Lynchburg had several very nice hotels, but your mother preferred to stay in Richmond. It was a short train ride, and Clark thought Beth would enjoy seeing the city and staying in the hotel there," Kinsey said. "I went with them at Clark's invitation."

"You did?"

"He knew how close Beth and I were. I lived in the home he bought for her," she reminded him.

Jared shrugged. "Clark never mentioned you at all. His letters were mostly about work and how happy he was with his wife."

"I don't suppose your mother mentioned to you that I was in Richmond, too?"

Jared thought for a moment, then shook his head. "No. I'd have remembered."

"That's because Amelia and I were never formally introduced," Kinsey said. "But I came to know her very well by accidentally overhearing her conversation with Beth."

Jared didn't say anything, so Kinsey went on.

"Beth and I were very excited about going to Richmond and staying at such a beautiful hotel. We'd never done anything like that before. Clark let both of us buy new clothes, lovely clothes, for the trip," Kinsey said. "Beth was very nervous about meeting your mother, of course. Worried that she'd do or say the wrong thing. Make a bad impression. She didn't want to embarrass Clark. He'd planned a special supper at the hotel where Beth and your mother would meet."

"From the things he said about Beth in his letters, she could do no wrong," Jared said. "Clark wouldn't have cared what our mother thought."

"Beth cared." Kinsey drew in a breath, forcing herself to continue. "Amelia came to our hotel suite the afternoon before the supper. Clark wasn't there. She told Beth in no uncertain terms how disappointed she was in her son's choice for a wife. She knew that Beth wasn't from your social circle, wasn't born into a prominent family of means, had no political or social connections. She refused to give her blessing to their marriage."

"That sounds like my ma," Jared said. "She's got a real determined streak in her."

Kinsey didn't point out that, to her way of

thinking, Jared had the same trait. She suspected he already knew it anyway.

"I was in the bedroom of the suite. I overheard everything," Kinsey said. "Beth was completely devastated. I don't know how she got through supper that night or the rest of your mother's visit."

"Why didn't Beth just tell Clark what happened?" Jared asked. "Hell, we all know what our mother's like."

"For the same reason I would have never told you these things if I hadn't been forced into it. Amelia is your mother. She deserves the respect that's due her."

Jared shook his head. "Beth should have told Clark. He would have understood."

"She was afraid. Afraid that if she spoke ill of your mother, Clark might turn on her. That he might resent her for coming between them. That he might decide she was too much trouble. Beth was afraid, afraid of everything. But most especially, afraid of losing Clark."

Jared was quiet for a few moments, taking in what she'd said. "What does this have to do with Clark's dying?" he finally asked.

"A few months later, Clark wanted to go home to New York. He wanted to take Beth and introduce her to the rest of the family. She didn't want to go. Clark didn't understand why. They fought about it."

"Married people disagree about things sometimes."

"No, not Clark and Beth. It was the only time I ever heard them upset with each other about anything—anything. Clark actually raised his voice at her. Beth collapsed into tears. Clark was so frustrated with her that he left the house, went to the construction site, and…"

Jared winced and turned away. "And he was distracted, worried about his wife. He wasn't paying attention…"

Kinsey went to him and touched his arm. "Maybe I should have stepped in, told Clark what was wrong. Beth had made me promise I would never tell him what your mother said to her. And, really, I didn't think it was my place to interfere with their marriage. But looking back…"

They were both quiet for a long while, the silence in the room hanging heavy around them.

Jared turned to her. "That doesn't excuse what I did, or the way I treated Clark."

"But you see, don't you, that it wasn't your fault. You have nothing to make up for. Nothing to redeem yourself for in Clark's memory. You can leave Sam here, where he's loved and happy, and not feel guilty about it."

Jared just looked at her.

"Beth tried to live in a world where she didn't belong," Kinsey said. "She knew she shouldn't have married Clark, but she loved him so much she gave it a try. And see how everything turned out? I'm not going to make the same mistake she did."

"Things will be different, if you come to New York. It won't be like it was for Clark and Beth," Jared insisted.

"Yes, it will. Only worse. Amelia wouldn't accept Beth and she was Clark's wife. What will it be like for me? I have no standing at all in your family."

Jared shook his head. "I won't let my mother treat you that way."

"And how will you manage that when you'll be in Maine?"

"You can't let anyone—certainly not my mother—control your life."

"I control my life," Kinsey said. "That's why I won't go to New York with you. Why I won't live in your family home, or even nearby. And why I absolutely won't have Sam raised by your mother. She didn't like Beth. I won't have her poisoning Sam's mind against his mother. Beth was afraid she'd do that. Afraid your mother would take him away from her. That's why she ran away."

"Even after everything you've just told me, I still can't leave him here."

"And I won't let you take him from me."

Jared squared his shoulders. "Come Monday, I'm leaving on the stagecoach and I'm taking Sam with me. You've got until then to change your mind."

Chapter Twenty-Six

It was the first time Jared had begun a construction project with a prayer, but he figured Reverend Battenfield's request for favorable weather, a safe day, and the good Lord's blessing on the work couldn't hurt.

Just after high noon, the men were heading back to work. The women in town had prepared a hearty meal fit for the dozens of workmen, and served it on the trestle tables that would be installed in the fellowship hall before the end of the day.

Miss Patterson was expected shortly, and Jared had already gratefully stepped aside and told Caleb he could give the woman a tour of the hall that would bear her name, along with the sign that grew larger every time it was discussed. Caleb's work on the project had elevated Bess Patterson's opinion of him. So much so that he'd confided in Jared that he intended to ask the woman if he could escort Sarah to the social after church tomorrow.

The women took turns watching the babies and small children, playing games, keeping them occupied away from the construction work. Sam was among the group of boys running in a relay race under the scrutiny of the reverend's wife.

Jared watched him, feeling a swell of pride as the boy ran faster than the others, beating them all to the finish line. Sam threw out his arms in celebration, then circled back to be with his friends again.

Suddenly he looked a little taller to Jared, as if he'd grown just last night. Hard to believe this was the same boy who had to be rocked to sleep each night on his mother's lap.

That would change soon enough, Jared knew. Sam seemed to have matured in the short time Jared had been in town. Pretty soon, he'd be grown.

He turned then, finding Kinsey among the crowd of woman cleaning up after the noon meal. Anger surged through him. She was washing dishes. Again.

Every time he saw her, it seemed, she was working, usually washing dishes either at the boardinghouse or at the White Dove Café in town. She worked too hard and it bothered him.

Everything else about today was going well. Progress on the church and fellowship hall was continuing, going smoothly so far. No construction problems, no fights among the men, no shortage of supplies. The easiest construction job he'd ever overseen. Of course, it wasn't complicated, just the big shell of a church and an attached fellowship hall, and more than enough volunteers to have it completed before dark.

But it was more than that, Jared realized as he watched the men nailing boards into place on the church. Much more.

When had his life turned from the enjoyable work at the lumber mill or at a construction site to worrying over the details of so many large, complex projects?

With no wife or children Jared's job was the most important thing in his life. It was the natural progression of things, he realized. A man had to move on, move up, accomplish more, accept challenges and overcome them. It was expected of him, and of his brothers, and Jared had eagerly set out to prove he could handle anything and everything that came his way.

But now, standing under the shade trees, listening to the ring of hammers and saws, watching the simple building he'd designed grow before his eyes, Jared realized that he'd done all of that. He'd taken on the biggest and the toughest, and he'd succeeded in it all.

For the first time ever, Jared wondered: what now?

His gaze found Kinsey again, still washing dishes at the tubs atop one of the trestle tables. She was smiling, talking with several other women.

It was nice, he decided, being able to look over at her whenever he chose. She'd caused him more headaches than any other person in his life, but still, there was something about her.

Kinsey dipped a plate into the rinse bucket.

Just what that "something" was, Jared couldn't name. It had nagged at him since he'd arrived in Crystal Springs and seen her outside the general store across the street from the stage depot.

Kinsey passed the rinsed plate to one of the other women. It slipped from her fingers to the ground. She bent over to pick it up and Jared's throat went dry.

She stayed that way for a fraction of a minute, her dress hiked up just a little, her bottom in the air.

Want and desire flooded Jared, bringing with it predictable results. Yet something more happened. His heart beat a little quicker. It seemed to swell. Everything else at the churchyard faded and all he could see was Kinsey.

He wanted to go to her. Take her into his arms and hold her, kiss her, make her his. The need to take care of her, protect her overwhelmed him. He could imagine nothing more important.

But how could he feel this way when he was leaving town in two days?

And why was he still here? The question slammed inside Jared's mind like a mule kick to the gut.

He could have left weeks ago. He could have taken Sam and headed back to New York. The boy was rightfully his. A blood relative. Jared had all the documents to prove it. Nobody could have legally stopped him.

The church project hadn't kept him here. He could have walked away from it. The situation with Isaac and Lily, Caleb and Sarah was troublesome, but really, nothing that should have prevented him from leaving.

So why was he still here?

Jared looked at Kinsey again and the ache in his chest, in his belly and in his soul grew stronger.

Whatever the reason, he only had until Monday to figure it out.

"Damn it, Kinsey, would you stop washing dishes?" Jared demanded.

She looked up from the washtub that now sat in the spacious, well-appointed kitchen of the Bess Patterson Fellowship Hall. Emma Foster, standing next to Kinsey, looked at Jared with raised eyebrows, but Kinsey smiled.

"Is that an offer to help?" she asked.

"Yeah," he grumbled, taking the linen cloth away from Emma.

They were the last people left. The work was done, the buildings complete and outfitted, and everyone else had gone home.

"I can't leave you two here with this work left to do," Emma insisted.

"We'll be fine," Jared told her, and managed to sound pleasant.

He was tired. He wanted to go home. But he wasn't leaving without Kinsey.

"Well, all right," Emma said, taking off her apron. "I'll see you two bright and early in the morning."

"Good night," Kinsey called, as Emma left the

kitchen. She passed Jared a dripping plate. "Here it is my night off from the White Dove and I'm still washing dishes."

"I wish you'd quit that job," Jared said.

"You don't act like a man who just designed, organized and oversaw the construction of the town's two most important buildings today." She looked up at him. "Congratulations. Everything is perfect."

Jared couldn't hold back the proud smile that tugged at his mouth. Everything had been completed, inside and out, and he couldn't have been happier.

"Where's Sam?" he asked, looking around.

"Dora Gleason took him home with the other children. He wanted to stay but he was too sleepy."

They worked together to finish the dishes, then Kinsey got her wrap and handbag and they walked back to the boardinghouse. The town was silent, everyone exhausted from the long, hard day, it seemed. A lantern burned in the kitchen as they walked inside and stopped at Kinsey's bedroom door.

"Well, good night," she said softly.

"'Night," he said, then looked past her and saw

that her room was dark. "No lantern for Sam tonight?"

"He's next door with the Gleasons," Kinsey explained.

Jared's blood surged. "All night?"

"Dora will bring him over in the morning in time for church."

"Oh…"

"Well, good night."

Kinsey slipped into her room and closed the door, then felt her way to the bureau and lit the lantern. She undressed and washed, then put on her nightgown.

Above her head, she heard Jared moving around in his room. From the door to the washstand in the corner, but not farther.

How many more nights would he be up there? Only one. Her heart ached, feeling the loss already. She couldn't bear the thought of him leaving, returning to New York.

Kinsey plucked the pins from her hair and shook it loose.

She was in love with Jared. How could she let him walk out of her life? And take Sam with him?

Should she go to New York, as he asked? Take a chance that she could find happiness with the Mason family, even though Beth had failed so completely?

But would she resent Jared for forcing her into a move she didn't want to make?

And if by Monday she couldn't convince Jared to leave Sam with her here, should she go with him, to take care of him?

Kinsey's heart suddenly ached. What would happen when Jared headed off to Maine for his next project, leaving her alone?

And how would she manage when Jared selected his wife, one that would satisfy his mother, one he could tolerate?

She turned her gaze upward to the ceiling, imagining Jared in his room. His footsteps continued back and forth, then faded. A moment later, she heard them again on the back staircase. He was coming downstairs.

Kinsey held her breath. A knock sounded on her door. She opened it and Jared stood there.

He just looked at her, his gaze burning hot. Kinsey felt it sear her. There was no mistaking the look in his eyes. Innocent and inexperienced as she was, Kinsey recognized it.

"Can I come in?" he asked, his voice low and husky.

She stepped back and let him into her room.

"I bought this for you," he said, and held out a large box wrapped in paper and tied with a pink ribbon.

Suddenly she felt foolish. Had she misjudged the reason for him coming here?

Then she saw his gaze dip, running the length of her. His nose flared and his chest expanded.

No, she wasn't wrong.

Jared dropped the package and pushed the door shut as he stepped forward and took Kinsey in his arms. He locked her against him, almost pulling her off the floor as he looked into her eyes. Then he lowered his head and kissed her.

He took her breath away. Kinsey moaned as his mouth took hers and his tongue pushed its way inside. Their bodies melded together. His kiss became more intense. She rose on her toes and twisted her fingers through his hair.

Jared broke their kiss and buried his lips against her throat. He smelled clean, like soap. His jaw was smooth, unlike when she'd seen him earlier.

He kissed her again, panting hard against her mouth as his palm covered her breast. Kinsey pressed herself against him. Her knees weakened as he plucked open the buttons on her nightgown and slid his hands inside.

Jared groaned and pushed her nightgown off

her shoulders. He gazed down at her. "You're…
you're beautiful…"

She reached out hesitantly. "Is it all right if
I…?"

"Oh, yes…please…"

She touched his chest, then splayed her fingers
against his tight muscles beneath his shirt. Jared
gasped, then dipped his head and kissed a hot
line down her throat. He tasted her breasts.

Kinsey collapsed against him. He held her with
one arm and braced the other against the wall to
steady them.

Jared panted in her ear. "If you don't want to
do this…now's the time…to say so."

"Now?"

"Well, a few minutes earlier would have made it
easier to quit," he said, "but if you want to stop…"

Kinsey pressed her palm to his cheek, gazing
into his dark eyes.

In two days, he might be gone. She might lose
him. But she had tonight.

"I don't want to stop," she whispered.

Jared swept her into his arms and carried her
to the bed. He laid her down, then pulled off his
clothes and stretched out beside her. Kinsey's
heart pounded with the certainty that what she
was doing was right.

He kissed her gently as he lifted her nightgown and pulled it over her head. His hands slid over her curves. She touched him, surprised by the power he possessed and the gentleness of his touch.

Their kisses and caresses grew more frantic. Jared moved above her, between her thighs, and pressed himself against her. Kinsey clung to his shoulders and lost her breath as he moved within her.

An urgency, deep inside, grew too demanding to resist. She moved with him. Jared moved faster, driving her until great waves of pleasure filled her. She pushed her hips hard against his and he drove himself into her, moaning her name.

Kinsey awakened to find herself alone in her bed. The lantern, burning low, sent shadows across the room. She saw Jared standing at the window, gazing into the yard.

He was naked. Long limbs. Muscles. All male. She loved him with all her heart.

Could she let him walk out of her life?

Jared seemed to sense that she was awake. He turned from the window, the lantern glowing against his skin, neither ashamed or disturbed by his nakedness. Kinsey's cheeks heated up at the sight of him.

He walked to the bed and looked down at her.

"Forget what I said earlier about New York," he told her, his voice low and tense. "There's no need for you go."

Chapter Twenty-Seven

Kinsey pulled the covers up around her and stared at him, hurt and confusion racing through her.

"There's no need for me to go to New York with you?" she asked, repeating his words of a moment ago. "I—I don't understand."

"I'm not taking Sam."

Just weeks ago these would have been the words Kinsey most wanted to hear from Jared. But no longer. Too much had changed.

"You're leaving, but you're not taking Sam?"

"Ever since I got to Crystal Springs, nothing has gone as planned," he said. "I didn't expect to stay here for so long, didn't expect to get involved with the town. And I sure as hell didn't expect to fall in love with you."

"You—what?"

"I'm not leaving. I'm staying." Jared sat down

on the bed next to her. "I finally figured out what I've been so confused about. I'm in love with you. I'm going to stay here in Crystal Springs."

She sat up straighter. "But what about your family? What about your business? Your project in Maine?"

He waved his big hand, dismissing her words. "I've got three other brothers. Any one of them can handle it."

She shook her head. "This isn't like you."

Jared thought for a minute, considering her words.

"I've never been more sure of anything. I want my life to be here in Crystal Springs, with you. If you'll have me, that is."

"Are you asking if I'll—"

"—marry me," Jared said. "Yes, that's what I'm asking."

Kinsey stared at him, too stunned to speak. Never in her wildest dreams did she imagine she'd hear these words from him. And now that she had, could she believe him?

Doubts crowded her thoughts.

Did he really love her? Or was this a ploy to get Sam?

Despite what he'd just said, after they were

married would he leave for New York and, as her husband, demand that she go, too?

"I love you, Kinsey," Jared said. "You believe that, don't you?"

She smiled, pleased by the warm glow in the pit of her stomach that his words evoked.

"Yes, I believe it," Kinsey said. "And I love you, too."

Jared didn't smile. He knew her too well.

"But…" he asked.

Kinsey hesitated, yet in her heart she knew she must be truthful with him.

"I'm not sure I believe you've really changed. That you intend to live here in Crystal Springs. Your life in New York is so different."

"I found something here I like better, something that means more to me than anything else." Jared touched his palm to her cheek. "I've found you."

Tears swelled in Kinsey's eyes. How she wished she could ignore her doubts, accept what he said and revel in the joy of their shared love. How she wished that now, at long last, her dream of having her own family and home might really come true.

"What about Sam? What about you wanting

him to live with your family, know what sort of life the Masons have built?"

"None of that really matters, does it? What matters is that Sam is raised by people who love him." Jared's gaze softened, as if reading her thoughts. "You don't trust me."

"I want to," she said, wishing with all her heart that she could. "But Crystal Springs is a small town. New York is a big city. Building projects here will be small, nothing on the grand scale you're used to. I'm not even the kind of wife you intended to marry."

"I love you. You just said you love me, too," Jared told her. "That's all we need."

Kinsey shook her head. "Clark and Beth loved each other. Isaac and Lily love each other. But that doesn't mean two people can make a life together, that they want the same things, that they can get along."

Hurt clouded Jared's expression but then he drew in a breath and nodded.

"I'm staying. I love you. And, in time, you'll see that we should get married."

He sounded so sure, so convinced that, for a moment, Kinsey almost agreed with him. She wanted to. Yet she didn't dare.

"Here," he said, presenting her with the package that he'd brought to the room with him and dropped on the floor. "This is for you."

Jared hadn't thought so many prayers were needed to dedicate a church and fellowship hall, but Reverend Battenfield and the good folks of Crystal Springs saw it differently, so he went along with it.

The reverend's first sermon in the new church had been one of giving thanks, of following a higher purpose and of loving your fellow man, all of which had been in praise of the townsfolk for completing a task so large and so necessary.

More prayers had followed after the sermon as everyone gathered in the Bess Patterson Fellowship Hall. The reverend spoke, then Mayor Fisher got up and delivered a speech that was, mercifully, short. He called on Jared to get up and say a few words.

Standing in front of the townsfolk seated at the tables in the fellowship hall, Jared assured everyone that he hadn't done it alone. Everyone in Crystal Springs had helped. He made a point of acknowledging Caleb Burk's contribution.

"I'm truly grateful for the friendship everyone in town has shown me." Jared gazed at Kinsey seated between Lily and Sam. "I feel like I belong here. So I've decided to stay. Crystal Springs is my new home."

After a round of applause, the Mayor's wife urged everyone to go outside for fresh air while the ladies served the meal. Voices rose as people made their way toward the door and kitchen. Sam scooted out, surrounded by the Gleason brothers.

Jared waded through the gathering toward Kinsey.

"You look beautiful," he said softly.

She dipped her gaze, trying desperately not to blush. How could she not after the night they'd shared?

"I love my new dress," she said, touching the skirt.

It was made of the fabric she'd admired in Hudson's Mercantile, the surprise that was in the box he'd brought to her room last night.

"I can't believe you and Maggie conspired to have this made for me," Kinsey said. "And how did you ever get Mrs. Hartwood to agree to make it? She's so busy with her own family, she never sews for anyone else anymore."

"She was glad to help out," Jared said, "after I *explained* things to her."

Understanding dawned in Kinsey. "Oh, Jared,

you didn't. You didn't pay her an extravagant fee for sewing this dress for me, did you?"

Jared smiled. "Worth every penny."

"I love the dress. It's beautiful," Kinsey said, and gestured around her. "As beautiful as these buildings—"

She eyed him sharply. "Did Reverend Battenfield really have enough money in the building fund? Or did you…?"

"I made a small contribution," he admitted, then nodded across the room. "Looks like it's paying off for Caleb."

Kinsey saw Caleb standing alongside Sarah and Bess Patterson. All of them were smiling.

"Maybe the two of them will be the first couple married in the new church," she speculated.

"I've got another couple in mind for that honor."

Jared gazed into her eyes, causing her to flush with warmth. She knew that he meant the two of them. More than anything Kinsey wanted to throw her arms around him right here in the fellowship hall, shout to the town that she loved him and that she would marry him.

Yet doubts lingered. Not about her love, of course. But about whether they could truly have a marriage. She didn't see how Jared could possibly agree to give up his entire life—just for her. It was too big a leap. Too much to manage.

She wished she were as confident as Jared that he would be happy here in Crystal Springs.

"I'd better get into the kitchen," Kinsey said.

Most of the other women were already inside. Rich smells of food already drifted out.

Jared frowned. "You're not washing dishes today, are you?"

"Of course," she told him with a smile.

Jared watched her go, his mind set. He'd convince her that he'd decided to stay here, make this place his home. Somehow.

He headed outside. Most of the men were standing around, talking about yesterday and the work they'd all done. Jared checked on Sam and saw him playing with the Gleason boys under the shade trees.

He saw Isaac standing alone, gazing toward the fellowship hall. More than likely, he was thinking about his wife inside. Thinking, too, that tomorrow she'd be gone.

He didn't know how Isaac would stand it. Jared's feelings for Kinsey were strong. He loved her with all his heart. He couldn't imagine how Isaac would let Lily walk out of his life, knowing he'd never see her again.

Jared strode over to where Isaac stood.

"Lily's a good woman and you two love each other," Jared said. "Are you just going to let her leave tomorrow?"

"I don't know what else I can do." Isaac shrugged helplessly. "Got any ideas?"

"Hell, yes," Jared told him. "I'll tell you exactly what I'd do."

"Are you sure, Lily? Absolutely sure?" Kinsey asked the next morning as the two of them headed toward the stage depot, each carrying one of Lily's satchels.

She'd asked Lily the same question several times since leaving the boardinghouse, and each time, Lily had given her the same answer.

"I can't stay here. There're just too many bad memories," Lily said.

"Isaac isn't a bad memory, is he?"

"I'll always love Isaac. No matter what."

"And you don't doubt his word about Dixie?"

"Of course not. I know my husband," Lily said. "Even if I'm leaving him."

Lily kept walking and Kinsey hurried to keep up. Now that Lily had made up her mind and the day had arrived, she seemed anxious to leave town, get it over with.

At the stage depot, Kinsey handed the satchel to the stationmaster while Lily bought her ticket. On the boardwalk out front, the stagecoach was already there, the six-horse team hitched up, ready and waiting. The driver and shotgun rider were up top. Two other passengers milled around in the early morning light.

"I'll miss you," Kinsey said. "Sam will miss you, too."

The stationmaster stepped outside and consulted his pocket watch. "All aboard!"

Lily took Kinsey's hands. "Maybe you can come to Baltimore for a visit one day? You and Sam—"

Lily's eyes widened as something across the street took her attention. Kinsey turned to see Jared walking toward them. Beside him, was Isaac, satchel in hand.

"What are you doing here?" Lily demanded.

Isaac looked at her. "I'm coming with you."

"You're—*what?*"

"I'm coming with you," Isaac told her again.

"All aboard!" the stationmaster shouted.

Lily's jaw sagged and she shook her head. "I'm *leaving* you, Isaac. You can't *come with me.*"

"Well, I am." He dropped his satchel at her feet. "If you can't live in this town anymore, then so be it. We'll live any place you want to live, any way you want to live."

Tears pooled in Lily's eyes. "But, Isaac…"

"If you don't want us to try and have a baby of our own again, that's all right with me. We'll go to an orphans' asylum and get us as many babies as you want."

Lily burst into sobs. Isaac stepped closer.

"I love you, Lily. My life is nothing without you. I don't give a damn about my job, this town or anybody in it,"

Isaac said. "So I'm coming with you and that's that."

Lily kept crying as Isaac slid his arm around her shoulders and pulled her close.

"Everything's going to be fine," he said softly. "As long as we're together."

The other two passengers already on the stage, the stationmaster, the driver and shotgun driver were all staring as Isaac helped Lily into the coach. He paused and offered Jared his hand.

"Best advice I ever got," he said. "I appreciate it."

Jared nodded and shook his hand. He stepped back next to Kinsey as Isaac climbed inside and settled on the seat next to Lily and the stage pulled out.

Kinsey stood watching the street for a long moment, then turned to Jared, her emotions running high.

"You gave Isaac advice about his marriage?" she asked.

"I told him that if my wife was determined to leave, and I truly didn't want her to go, there was only one thing to do," Jared said. "I'd go with her."

Kinsey burst out crying, as so many things came clear to her.

Isaac had given up everything he worked for so he could be with the woman he loved.

Clark had turned his back on his family, his home, his social circle, because he desperately loved Beth.

Maybe it wasn't so hard to believe that Jared would do the same.

Kinsey swiped at her tears. "You mean it, don't you. That you can live here in Crystal Springs and be happy."

"Hell, yes." Jared folded her into his arms and pulled her against his chest. "As long as I have you. That's all that matters."

She cried, soaking up his strength, feeling the love they shared. When she finally stopped, she gazed up at him.

"So will you marry me?" he asked.

Another tear rolled down her cheek. "Oh, yes."

Jared leaned down and kissed her lips, then wiped her tears with his fingers.

"We need to get a few things straight first," he said. "You're not working anymore."

"Oh, but Jared, I have to—"

"I'll take care of you. You and Sam. So, no more working. And no more washing dishes," he told her. "I bought Isaac's house from him. It's small, but just big enough for you, Sam and me. I'm hiring a girl to come over every day and clean and wash the dishes."

"Jared, I can't sit around all day and do nothing," Kinsey insisted.

"Then open a dressmaking shop. I know you'd like that," he said. "Or do whatever else you'd like."

"What about you?" she asked.

Jared looked thoughtful. "Crystal Springs is a growing town. I figure I can build myself a construction business here. I talked to Caleb about it. We're throwing in together on it."

"That sounds like a wonderful idea."

He raised an eyebrow. "So we're settled on everything?"

"Just one more thing," Kinsey said. "Your mother. She wasn't happy about having Beth for a daughter-in-law. I know she won't be happy with me either."

"Don't give my mother another thought," Jared told her. "She might be hardheaded and determined, but she knows when she's wrong. It's a family trait. You might have noticed?"

Kinsey smiled up at him. "I love you."

"I love you, too."

"Even if you didn't find the sort of wife you were looking for?"

"I didn't find a wife I could live with," Jared agreed. He leaned down and kissed her softly on the lips. "Instead, I found one I couldn't live without."

* * * * *